The Secrets She Keeps

BY THE SAME AUTHOR

My Summer of Love

The Secrets She Keeps

helen cross

BLOOMSBURY

First published 2005

Copyright © 2005 by Helen Cross

The moral right of the author has been asserted

Bloomsbury Publishing Plc, 38 Soho Square, London W1D 3HB

A CIP catalogue record for this book
is available from the British Library

ISBN 07475 7624 6

10 9 8 7 6 5 4 3 2 1

Typeset by Hewer Text Ltd, Edinburgh
Printed by Clays Ltd, St Ives plc

All papers used by Bloomsbury Publishing are natural, recyclable
products made from wood grown in well-managed forests.
The manufacturing processes conform to the environmental
regulations of the country of origin.

www.bloomsbury.com/helencross

For Andy and Kendra Rose

Chapter One

I fell in love with Hepsie Vine on a snowy December afternoon. The day I went for my interview at Miss Moore's London mansion, Chessington Vale. I admit that I'd hoped for fans outside the house: a sway of chubby milk-faced girls and boys rocked on screams. I expected bed sheets sloganed with raw adoration. I wanted stalkers. Flowers. Love-struck graffiti. I wanted screaming vulgarity. Slender cars. I longed for glittering lights, a gaudy lustre of energy, money, passion and, high above, stars – thrown into the night by an admirer like a handful of jewels to twinkle for ever over Miss Moore. I'd imagined taxis. Their engines running clockwork thunder as they ejected the fitter, more fashionable, those richer, slimmer, those London beauties silvered as lightning.

For the interior of Chessington Vale I envisaged a breath-taking grandness. A place Miss Moore had designed herself that glowed far off in the moonlight. A palace, floating in a park of loneliness and riches, sickeningly vulgar, based on the only homes she'd ever known: hotels. There would be those same blind hotel corridors, a row of endlessly closing doors, the familiar scuttle of faceless staff peeping awestruck upon the lives of those greater than themselves. Perhaps a fountain. Certainly a white stone staircase of Hollywood proportions. Bathrooms like igloos. A pretty, bored PA filing her claws in the front hall. A heady scent of new wood, fresh leather, perfumed linen. But most discernible of all would be a mumble that sobbed across the night air and spoke only to me. 'Oh I have all of this, John: money, men, beauty, fame, and still I am unhappy.'

And all the time the snow would keep falling, in tiny white bells.

Sex didn't come into it; it was all romance.

So, I was nineteen then and wanted overwhelming gaudy misery in a majestic setting, but what I got, as you may already know if you read the magazines, was a huge red-brick box around which security was so tight that the whole place resembled a private clinic. A tubby uniformed guard circled the perimeter regularly. Four new CCTV cameras swivelled nimbly on each corner of that enormous but deeply ordinary modern house. And my interview was not for starry midnight, but for an early Wednesday afternoon on 27 December 200 –. On a day so mushroomy and thick that the sky hung above me like a sodden grey overcoat. Still, I expected a thrilling crassness, and to end my contract laughing about my time with Miss Moore.

In those distant hours before my interview, before I'd ever met Hepsie Vine (six long months before I briefly set up home with the girl), I loitered for a long time outside the high gates entertaining all manner of amorous dreams – for those were the years when I longed to be a movie director, or perhaps a playwright, a poet maybe, or a painter, and when I thought that whatever I longed for I would have –

and when getting fried alive in trashy TV was the furthest thing from my mind. My heart quickened and my brow glistened at the thought of my first meeting with a glamour model, and a millionairess. I'd spoken to Miss Misty Moore very briefly on the telephone before my appointment, but because she, or rather what I think of now as the *resemblance* of her, was regularly in the papers around that time I held the exciting image of Miss Moore long before I'd actually met her.

By the living-room window a perfectly dappled pony with leather reins and silver stirrups snorted and spun on its rockers. By the huge pink fireplace teddy bears warmed themselves by the flames. I can tell you nothing more about how I actually got into the Chessington Vale mansion that damp December day, for I feel now that I entered with as much conscious will as if I'd been sucked down a tunnel. A Christmas tree, so splendid I imagined it pinched that morning from Trafalgar Square, hovered in a shower of red-green-yellow stars. It had indeed started to snow. Everywhere, as though we were the embarrassed visitors of corpses, were fragrant pink blooms.

'Oh,' the woman said when she saw me, and her sigh did seem to tinkle the tinsel-hung chandeliers and send a ripple of cream over the diamond-spun buttermilk walls. The woman coughed and waved her hand – until between two fingers, like a tiny white wand, popped a cigarette. 'Isn't this just too amazing?' she said. I nodded keenly. 'It's what I've always wanted,' she smiled. Then she twisted, so she lay across the sofa in a way that suggested both illness and indolence. She was pale as one should be after childbirth. Her limbs were heavy with exhaustion. Like the entire room, she too seemed sunk under the weight of riches.

By the side of the floating woman stood a person, male, but no more a man than that plastic groom speared into the icing on a wedding cake is a man. A slender well-dressed black guy in his twenties. Gems of light from the tree glittered his features and as I looked in his direction he blew smoke high into the air, creating a grey cloud of stylish misery.

'So,' the man said, leaning rakishly against the pink-bloomed marble fireplace, 'welcome to the divine abode of the intensely private Miss Misty Moore.'

'That's a joke,' the woman said. 'It's just something they said in a magazine yesterday.'

And I knew that, to this girl, for increasingly as I stared at her she seemed more girl than woman, *something said in a magazine yesterday* was the absolute height of tedium.

'So I'm supposed to be having this media career,' the woman reclining on the sofa continued, and she sighed and stretched and I held out my hand, which she shook.

'Lovely to meet you. How are you feeling?'

'All right.'

'Oh good,' I smiled. 'You never know how it will be, I imagine.'

'What,' she said sadly, 'do you mean?'

'Having a baby,' I smiled.

The pair looked at me for a long time.

'Oh no,' the plastic man by her side said eventually. 'No, no. You're thinking of Miss Moore.'

This black man's syrupy voice, the practised lazy fall of his eyelashes – perhaps it all affected me so completely because, despite my single year at university, I'd lived without intoxication, an indulged only child raised under anaesthetic in Tunbridge Wells by middle-class, middle-aged parents who, because of my father's snoring, slept in separate bedrooms.

'She's not Misty, darling. Not by a long way.'

'Oh no,' the girl said, with that snap of 'ha!' in her voice, 'I'm certainly not Misty Moore.' I looked again and she was smiling a look of sad mischief at the misunderstanding. 'Though once upon a time long ago I did have a picture of her on my bedroom wall.'

And from that small smile I knew that she alone had invented lips.

'Isn't that funny? I used to be a fan and now here I am sitting in her living room. But no, I'm definitely not *her*.'

Of course not. This girl spoke with a creamy burr. She was young as a pup. Before my interview I had exchanged a few nervous lines with Miss Moore on the telephone and the millionairess had the smarter, chillier clipped vowels of a radio presenter.

'Did he tell you you would be going to live in the country some of the time?' Miss Moore had said before she even asked my name.

I replied that I did know this. The day a man had approached me in Old Street's famous *Madame Baguette* where I 'designed' expensive buttered sandwiches for portly bankers, he'd explained that the contract would be to work for the family not only in London but also in a small village in Yorkshire for six months. There I would look after two children, a boy and a baby.

'Good,' Miss Moore said flatly, and then she howled that strange long animal laugh, the one I have since decided allowed her to slip out of her real self, and into something more comfortable: her copy of herself. 'I bet you think it's

5

my idea we have a male,' Miss Moore said eventually when she had stopped laughing. 'Well, actually, it's not.' And she laughed again.

'You make me sound like a tom-cat,' I said, flirting without ever intending to, for she had this way.

'*Hello?*' the girl called then. 'I'm Hephzibah.' Hephzibah spoke as though reminding herself of her name rather than imparting the information to anyone in the room.

'And she's just leaving,' the plastic man said, and made a high stretch, which revealed a belt of hard black flesh around his waist. He wore his hair close-cropped so his pretty head resembled a tight fist, and he followed me with that quick cold eye.

'Everyone calls me Hepsie. And, as I was saying, I'm supposed to be having this *media* career.' The girl before me sighed again – as though she had known the man and me for years and we had all discussed every topic through endless violet nights and now there was nothing else in the world to say. Not only were her eyes and lips bigger than is average on a young woman, but they had that dark-purple hue as if just snipped out of twilight.

'What do you know about her?' the man asked. Twinkles of fairy sapphire danced over his face.

That her hair was blue-black as the last blaze of midnight. It had such a sheer sheen, a deep, almost purple, gloss, that it reminds me still, to this day, of a freshly rubbed plum. So fresh that if I'd, and oh I do so wish I had, dared lean towards her and stroke my trembling fingers through her curls I'd've come away with hands dripping with a permanent inky blue.

'Not *her*,' the man sighed, 'I mean Misty Moore. What do you know about *her*? I mean, apart from the fact that she has a new baby, huge titties, is very famous and is a millionaire.'

'I'm afraid not a lot,' I confessed. 'We spoke on the phone briefly, but I can't say that I've caught her on TV recently.'

'Ah, then you've not been staying up late enough,' the man replied with a smile that was hard to read.

'Don't be unkind, Brian,' Hepsie said, punching the man playfully on the arm. 'I used to think she was a goddess. In fact she's probably what made me want to run away to London in the first place.'

I felt a searing flush of embarrassment as the pair eyed me coolly through the incessant flashing of tree lights. Neither one of the couple who watched me that winter afternoon had mastered Misty Moore's gift of gazing on strangers as though they were the most precious treasure in the room. I continued to stare at Hepsie, and I saw that in her hair she wore a sprig of holly.

Amidst those thick black curls three holly leaves appeared, glinting like emeralds in a pile of sun-shot coal. Three dark leaves, two red berries and a thick khaki nub of stalk. The scarlet fruit was dark and trembling as a just-oozed dot of blood. This silly adornment, perhaps a nod to Christmas, or that season's popular girl-as-fey-child fashion, would have seemed spikily coquettish on any other girl (would there later be a ridiculous routine whereby she pricked her finger on a thorn and fell into a snooze for a thousand years?) but on Hepsie Vine it just enhanced the feral whiff of a creature who has slunk through the undergrowth to be with you. She had the wilderness in her eyes, and though she was devastatingly fit I was certain the only heat that had ever warmed her skin was the sun, and the only wet that had ever licked her was the rain. She was both dirty and fresh. That's as accurate as I have ever been able to be about her. And it's enough for any man.

And perhaps this was the reason why, despite her modest dress, a white baggy T-shirt over jeans, and freshly scrubbed appearance, I sensed immediately trouble between Hepsie Vine and Misty Moore. Or, to put it more bluntly, I felt sure that Hepsie was being fired. Why? She engaged in none of the nanny's usual flirtery and flattery, that essential and tiresome jollity required to cajole one's employers into believing you are a kind and harmless person. Misty Moore had, I assumed on that December day 200 –, got rid of blistering Hepsie, and, just by arranging for that man to walk into an exclusive sandwich bar in Central London and ask a total stranger if he wanted a job, replaced her with a more pliant model: me.

'So,' I said, unable to bear the flashing silence a moment longer, 'is Misty here?'

'She's upstairs,' the man replied coolly. 'With her baby.'

'So, yeah, this bloody media career. Apparently it's just TV presenting or something.' The girl sighed, and despite her fatigue I felt sure she had determined to keep me a while longer from the legendary Misty Moore. 'And then there's the modelling too.'

'That's marvellous,' I smiled. 'Sounds like a dream come true.'

'Is it?' she replied, looking at me suddenly as though it was the first time she had ever seen me. Hepsie wiped one fat tear from her cheek. 'You think it'll all be worth it?'

Then she gave me a curious look, as though the only news she could think to tell me was bad news, and so instead she sighed and stretched and I saw a naked girl walking through a deep yawn, in her high hand a brand of fire, the light of which cast an orange glow down over the slender, almost boyish body. No, not boyish, not in December. That was later. Hepsie, in 200 –, was not thin. Perhaps for this reason Hepsie at eighteen seemed older than her employer. For at thirty-eight, Miss Misty Moore, singer, actress, model, millionairess, was distinguished, despite her renowned ballooning breasts, as being as tall, hard and slender as a nail.

And yet, I hardly need to say this, there was something about Hepsie, being eighteen, that Miss Moore, being thirty-eight, could never touch. And on that day I went for my appointment at Chessington Vale, it smelt like teen fury.

'Ooops, I need to go get sugar,' the man said, and the sound of his high voice startled the thin muslin curtains so they billowed like a bride in flight. 'Or are you sweet enough?' and laughing he stood and exited the room stage right.

'Don't worry,' Hepsie said when we were alone. 'It'll just be you and Misty in Wychwood. I mean Brian needs the discos and the drugs too badly to go to the country for six months. Though she has asked him to help you with the baby. If necessary.'

I asked Hephzibah then who the strange man was.

She told me he had a style column in a Sunday newspaper and he was Miss Moore's friend. She bit her lip in excitement as she spoke. 'Sorry, I mean he's her *style adviser*,' she said. 'Incredible, eh? He has clothes, sorry, I mean *haute couture*, draped like starved corpses all over his flat, sorry, his *apartment*,' she said. 'That's his real job.'

'Wow. I've never met anyone quite like that before,' I smiled. 'It'll be fascinating.'

'Yes.' Hepsie nodded rapidly, and we beamed at one

another in eager anticipation until there was a far-off sound, which gradually got louder and was as unavoidably obvious as fierce arguing. 'Have you been to the North before?' Hepsie asked quickly, surely to cover the argument growing overhead.

'Not very far. In fact I'm sure when I get past a certain point on the M1 I'll get vertigo.'

'Not vertigo,' she said, 'but something odd might happen to you up there.'

'She's only teasing,' Brian interjected, bursting back into the room brandishing a squat silver sugar bowl. 'Take no notice of her.'

But a certain look had passed between the strange pair, which twisted my next sentence to a stutter. 'How long have you been in London?'

'Oh, millions of years, trillions,' the girl sighed. 'Longer than Big Ben, Nelson's Column and St Paul's Cathedral all put together.'

'You're obviously quite an attraction.'

'It's bloody tiring. But I'm sure in the end it's all going to be worth it.'

'And you must miss your family.'

'Well, my dad and granddad shot themselves last year.'

'Hepsie!' Brian said curtly. 'Please. The fine gentleman doesn't want to hear of such troubles.'

'Which is partly the reason I'm here, John,' she said softly. 'Partly to get away from the misery of my home, and partly because I thought I really could be famous.'

It seemed like we all gazed at one another then for a long time. Suspended, shocked, unnaturally still, three tiny face-less figures in a glass-domed snow-globe, waiting to be upturned, flung and stunned.

'Don't look so scared,' she smiled. 'The suicides were a while ago now.'

'I'm not scared,' I croaked.

'It's only because you're from the city and you're not used to it. In the countryside killings, slaughterings, butchery – all kinds of deaths – happen all the time up there.'

'Well, I'm sure young John'll have plenty to do,' Brian said cheerily, eyeing Hepsie with a frown, 'without thinking of death.'

'That is, of course, if I agree to take the job,' I said. The sky was snow-white now, and dampened in patches with smoky blotches of grey.

'Oh you'll agree,' Hepsie muttered. 'I knew you'd agree. You've no idea how much I want this to work.'

'Honey, it will work,' Brian said harshly, 'if you shut up and calm down.'

'She'll have her own show within the month, I'm sure,' I replied. There was an intimacy flaring between my interrogators that uneased me.

'Because really,' Hepsie said, another edge of sudden tearfulness in her creamy voice, 'it's nothing to do with Misty. Not now. At the end of the day it's all down to me. That's what everyone says about success, isn't it?' And she glanced up at the silver tinsel hung over her head in thick clouds. She was edgy, over-emotional, prone to wild mood swings. The thought was growing in my mind that my beautiful predecessor had been kicked out of the employ of Misty Moore because of some addiction. ' "It's all possible, but it is down to you now." That's what everyone says.'

'Being so beautiful must help,' I said, before I had time to stop the words.

Brian flinched in imitation of astonishment and somewhere in the house there was a sudden burst of temper like a far-off explosion.

'Yes, apparently the world's my lobster,' she said, turning on her side and arranging her limbs so the left leg was outstretched and the right leg bent at the knee and rested above it. This was the first indication I had of an important lesson I was to learn in 200 –: some women spoke most eloquently in gestures rather than words.

There was a loud crash from upstairs and Brian excused himself from the room. When he was gone, simply to fill my lovestruck silence, I made the mistake of asking the lolling beauty if Brian lived at Chessington Vale with Miss Moore.

'No, I told you,' she cried, 'he lives alone in a flat, an *apartment*. In a warehouse.'

'In London?'

'Ha!' she exclaimed. 'Yes, exactly.'

Then, 'Have you ever done things you regret?' she said quietly. But, by the time I had absorbed the question, she'd waved a hand over her face and said, 'Oh never mind, forget it.' She moved towards me silently whispering, imploring me to understand some terrible thing that had happened to her. 'It doesn't matter now. As long as I can make a go of it here in London it's all been worth it. You've no idea how long I've dreamt of this.'

Troubled. That would rather accurately describe my attitude to women at the time. Six months previously I'd been abandoned by Clare, my first serious girlfriend. We'd only been together six months, but I was a weepy sensitive guy then and I loved her; some people die from eating a single peanut.

Hepsie's eyes were still dark, but for a tiny pine-green crescent moon, which was a single light cast over from the tree. 'Never mind,' she said deflating, instantly disappointed in me. 'I don't expect you to understand.'

'I want to try,' I begged.

'Oh, it's not complicated. It's just that no matter how much I want it – and God knows I do really really want it – there's always gonna be this problem. Think of the difference between: *He lives alone in an apartment in London* and *She lives with her family in a caravan in Yorkshire.*'

I smiled and said no more, though the outburst hung in the room, mad and dangerous as though we had just unleashed a swarm of invisible bees.

'I don't imagine Mouse will be much trouble,' Brian said, reappearing with a grin.

'Poor thing,' Hepsie said quietly. 'The medication has right affected his appetite. It's one of the side effects. And the homesickness doesn't help.'

'He might eat more if he comes off the drugs,' Brian added.

'The drugs?' I said, and I was sure then that the pair glanced at one another and tightened their lips to suppress a giggle. 'Is there something I should know?'

'So Mouse, the boy, is . . . ?' I asked and the pair looked at me blankly. 'Why's he called Mouse?' The pair shrugged. 'Is his name Mickey?' I asked. They looked at me without smiling. I asked more bluntly who the boy was and Brian told me he was seven years old and was the child of Misty's former lover. His father had recently split up with Misty and moved out and his mother was still in America.

Later I would feel breathlessly anxious about caring for the abandoned pill-popping boy, for I had no childcare experience at all, but in the daze-dizzied moment I just tried to mask my panic with a smile and said, 'They both left him?'

'Oh,' gasped Hepsie quietly, and my perfect little beauty rose up suddenly, like she'd been carried off on the wind, blown to the door and, like a breath of smoke, had vanished.

Suddenly that room belonged to the furniture in that gaudy millionaire's house in London. Without Hepsie the absurd overblown pine wept down a puddle of needles. A tasteless moulded fireplace groaned under the weight of pink buds. I tried not to think of the lonely boy alone with me and instead, for the first time, I noticed everything, from the marble dolphins supporting each corner of the smoked-glass coffee table to the life-size colony of terracotta penguins waddling around the chrome cinema-size television. It's all too gluttonous to describe now, and anyway as you will begin to see I am uninterested in the description of riches. Truly, all that sticks in my mind of any meaning are the spoons Brian served with tea, perfect and sad as snowdrops.

When at last Hepsie blew back into the room I tried to continue the conversation about the children by saying, 'And I'll also be responsible for the baby, right?'

'You mean stuff like bathing, changing, dressing, feeding her?' Brian said.

I nodded.

Then Brian and Hepsie glanced over the white garden, their young foreheads corrugated with frowns. I looked out too, and suddenly, yes, there now in the garden, before the window, was a perfect, mid-sized, carrot-nosed snowman, a line of black-coal lips curled up in a smile. A cerise cashmere scarf knotted around its thick white neck.

'Well,' Hepsie said slowly, 'she certainly, definitely, absolutely won't be breastfeeding, will she?'

Brian shook his head slowly. 'No. Alas, not. For all the obvious reasons.'

'Well, it will be an amazing adventure,' I said quickly. 'Who cares who feeds the baby.' I was embarrassed at having, so thoughtlessly, already engaged in what seemed like lurid tabloid speculation. 'How old is it, the baby?'

'Two weeks,' Brian replied.

'Two weeks!' I exclaimed. 'But I had no idea. You're joking, right?'

'Hmm,' Hepsie said softly, sucking on the tip of her little finger, her pretty face twisted sharply away from me. 'Two weeks exactly.'

'But is it right for a baby that young to be cared for by – me? What about the baby's father?'

'Look,' Brian said with a sigh, 'you just put the food in one end and wipe it out the other, OK?'

Who were these people?

After some time, when still neither of my companions showed any sign of urgency, I said, 'OK, do you know what time my interview is?'

'Interview!' Brian exclaimed.

'What on earth do you mean?' Hepsie asked with a higher laugh than I'd heard before.

'I should have said earlier,' I smiled. I'd no idea why the reason for my visit had not already been mentioned, by me or them. 'But I was to have an interview at 2 p.m. about working for Miss Moore as a nanny. And now I know about the age of the baby, I need to make it clear that –'

'But this is it,' Hepsie exclaimed with another little giggle. 'You're having your interview *now*!'

'I don't even know if the baby's a boy or a girl,' I said, when I had drunk on Hepsie Vine so long I was intoxicated and emotional and overtired. 'Is it really only two weeks old?'

'She's called Jewels,' Hepsie said. 'You'll meet her soon enough.' And she sighed.

I thought how an outsider might watch the windows growing rosy, imagine the slow blush of evening secrets spreading throughout the huge humming house. My rich lonely bankers at *Madame Baguette* would long to be deep in the warm heart of a family home at Christmas time. Then Brian flew me outside, past the snowman and into a purpling courtyard where he showed me a low yellow sports car with a black felt roof.

'It's the top of the range,' he smiled. 'One of the most expensive models on the road today.'

'God yes, I can tell. It's astonishingly beautiful.'

'And brand new. 0–70 in seven seconds. I bought it for you. For when you're in the country,' he cooed, and we stroked our hands over the smooth cool bullet of gold.

'I just hope I'll be able to live up to the previous nanny. Hepsie seems very committed,' I said, still rubbing at the sports car.

'Oh yes,' Brian nodded. 'She's been totally committed.'

And when we fluttered back indoors Hepsie, tear-stained, exclaimed, 'You've no idea what it's like for everything to rest on how you look! I mean, yes I do want to get to the top, more than anything, but I guess I'm afraid too. Everything doesn't rest on beauty for you, John.'

'Oh Hepsie!' Brian said harshly. 'Shut it, babe!'

'I mean, yes, you are tall and strong and handsome. And of course that's one of the reasons I liked you, from the first minute I saw you, in fact, in all honesty, it was probably the *main reason* I picked you, I can't deny that. You kind of look like a darker, more handsome Prince William. Has anyone ever told you that before?'

Something had changed. Our snow-globe had been turned and Brian, Hepsie and I tumbled helplessly hither and thither, shaken to mindlessness through the white whirl.

'That's just the way he blushes all the time,' Brian smiled dizzily, brushing the snow from his shirt and stumbling to regain his calm, 'and the way he flirts up at you through his fringe.'

'I know. And of course handsome's always good, but . . . it's not good if the *only* thing you have to sell is your body or your beauty. That's why I have to make sure I get into presenting, then acting, as well as the modelling. Because, you see, the thing about beauty is, *it wears out.* I mean, my mother and grandmother were beautiful once, and look what situation they're in now . . .'

Brian coughed and poured another cup of tea. 'Hepsie, toots, calm down for Christ's sake,' he muttered.

'But you are beautiful now,' I exclaimed. Tears were coursing down her pretty face and I felt a rush of terrible helplessness. I wanted so badly to hold her and kiss her then, and if Brian had not been gazing upon me like I wore the taint of a madman, I may have done just that. 'You are. You're beautiful now.'

'I guess that's why I have to not let anything get in my way,' she said, and blew her nose on a tissue. Then she smiled, first at Brian and then at me, with a sly lifting of the chin. For a moment it was hard to tell if the conversation had been one huge yell for attention.

I rested back in my chair and exhaled slowly.

'Oh do that again!' she cried. I must have looked at her with extreme puzzlement because she clarified immediately. 'Do that thing where you stroke your hand slowly over your chin while frowning. It's so sweet!'

'I remember seeing you do that through the window of your café,' Brian smiled.

'It's one of the first things I loved about him. Look, Brian!'

'Wow.'

'I imagine it was when some poor City secretary asked for a particularly tricky filling, you looked so perplexed, but totally concerned with getting it right for her! You looked so gentle and kind and shy. It's what got you the job above everyone else we'd watched.'

And though ten years on I cringe at myself now, that snowy afternoon in December 200 – I did actually as young Hephzibah Vine asked. I sat there in a millionairess's leather armchair, measled with fairy lights, frowning and stroking my chin. Until the fit little honey I'd known for just a few hours was smiled back to sweetness.

Chapter Two

I had been driving for four hours when at last I came upon a wider road, on either side of which loomed a tall wall of woodland. Weak with anxiety I stopped the car and watched soft white fluorescent scraps spangle in the head-lights. Then settle on the windscreen in a felty heap. Beneath the trees I could see thick toothy fronds, but nothing distinctive to aid my navigation. Over the verges the snow still lay like a white bandage and there was no sign of anyone to ask directions.

I listened to the fierce engine purr and suddenly loved that car as much as I'd loved anything in my entire life. On the map, which I'd consulted in growing frustration several times, there was still no mention, on any of the pages, of the village of Wychwood, though I'd exited the motorway according to my instructions and threaded through narrow lanes, taking the lefts and rights as directed. I should be there. According to the milometer we were 210 miles from London. The in-car route planner had estimated my jour-ney as 219 miles. I was lost.

In the rear-view mirror I saw Mouse and Jewels safe and sleeping. The rise of that tiny chest indicated the baby was still breathing. Though the children did not look at all alike, one was dark and one was light, I assumed the pair had the same vanished father. Even with his eyes shut the boy was odder than I could have expected. He was small and thin and his skin had the fogged translucency of skimmed milk. He wore a black woollen balaclava over his white hair, which, Brian had wearily explained, was only ever removed when the boy was alone. The kid needed a psychiatrist, not a bogus boy nanny. Furthermore he seemed smaller and more frail than a seven-year-old and Misty would later explain that weight loss was one of the most common side effects of his medication. The other was insomnia. The positive effects were increased concentration, euphoria, greater self-confidence, heightened energy and new levels of focus. He was intelligent, but shy. No one knew how long Mouse would remain with Miss Moore, and for this reason it had been decided that he would attend the school in Wychwood, rather than enrolling in a private school elsewhere. I got the distinct impression that Mouse was a lunatic. A hindrance to all concerned, and the real reason he was going to attend the Wychwood school was because no one could be bothered to sort out anywhere else.

I drove on. Lost, and minutes away from losing my nerve. I passed isolated cottages on the roadside, windows still waxed with a blur of Christmas lights, chimneys chugging grey ringlets into the moonlight, all doors firmly bolted against Southern strangers. Then, on the black verge, I saw a glimpse of blue. It was a child, or a very small person. Trembling, I rolled the window down and called out. 'Hello, can you help us? We're lost.' Snow flew into the car like a whirl of ice butterflies. My words skidded away on the winter air. The blue faded and the child melted to branches in the velvet dark. Then in the space where the small body had just vanished I saw a snow-capped sign appear: *Wood Scorpion*.

It was almost 11.30 p.m. and it was New Year's Day 200 –. As I came into the village Jewels began to whimper and Mouse made repeated low moans through his druggy dreams. I had to give the baby a bottle at midnight; I must not forget. Mouse moaned again. That afternoon Brian and the children had been waiting for me in the hallway, silent and staring as a group of orphans. 'Hi,' I'd said, bending to greet Mouse for the first time. 'It's really great to meet you.' His head was a ball of black wool. His mouth was twisted away from the opening in the balaclava, so only his pale eyes and a nub of white chin were visible. 'You want to tell me why you're called Mouse?' I laughed.

'Hey, don't go berserko – you just have to act as if you like me, yeah?' Mouse replied in a calm muffle. 'You don't, like, have to really feel it.'

If I'd not been so unnerved by the look of the boy I'd have thought him a sarcastic brat, but there was a blue sadness in his eye that made me fear for both of us. 'Well, we'll have great fun,' I'd smiled at the boy as I shook his cold little hand.

'Sure,' he'd said blankly.

The baby had lain there like a poor pink rodent, silent and blinking. She didn't seem a particularly attractive baby. Her face was wrinkled, red and blotchy. Her temples were indented giving her long head the comically pinched look of a peanut shell. 'Forceps birth,' Brian had whispered with a grimace.

Soon ahead was a pub with the sign *The Lady* blowing madly in the white snow-wind. Was I aware of anything odd as I drove towards Wychwood? Did I notice for one minute a trick trembling in the air? Not at all. I was deeply panicked about being lost in the dark countryside and alone with those fragile children, but nothing more. As I've confessed, I'm honest and privileged and despite a shaky start with girls I have lived nearly all my life in the sunshine. I believe only in the rational. Everyone I've been close to in my life has treated me well – even the girls who dumped me did it very nicely. I am optimistic. I like the world as it is. England in 200 – was a great place to be a young man. I did not foresee trouble or failure. Still, it shocks me when it comes. That sunny winter morning as I sped from London to the North I was simply thrilled at the thought of imminently entering a splendidly sordid world of pure glamour. I'd felt nothing more disquieting than a lingering snarl of lust for Hepsie Vine, and a constant flutter of excitement about at last meeting my millionairess. I certainly had no sense at all of being followed.

I drove slowly along the main street of Wood Scorpion, watching as from the door of The Lady a few bent drinkers shot stumbling towards the new year, their faces pressed to blue stone against the ice. Either it was the violence of the weather, my too-gentle Southern accent, my anxious hesitation, or my ostentatious glittering car, but when I rolled the window down to call out to these people asking for directions there was not so much as a backwards glance. Perhaps some laughed; most just hurried onwards. One certainly shrugged. Behind me Mouse twisted his face round inside his balaclava and ached out another helpless drug-stricken moan.

Then, when I was about to drive on in even greater despair, a woman, late middle-aged, it seemed, and dressed entirely from neck to ankle in a pale-grey coat, came out of the pub. She stood for a moment turning in the moonlight like a swan on an icy lake. She was made small-faced by a large black hat, and sheathed round the neck with a thick grey scarf. I saw immediately that her eyes were so bloodshot pink – veined with that look that spoke of a thousand all-night troubles – that if she were to cry her tears would be tiny red berries.

Interplanetary. That is the word for those eyes that caught me that night.

Still, any unease at meeting with such a stranger was outweighed by the prospect of reaching my destination. 'Excuse me, can you help me? I've been lost for hours,' I shouted. Then, as though I'd slept for a few seconds, she was there, leaning in at my open window, speaking into my ear. A voice that was little more than a trickle of cold water. Her mouth was cosmically wide, and her teeth were a perfect pearly crescent. I could hear the wet slap of her heart. I sniffed for drink, for there was something about her distraction and sudden shivering that made me think of Hepsie and drink and drugs, but this woman's panted breath was as fresh as the coming ice: she was sober and sharp as a whistle.

Immediately my heart was racing, but I decided this was due to the constant drone of panic I felt about the two-week-old scrap who sat alarmingly silent in the car seat behind me. I'd held the baby for the first time when I put her into the car. I'd felt her tiny vertebrae light against my fingertips: terrifyingly fragile, terrifyingly my responsibility.

Bewitched, I asked the woman to speak more loudly. It turned out that she was going in the direction of Wych-wood herself.

'Shall I give you a lift?' I yelled.

'Yeah, if you . . . don't . . . ' she said, 'the weather's . . .' and her shoulders slackened and her face melted into a laughless smile. I felt suffused with relief and wildly happy that this was the kind of trust in operation in country parts.

'Is it safe for a woman to be wandering alone?' I asked as she got into the low yellow car with a gentle thud. I glanced at her then, but in my eyes she was hazy, all her hard edges blurred to trembles.

'I'm too old to be jumped,' the shaking woman said, settling herself and securing her seat belt. 'Though I imagine round here that being jumped probably isn't the worst thing that can happen to a woman.'

'You mean ghosts and ghoulies?' I laughed.

As we drove I spoke cheerily about the beauty of these hidden villages. How perfectly they had preserved their ancient authenticity, though in fact the landscape we were travelling through was far from picturesque. I speculated about how what often looked like low hills were in fact a range of Neolithic burial grounds.

I was relieved to have a passenger. Even more so to be safe in the company of a woman who, if things suddenly went wrong with Jewels, could instantly take over. A woman who, now that I was close by her, I found rather attractive. I informed her about how in England in the sixteenth century men were tried for being werewolves as often as women were tried for being witches. The interesting thing about the wolf, I continued, was that the animal was a scavenger as well as a hunter. And yet nowadays the poor wolf was becoming extinct and was, in fact, included in the Endangered Species Act. (I cringe at my nineteen-year-old self now, so naively boastful of all the trivia I knew

– especially in the company of women. Anyway I guess my passenger saw through my adolescent bragging for she said nothing, just looked away from me, out over the new year's dark.)

Nerdy ignorance of the female lot was another of my defining adolescent traits. 'You don't understand me!' Clare would wail, and she was right.

The snow was falling thicker now and faster and I wanted to keep close for another moment to this new stranger-warmth. In the rear-view mirror I saw the children sleeping, breathing. I told the woman how the tale of Little Red Riding Hood was just one example of how deeply the wolf was seeped into the human subconscious. Then I speculated confidently as to how people had perhaps been living in these parts for hundreds, perhaps thousands, of years, and how many areas of the land may not have changed since ancient times. 'It's wonderful!' I exclaimed.

My passenger had given no clues during the drive as to her local knowledge but soon we did reach a spot, which the woman informed me was Wychwood.

'Stop here,' she said suddenly, though we were driving along a narrow lane and did not seem to have yet reached the centre of any village. 'This is it. This is where I have to get out.'

'There's nothing here,' I said.

'Yes, there is,' she replied quietly, 'there is an old farm-house behind this wall. I must get out here.'

I saw now that we had indeed come to a halt alongside a stone wall, bricks like boulders, blackened from many inky Wychwood nights. Behind the wall I glimpsed a sizeable old property standing some way back from the lane. 'Thanks for the directions,' I said. 'I could have been driving all night.'

'I wouldn't have minded that,' she replied with a small laugh that was, I later imagined, closer to a sob.

'Well, my employer might,' I grinned. 'I'm starting a new job tonight and I'm hours late.'

'Well, just tell them that you gave a lift to a lonely old woman.'

'I don't know if you've heard of her but I've just got this job with Misty Moore,' I said. 'She's moving to this village for a few months.'

'Misty Moore?'

'That's her stage name, I guess,' I laughed. 'I don't suppose she was christened that.'

'Really?'

'You've heard of her?'

'Yes.'

'It's quite a stupid name, I suppose, but you get used to it.'

'Yes.'

'I'm actually rather thrilled to be meeting her. She gets in the papers even now.'

'But I'm Misty Moore.'

Was I right in imagining all the time she was looking at me as though willing me to challenge those words? Expecting me to burst into mad laughter. *But I'm Misty Moore!* Could I have changed the course of both our lives if I'd clapped my hands then and laughed incredulously at the suggestion? *You! Misty Moore! No way, Mrs. Get outta my car!* But we just stared at one another for a long moment, until I blushed with humiliation and astonishment. Had she been pretending not to recognise me, or the children?

'What were you doing out there?' I asked quietly.

'I was about to find a cab. Then you called out to me.'

She certainly seemed older than I'd imagined and her skin on that winter's night was rough and sore – as far from flawless as sacking is to silk, but she was remarkable in one way: those interplanetary eyes, and when she spun that ruby-sapphire gaze upon you it was as though every other man in the world instantly vanished. Leaving only you – and her. I twisted in my seat to conceal my erection.

'And that, you see, is Long Meadow End,' she said flatly. She was pointing at the huge farmhouse. Restrained by her wealth and beauty, cowed by her twenty more years of worldly experience, I repressed all doubt about our meeting and just looked to where she pointed.

Long Meadow End was not exactly the kind of place that in another age would have been shipped brick by brick to America, but almost. I pictured bats the size of businessmen and beetles big and shiny as hearses.

'What,' Miss Moore continued, 'do you imagine the woman who lived there before us was like?'

She looked at me eerily then, from the corner of those strange eyes, and for a moment we were held in a bubble of warm silence as if in the very palm of *the woman who lived there before*.

'How about a decayed old spinster, a headless horse-woman, a murderous farmer's wife?' I laughed.

'Yes, perhaps you're right,' she said sadly. 'I guess now she's gone she's just whatever we imagine her to be.'

But already I was thinking how we would have to carry knives and light candles, flicker through Long Meadow End lost as murderers.

'They're right, of course,' she laughed eventually.

'There's no point me being in London, I mean, while I try and get over the birth. This is a much better plan.'

Suddenly, looking at Misty Moore reminded me of something Hepsie had said. 'Has it been amazing working for Miss Moore?' I'd asked the strange girl the previous week, on that unforgettable December day.

'It's been . . .' Hepsie replied, smoothing the thick black hair from her perfect face with both hands, like one who has just come up from underwater. It was a gesture of pure weariness, but one I found most endearing.

'I mean, you must have met all kinds of famous actors, pop-stars, film people . . .'

'Oh yes,' she said, again with that sudden little 'ha!', which then was so hard to read, but which now says absolutely everything, 'but then you realise that's the trouble. They're all amazing *actors*.'

I could hear the baby's breath, pure and delicate as a trickle of water. Again the horrible, incredible, realisation came: it was just me and this strange deceiving mother – who had pretended not to recognise *her own child* – who would ensure the baby stayed alive.

Curtains thin as cotton dresses had been dragged roughly, perhaps hastily, across each window of Long Meadow End, and though there seemed to be no light within the house there was a crepuscular glow strumming at the window's edge.

'Could I ask you one thing, John?' Miss Moore smiled, gazing up slowly over my knees, over my groin, my chest, my neck, to focus for a long minute on my lips and then land her incredible look, wide as a tiger in the snowlight, on my eyes. 'Could you be any sweeter?'

It was true! I was alone in a top sports car with every

schoolboy's dream stroking my left knee. So far she had not mentioned, or even looked at, the children, but then as though the repetition of some catch-phrase had allowed a spell to be broken she reached into the back-seat pool of dark where her daughter and the boy slept. With a sudden gasp Miss Moore stroked her hand over the baby's dark bud of a head. Then glanced uneasily at the boy in the balaclava.

'She's gorgeous,' I said. Again I was blasted with horror as I looked at the delicate scrap.

'Oh isn't she? But, you know, John, if she had to be a girl I almost wish she'd been a complete fright, for her own sake.'

'Well, I'm sure she'll have a very happy life,' I cooed.

My boss stared at me open-mouthed. Was it ego or was it paranoia she was displaying? I had no idea.

'Why do you say that?' my passenger said sharply.

'Well,' I said, embarrassed. 'I imagine she'll have every advantage.'

'Oh but, John, that's the *curse*. For a girl. At least if she'd been a boy she could've enjoyed the sports cars and photo shoots and the foreign travel while screwing around to her stony heart's content. I mean, you can have as much fast dirty sex as you like, can't you?' I coughed, twisting again to conceal my groin. I was in complete hormonal agony much of that first month. 'Being rich, pretty and female is very different.'

Together we looked at the tiny quiet baby. I tried hard to envisage what horrendous future of beauty and riches awaited her.

'And this must be the new sports car Brian bought you,' the woman continued quickly, as though fearing she had revealed too much. She was stroking at the leather seats with a heady smile and then gazing back over me.

'What were you really doing? I mean, out in the snow?' I whispered.

She did not reply but a half-wink in her eye suggested, as a certain look had with Hepsie Vine, that our whole meeting had been an elaborate joke. She was definitely not drunk: in fact in the six months we would spend together I would never see her drunk once. I wanted to force her to answer my questions, but her superior beauty was of the glacial kind that instantly freezes unwelcome intrusion to icy silence. Mouse had buried his head back in the car seat and started a wool-muffled cry.

'I think someone's watching us,' I said suddenly.

'Probably,' Miss Moore said, sweeping that cool sapphire stare back over her children. 'I don't imagine they see many tall, strong, handsome young men in sports cars in Wychwood, do you?'

I'd been sure it was a woman's face, but now I looked again the phantom had gone. I was conscious that it was very dark outside. A horse-chestnut tree was tapping the tip of its bony branch against the hood of my expensive car.

'And so that, is Long Meadow End,' she said, 'and isn't it just . . .'

'Yes, it's . . .'

'Though by now the place will be full of insects,' she said, 'and mice.'

'We'll set traps,' I said with a high laugh, for I was both frightened and thrilled by the place. And both frightened and thrilled by Misty Moore.

'Oh yes, sweet John,' she giggled harshly, chewing more quickly on her thumbnail, 'we'll resolve to murder everything with a furry face. Then we'll be absolutely fine.' Miss Moore's head had fallen slightly to the left and her plump lip lolled.

'Oh I'm sure everyone'll be very welcoming.'

'You don't think they'll be barbarians?'

'Barbarians?'

She began to chew on her thumbnail thoughtfully. 'I'm so glad you're with me this time, John,' she said suddenly, and turned to gaze on me sharply.

See, she was a woman who spoke two languages simultaneously: a sugared sweetness from her plumped lips and a darker silent lingo of looks, wiggles, smiles and steps. And I was too young to know the terrible complexities of that purely female language in 200 –. I thought of it as nothing other than simple natural childishness.

'And you really are terribly handsome,' she giggled, 'just like they said you were.'

Of course, I hoped it was all just a mutual aching for sex. As Brian would soon explain to me, the relationship between a nanny and their opposite-sex employee is always fraught with an element of sexual tension. Brian said it would be naive to expect anything else. 'That's why the husband always wants to bang the nanny,' he explained.

'In your situation Miss Moore's just thinking of you like a helpful, homely husband – and even better, one who is paid to do absolutely anything she says. Half husband, half slave. Surely the most sexy sort.'

'. . . and then I went back to America again, which as you can imagine is a training in itself . . .'

But as usual Brian was not quite right. It was not just sex. It was fear too, for that New Year's Day Misty Moore and I were no more than strangers plucked from the night, yet we were soon to spend every day in one another's company – or so I assumed. Alone but for a fragile newborn – who just a moment of neglect, of innocent forgetfulness, could kill outright – and a balaclavaed delinquent child.

Anticipation misted my hot teenage breath to blooms on the windscreen. If Misty and I were to . . . together . . . perhaps . . .

'. . . and then it just took off! Amazing! Of course I could have stayed in Paris, but as you can imagine, Paris is one of those cities where . . .'

I realised she'd been speaking, and when she saw me looking at her she stopped suddenly and returned to biting her thumbnail. Then we both turned to peer through the left-hand window. Nettles, brambles and thorns barbed the iron gate. I edged the car forward. It became possible to see right through and to stare directly at the farmhouse.

'No fair maiden's hand has soothed the End's troubled brow,' I said in a deliberately Gothic manner to try and lighten the anxious mood that had settled in the car. 'No sweet smoke calls a welcome from the crowd of chimney pots.'

'But at least it looks secure,' Miss Moore said quickly. 'I told them that if they insisted on me coming here they had to guarantee it was secure.'

'You'd need dynamite to break in there,' I said. I guessed at ten upper rooms and instantly thought how seven of them would be empty all night but for the moan of winter weather, just bed linen gone damp and cold as midnight grass.

We fell then into a silence until my employer said quietly, 'Though it's funny isn't it, that a place this large and wonderful has been abandoned.' She eyed me curiously.

Again it was not a question, more a test of my willingness to collude. If she had worn half-rim spectacles she would have peered over the top solemnly. Yes, throughout those first months I remember her as so visibly dishonest, and yet possessed with that breathtaking glamour that meant you preferred her lies to your own truths.

'I guess it's because there's no work around here any more.'

'Oh yes, dear John,' she cried, 'that must be it absolutely.'

'And I guess it's expensive to heat.'

'Oh yes,' she exclaimed, clapping her hands in delight. 'Correct. That is it exactly!'

I saw myself in the house then. Striding through the winter cold that would bleed into Long Meadow End for months. I felt rigid with anticipation and domestic anxiety, and yet strong and manly too. By her beautiful side I was unafraid. I felt like a hero in a woman's romantic book or film.

'Well, if it turns out that you don't like it, we don't have to stay here, do we?' I smiled.

'Oh but we do,' Miss Moore gasped, turning to fix me with those space-ship eyes. 'I'm afraid, John, that's exactly what we have to do. Stay here.'

Misty took her hat off then. Leisurely unfurled her scarf. She undid the top two buttons of her coat. We had the car heater high and the wipers working in a fury. I could see a high rise of female flesh, which was the top of the sandy-brown bulge of her notorious breasts. It was all revealed very slowly, deliberately, to torture me.

Breasts so light and fluffy they might have loosened from their moorings and drifted up up up coming to settle against the roof of the car. Though I intended to laugh, I must have betrayed a moment of panic because she reached across the polished mahogany gear stick and took my sweating hand in her cold white palm. 'We just have to do what I always do in these situations.' I didn't have the heart to ask so I just looked at her and smiled as warmly as I could. Though her eyes were wide with worry, her fingertips wrinkled to a hard blue terror. She said quietly and sadly, 'Throw a load of money at it, John, then have a big party.'

Chapter Three

In my early weeks in Wychwood I was both intensely excited and constantly alarmed. It was not, at first, the burning village that troubled me: I feared picking Jewels up and I feared putting her down. The pink heat of her shocked me, as did her bird-like snappable bones. I dreaded choking if I fed her, and starvation if I did not. The shrill wailing scratched at my very soul, but the absence of it sent me racing to shake her awake in case she had expired in the crib. I was a wreck.

Worse, I had correctly assessed the End on that night we arrived: it was ancient, dark, damp and dangerous. But it was not, I sensed, a long-abandoned wreck, though in places it still snowed, though we were inside. Blizzard flurry had fallen through the roof and lay heaped like meringue on stairs, the tops of wardrobes, mantelpieces. Skeins of cobwebs hung like old wool along the skirting. There was electricity but it only served to illuminate the cold, and crackle a harsh cobalt wash over the cracks in the walls, and the ancient flies entombed in the bowled light-shades. Crusts of sauces were cracked in pats on the icy kitchen floor – still bright as if recently spilt. In the vast empty living room a bird's nest had shattered down the chimney leaving an explosion of shitty mud, twigs, leaves and feathers. There was no central heating when we first moved in. The weedy fires we made coughed smoke roomwards in rapid clouds. The heavy doors were painted a violent purple and in each lock was a large black key. The carpets were a threadbare riot of stained floral swirls. The furniture smelt as though it had just been dug up from underground. In the laundry room a twin tub rusted beneath the choke of bubbling damp. And in that corroded tub, on my third day there, I found several cold items of female underwear. Knickers, cheap but fashionable, distinctly modern. On the vast iron range, the open oven door revealed a scatter of droppings amidst the crumbs. On the scorched oak kitchen surfaces a few black hairs curled. It was not possible to say if these were of human or animal origin. But I sensed whoever had once lived in Long Meadow End, whatever woman, had not long ago left.

From the back rooms of Long Meadow End could be seen a sizeable garden. Wide soily borders marked each edge. Once heavy-headed roses would have thorned up through the weeds. There were four high elms and a weeping willow. Wintering in spikes and spines a line of gnarled gooseberry brushes ran down to the right of the lawn towards a distant sea of choppy fields. Beyond were tiny trees dense and green as broccoli. Despite her interest in the garden at Long Meadow End Miss Moore did not go outdoors. She refused to do anything but gaze from the window. Thrilled, I watched her watching. Frequently her stare suggested that something was trying to climb out of the earth and speak to her. At first I imagined her staring on darkness as a display of raunchy misery, but I came to realise that Miss Moore really did see all kinds of wonders out there.

Long Meadow End was also more of a farm than I had expected. Behind the house and to the left of the orchard, stood a barn, a row of straw-strewn stables, several blocks of dusty pens, a rusted tractor, harvester, and buckets, wheels, ropes and stinky wads of sodden hay. There were three collapsed sheds closest to the house containing five rusted bicycles, a climbing frame, the dismantled bones of a swing set, several blackened skipping ropes and at least ten pairs of rotting little shoes – modern shoes, not antique.

In the derelict stables I found time-smoothed tyres hooked over the saddle racks. Heavy rolls of dusty carpet looped over the hoof-marked stone floor. Two squat electric fires rusted like little dogs and three single beds were upended like big soft graves against the cobwebbed wall. Sallow light came in through a narrow window dappled with dirt. The radiance made shade by pale-yellow ivy. The disquieting sensation I'd had upon first entering the house came more strongly; despite the squalor inside and out I felt certain that the previous occupants of Long Meadow End had just left. There was a faint sweet smell, which reddened the musty air. Sweet, sticky, intimate odours that pressed up against you like strange skins.

Yet despite my enthusiastic retelling of such wonders in the farmyard Miss Moore did not want to go and explore. 'No, darling, I couldn't possibly, no, you go. You take Mouse and Jewels. I'd better stay indoors. Just to be safe. I have to rest after all.'

It was noticeable to me, but not deeply troubling, that Miss Moore took little interest in the children in those first few days. I excused her distance by thinking it was because she was rich, busy, tired and celebrated. I too had discovered childcare was largely tedious. My own mother had also found many better things to do with her time. I decided Miss Moore's wild aura of weary mystery was just a way of concealing that she was a regular lazybones.

So, the children were entirely my responsibility. Wildly Mouse ran through that strange grass like a rodent. I encouraged him to exercise, for I hoped activity might calm him and allow me to wean him off the drugs. Each morning I stood with Jewels in my arms and watched Mouse racing through the heavy sleet, cheering his wild kicks and turns. I began to feel a kind of pride whenever the boy ran faster or leapt higher than before. Despite his odd reserve I liked the kid, and would be sorry when he left. He had told me that he wouldn't be in England much longer: his mother would soon be coming from America to collect him. He might only be with me a few days more.

Though the poor drugged boy was indeed peculiar, often stern and glassy-eyed, I was pleased to discover a dark sense of humour. One morning in that first week Mouse and I wandered into the living room to find Miss Moore wearing a tiny sequinned minidress and a pair of enormous glittering earrings. The boy raised his hands to his face in imitation of childish excitement and cried, 'Gee, Pop, who put up the Christmas tree?'

'Look!' Miss Moore exclaimed as our gazes met late one night, phantomed in the dark glass of the window. 'Long Meadow End is perfectly in line with those lights up there on the hill. Isn't that funny, John?'

She gave me that familiar haunted look, the one that suggested she knew exactly the answer to the question. Still,

I was excited that she was a famous beauty and she was asking my opinion. As I stared harder I could see the precise point where Miss Moore was looking. Far away at the top of the meadow, which extended from the end of our garden for perhaps a mile, was a bar of light, a long oblong of flickering, made tiny by our distance, but still a terrific, unavoidable glow of cerulean blue.

'What is it?' I asked.

'You tell me, John.'

'Perhaps it's a factory.'

'Hmm. But isn't it a bit late for a factory?' she said, and began to bite her lip anxiously.

'A poultry unit. With night workers.'

'Yes, I agree. I think that's exactly correct.'

And she continued to stare at the lights, transfixed until late on in the evening. Over the next few months I realised that Brian was right when he said my employer was served in her lonely observances by a keen eye and vividly dark imagination. Just by looking out from indoors she had already discerned a lily pond in a thick patch of shadowy grass, an antique wooden kissing gate leading on to the grassland on the right, and several of Wychwood's most notorious former lovers walking arm in arm, touching cheek to cheek, biting, kissing, scratching, spitting, stroking, struggling under the cover of leaves.

Somehow around my excitement and unease we settled in. Jewels continued to breathe. Mouse did not overdose. Life went on – in what, I imagined, passed as normal for Miss Misty Moore.

I have been asked so often in the last ten years about what Miss Moore wore, how she lived from day to day, the casual things she said, and particularly about the exact nature of the endless luxuries she owned. How she spent her millions (rumours of her wealth fattened year on year). I will try to provide some of these exciting details, though I should admit that I am not a man of the greatest observational powers when it comes to the tiny details of female clothing, shopping or hairdressing. And also, much more importantly, the truth is that what she owned, and what she said, revealed least of all about Misty Moore. It was rather what she didn't have, and what she didn't say, that defined, and ultimately destroyed, her.

'So tell me what is happening?' Misty would gallop towards Brian.

I would be standing there holding the baby, red-eyed with exhaustion, every muscle in my body aching, smiling like a gargoyle, a dribble of sick down my shirt. We had been in Wychwood about a week. Miss Moore would circle Brian begging for news of life in London, as though the place were now a thousand miles away over stormy oceans. I still adored being around her but so unpredictable did she seem by the end of that first week that I began to wonder if it was the time of the month and she was bleeding.

'Nothing at all now you've gone,' our flamboyant, fashionable friend replied, twirling his slim, tall, beautiful pal round like he was her handsome dancing partner and their ballroom was the entire wintered world.

'Really? Has the news stopped utterly?'

Mouse watched us from the side of the room – his back pressed up against the cold wall. Often in those early days he seemed to wonder who we adults were – if perhaps we were all visions from an awful dream. I wanted to reassure the boy, but found it hard to know what to say of any comfort. 'What do you call Miss Moore?' I'd asked him. 'Do you call her Misty?' He shook his head vigorously. 'Do you call her Miss Moore?' Again he shook his head. 'Do you call her Mummy?' I asked hesitantly, and the boy let out a long laugh and said, 'Hello! That's totally a joke, right?' There had still been no news from his mother or father, and neither Miss Moore nor Brian seemed particularly concerned about resolving the situation, though Mouse had not been well. Sometimes, for no apparent reason, he shouted and kicked the walls.

At night things were worse for us all. I was awake for much of the night with Jewels and consequently exhausted. I'd been shocked to discover that it was expected I'd look after the children not only through the day but through the night also – Hepsie Vine had not informed me that this would be the case. It was outrageous to me that it was felt appropriate for a nineteen-year-old man to care for both a newborn baby and a disturbed seven-year-old through a long country night – every night.

Despite my best attempts at reason and comfort the boy seemed to sleep very little. As the baby whimpered in the crib by my bed and I lay imagining Hepsie, Mouse's melancholy sobs dampened the air. I heard him rising often to patter to the kitchen for milk, or furtively to carry a damp bundle of sheets down the long passageway to the laundry room. Bed-wetting was one of the effects of his anxiety, insomnia one of the side effects of the cure. Confusion was surely the root of it all. This saddened me, for I liked the boy. Mouse had been told even less than me about Wychwood or why we were staying at Long Meadow End.

'Is that guy, like, her new boyfriend?' he asked me one day.

'Brian? Oh no, he's just her friend.'

'Sure,' he laughed, 'he looks like a totally friendly guy, right!'

'Your dad was her boyfriend, wasn't he? And that's why you came to England. They were going to get married, Brian said.'

'Sure, and then my dad woke up.'

'I guess it's always hard when a new baby comes. Perhaps the idea of having two kids, you and Jewels, meant your dad . . .'

'But my dad's not Jewels' dad.'

'No? Oh.'

'No way.'

'So who is Jewels' dad?'

'Some other sucker, I guess,' he shrugged.

It felt good to have some information and I decided, with a tabloidy thrill, that Miss Moore and Mouse's father must have parted when she became pregnant by another man.

'How's it going at school?' I asked next, for I feared talking about the boy's parents was wandering into inappropriate areas.

'OK,' he said, itching at his balaclava as he did when particularly uneasy.

I knew that, as the new boy, Mouse was being bullied, and he was under pressure to swap his medication with older boys in exchange for compact discs and new trainers. Brian told me that in Wychwood boys as young as ten had been found stoned on horse steroids.

'You'd tell me if there was anything wrong,' I continued, and Mouse said nothing, turning away instead to watch the distracting pantomime of Brian and Miss Moore.

'Oh yes, toots, all the showbiz rags are printed with

blank pages now, because there's nothing to write about,' Brian said. He looked at Mouse and me, winked, then stared upon us a few seconds longer.

I really couldn't tell whether Brian loathed or loved me. I felt rather embarrassed for him, that this was his *life*, just making sure he kept the ball of her ego in the air, up up up endlessly. Who was this guy who popped in and out of our lives as smoothly as if he lived next door? Why hadn't he told me that Jewels and Mouse had different fathers? At first I thought it was a mark of loyalty that Brian was willing to drive the 200 miles from London to Wychwood several times a week. Of course I now know that Brian had devoted himself to those months for his own reasons, and the long drive, day or night, was in fact the very least of his challenges.

'Oh really darling? Is that truly true?'

'Absolutely. And all the magazines are half their former size.'

That night Miss Moore and I were together in the sitting room. It was both tremendously stirring and rather embarrassing to be alone, relaxing, with her. Miss Moore was sunk into her seat staring at the smoky fire, lost in deep thought.

Casually, to make conversation, I said to Miss Moore, 'Will Jewels be seeing her father?'

'Her father?' Miss Moore exclaimed, jumping out of her seat in alarm. 'Her father? When? How do you know her father?'

'No, no, I just wondered if he'd be around while she grows up.'

Miss Moore was standing up glaring at me, wringing her hands in alarm. 'Christ, I hope not!' she exclaimed.

43

'I'm sorry, it's really none of my business. I shouldn't have asked.'

'Heavens, for a moment I thought you meant you'd *seen* her father. You nearly gave me a heart attack.'

And she left the room quickly and I didn't see her for the rest of the evening.

'But does anyone in London really know I'm gone?' Misty begged Brian the next day, shivering in the warm living room.

'Honey,' Brian cried, 'they've declared a month of mourning from Hackney to Haringey.'

'Just a month!' she exclaimed, snapping her muscled arms akimbo in mock-fishwifery.

She towered there over us men like a statue (I have since thought on several occasions that perhaps there was nothing more to Misty Moore in 200 – than the simple fact of being very tall in an age that set great store by height). That morning she had bumped into me as she came rushing into the kitchen. All day I had been stained with the bright touch of her, marked by the moment as indelibly as if I'd stumbled up against a wall of wet red paint.

'No! Two months. Three!'

'It's true, I'm over!' she giggled madly, falling face down on the newly delivered Italian-designed sofa, which was still swagged with plastic. 'Oh Brian, drive me to London for lunch.'

I loved it when she laughed and all her curves quivered like a jelly in a storm. Even Mouse would look directly at her, open-mouthed, and often that silent amazement – astonished shock at the situation he had fallen into – spoke for us all.

44

'You know I can't do that, toots, you're *resting*. You have to stay here.'

'Aaaah!'

'What if someone were to see you? It would surely start a *stampede*.'

In response to the madness Brian arrived every morning, not only with an armful of clothes but with a new selection of oils, scents, candles, lotions, crystals, herbs and 'oh everything' that might ensure Misty did not need to feel part of the mortal world. And in turn at first she determined to be cheered by the dresses and magazines and photos and jokes that Brian brought for her, and his total unwillingness to admit to anything serious or sad in the world. I assumed she adored him. And that they had been friends for ever and ever. There was definitely a deep bond between them. They seemed so entwined in something urgent that I didn't like to ask for help with the baby, or even mention too much about Jewels. I struggled on, alone, with just Mouse's skulking slack-jawed silence and occasional witty comment for company. I think now I ignored everything because I was both nervous and conceited. I preferred the security of deferring to those richer, wittier and prettier than myself to the work of figuring it out alone.

A typical morning in late winter 200 – would go like this: after Miss Moore had done her morning exercises and meditations alone on the second floor, she and Brian would move along to the first-floor room across from the nursery, which she had designated as a dressing room. There the model millionairess and her fashion adviser would choose an outfit for the day. It seemed that even if Miss Moore was not to go out of the house for the entire daylight hours it was still vital she appeared the perfect cover girl. And I learnt on those bleached winter mornings, as the rain fell as iron tacks from a metal sky, and the baby mewled wetly on my shoulder, and Mouse dizzied around us in his balaclava, how a career could rise or fall simply because of the way you do up your jeans (consider badges, paper clips). Or how effectively you accessorise (try a magpie feather in a beret, a piece of genuine rat bone worn as a necklace, a scrap of vole pelt stitched to a lapel), and crucially how kookily you combine designer chic with the charity-shop tat that Brian called vintage.

'Did you hear that, sweet John?' Miss Moore laughed one day, patting me on the bottom as I passed by with a basket of laundry. 'Don't you dare ever, ever, wear vintage from a decade you actually lived through.'

Though I had both children with me she didn't meet their eyes but instead returned my adoring smile with that look – an empty stare that acknowledged how ridiculous – how humiliated! – she and this cabaret she called a life truly were. When she did gaze at the children, her incredulous stare indicated I had a newborn unicorn slung over my shoulder, and a dazed troll clinging to my thigh.

Then suddenly she began to speak about her career. 'I thought I'd become a dancer when I was a very little girl,' she'd said.

'Was it the tutus that appealed to you?' I'd smiled.

'It was the adventure. It was the travelling to Russia and Africa and . . .'

'But I always longed to be a traveller too!' I cried. 'I guess that's why I'm here with you.'

'When I was in ballet school years later I did an exchange with the Bolshoi.'

She twirled then around the room and extended that impossibly long leg high up on to the window sill so the thin bone stretched like a great white wing. Mouse began to shake his head and whistle long and low. It was hard to tell if he was impressed or appalled by the performance. Lick me, that's what the leg said to me, or stroke me, gently, higher and higher. I could see a tight white gusset.

'You danced with the Bolshoi!' I'd exclaimed, a round of applause in my eyes. 'They are simply the most beautiful dancers in the world.'

'Oh yes, aren't they?' she'd said, lowering the long lean bone and biting her pearly lip, her blue eyes sparkling. 'And beauty, and elegance and poise have always been something most important to me.'

I had, of course, only half believed her, and of course I'd never seen the Bolshoi dance, but more importantly I had wanted to believe her. Safety and warmth flooded over me. Self-obsession didn't bother me. She had danced with the Bolshoi and I, John Parks of Tunbridge Wells, failed romantic, aspiring writer, sandwich-shop assistant, BA Land Management drop-out, was now a gypsy lover sprung from the soil of old Europe. Friend of beautiful ballet dancers. I believed her lies, and added a few of my own. And because we both wanted to believe we were wonderful, briefly it had been so. Both of us. Us! Beautiful, young, handsome, rich people had rejoiced at the fortunate turn of events that had brought the two of us together. Me and this beautiful woman, this creature with the jelly wobble who looked good in all the right places, and had posed professionally for photographs with her vagina spread between her fingertips, and was a soft, kind ballet dancer.

'She danced with the Bolshoi,' I said to Mouse that evening. 'Isn't that something?'

'Sure.'

'It's true,' I smiled. 'Isn't it fantastic?'

'Right. But I've never seen a ballet dancer with tits like that before, have you?'

'She's a mother now. She's changed,' I replied firmly.

'No kidding. She's totally the weirdest mom I've ever met.'

'Do you know exactly when your mum's coming for you?'

'My dad left my mom and took me with him. So mom thinks I'm with my dad. But I guess now my dad thinks I'm with my mom. I think I was meant to go back to my mom when my dad went off. She'll be coming soon. As soon as she finds out where I am,' he said, and wandered off, shaking his head, into a cold dark corner of the house.

'It's going to be just fine,' I said to Brian one day that first week, exhaling with a long smiling sigh. 'The six months here will be great fun, I think.'

'Oh sure, it's a great village,' he enthused, with a now familiar edge of malice. 'So much to do. So many great people to meet.'

'Well, it's certainly memorable,' I laughed. 'I'm having the time of my life.'

Sex was slobbering around the room like a wet dog. Brian was of average height and slender-hipped but muscular, particularly around the shoulders and arms. He glistened as though his entire black body had just been buttered. Though I was the bigger in height and build, he was the more powerful – the prowling confidence with which he possessed the chair, the panther's spread of his athletic limbs at rest.

'Oh yeah. You'd come here if you had only six months to live, wouldn't you?' he said, turning to me with that high cruel chortle. 'Because six months here is gonna feel like six years.'

And off he went laughing at his own nasty joke. I admit I'd sensed there was a connection between his instinctive viciousness and his devoted friendship with my boss. I too had felt the buzz of that brutal curiosity – did we want to know her intimately just so we could expose her? Then hurt her?

But if I'd hoped for clues to our adventure in the press I was disappointed. I read nothing about Miss Moore for we took no papers (Brian said that Miss Moore had decided no longer to read about herself after she'd linked her daily vomiting with the arrival of the morning rags), and the days when she featured regularly on the TV or radio had long passed. If throughout the land newsvendors were singing out the name of Jewels Moore I'd not have known about it.

Around this time Mouse took to calling me Mummyman.

'How should we stop Jewels' crying?' I'd asked him one day when I was particularly desperate.

The boy had looked at me blankly for some time.

'Gee, don't ask me, you're the mummy, man,' he replied eventually.

And from there the name had stuck. 'Hey, Mummyman,' he'd shout out in the night, 'the baby's crying,' or, 'Mummyman, chill!' if I became particularly frustrated with my duties. 'You know, Mummyman,' he said on one occasion during the second week, 'you're worrying too much about the cooking. Remember none of us really likes eating.' I had discovered that meal preparation, not only for the children but for Miss Moore too, was to be another of my duties. Preparing the menus for the day caused me considerable stress. 'She only eats warm vegetables and a few torn leaves. It's no worse than looking after a sick rabbit. Relax, Mummyman, you're doing fine.'

'I'm sure I don't match up to Hepsie. I bet she was a brilliant nanny,' I sighed, as I baked another potato.

'Well, she can't have been that hot, can she?' he replied. 'Or I guess she'd still be here, right?'

'How did you get along with Hepsie?'

'I never met her, did I?' he said. Immediately I believed the boy was lying. I shook my head and let it go. I assumed Hepsie had been Mouse's nanny, that this was the job she had done for Miss Moore. 'Though I've heard them talking about her, sure.'

'What have you heard about Hepsie?'

He shrugged. 'That she got herself into some kind of trouble.'

'What kind of trouble? Tell me.'

'Man trouble, I guess. For a cute girl what other kind of trouble is there?'

'If you never met her how do you know she's cute?'

'I saw pictures. Brian brought round a whole lot of photographs of her for Miss Moore.'

'I think things will be better when we get the central heating in,' I said to Brian, after Miss Moore had seemed particularly unsettled and Jewels too had been whimpering through the night.

'Now just because our lady is shaking, John, doesn't mean she's cold,' he replied with that now familiar ugly smile.

He was teasing me. It worked. I longed to know more, and my craving united Brian and me in something exciting and dangerous.

Brian flirted with me relentlessly in those early days and seemed thrilled by my appalled nervousness in his presence. 'Nice trousers, Johnny boy,' he'd said on my first day in Long Meadow End.

'Thanks,' I muttered, turning away to busy myself with Jewels.

'Now do you mind if I test the zipper?'

By the beginning of the second week, when the snow had stopped, I ventured out with Mouse and Jewels beyond the house and garden. We went towards the village. I felt light and happy. There was an icy blue sky and a lacy day moon above. I wanted to give Mouse a sunlit English childhood of the kind I had enjoyed. And I liked pushing the expensive three-wheeler pram. I hoped my charges would thrive on fresh country air. But I was surprised to find, when the blizzard calmed, that Wychwood was not a pretty York-shire village. I was keen to explore and wandered for some time around the village.

It was a surprising choice for a therapeutic retreat from the metropolis. For though the place was indeed remote, the land was dull and flat, the village shabby and sparsely populated. The central bus stop, where no buses now stopped, was a dirty concrete cube. The children's play-ground was flaked and rusted, the grass a muddy patch. There was no post office, surgery or any other public service. Twisted cars speared upended from verges. Fre-quently the most recently mangled village boys were re-membered by forlorn bouquets circling trees and lampposts. There was a small estate of council housing on the northern side of the village; otherwise there was just a scatter of very ordinary grey cottages, some obviously abandoned. It was definitely not a place that attracted second-home owners or affluent commuters – in fact the unavoidable truth was that, just as Brian had predicted, this was the kind of English village you stayed in only if you couldn't get away.

Chapter Four

Days passed and I got used to our strange location. Though the windy drizzle muzzled at our faces like sneezes Mouse and I soon took pleasure in walking wildly into the Wychwood fields. There the winter sun knifed over the black branches and fell to gloss the mud with a rich teapot-brown. Those winter afternoons the Wychwood sky glowed as polished iron, rising some days to that magnificent brittle pink-blue of thistle whiskers. I'd noticed this mundane village often seemed totally to change colour. In fog it was lilac as a young plum with a misted breath of pearl on top, in sun a sudden Mediterranean white, in rain this iron purple-blue.

Maybe sex and nature were enough for me. Perhaps I didn't need to be an artist; if I could have my pick of pretty young women and a few good walks maybe it was possible I'd be happy in life.

On the day in question Mouse and I had been walking back home to Wychwood when, because a black-and-white dog, brilliant as a zebra, crossed our path and vanished up a hill, I agreed that we could prolong our outing and take a longer walk. The two of us were alone for, to my surprise and great relief, Miss Moore had, for the first time, requested a private hour with her daughter. Now that we took regular walks the boy was far less anxious outdoors. His frequent tendency to kick and scream when panicked greatly lessened. Usually we talked about dogs – 'what breed could definitely kill a guy' – but that day he spoke gently about his mother. 'She's gonna get a lawyer, Mummyman,' he said. His little hands were clenched into pumping fists. 'Then she's gonna come to England and get me back real soon.'

'You must be missing her. And your dad.'

'I sure am. It's been a long time. I'm starting to totally not remember what they look like.'

'I bet they're missing you too.'

'Wonder why it's taking her so long to find me then.' I could not think what to say. 'Well, I won't be here much longer now. Probably just another week.'

I didn't like to press him for fear of worsening a wound, so instead we chatted once more about nature, weather and dogs and, even if our communication was not exactly fluent, there was a manly pact to our silences.

I remember I was preoccupied that morning because we'd just had an obscene postcard delivered. It was postmarked London. On the front was a beaming picture of angelic Princess Di, complete with pearly teeth and a tiara. The insults were written in green ink. After a string of pornographic invective it said, 'Now why don't you piss off, you thick bitch!'

'Don't worry about it,' I'd said to Miss Moore, when I found her alone in the sitting room staring at the postcard. 'It's just some creep who wants to imagine he knows you.'

'Knows me!' she cried. 'I want to know me!' and with

that she ran off to the dressing room where Brian was insisting she try on a new winter fur bikini.

Mouse and I walked on, across the vivid village green, perfect as an emerald pool, past Wychwood's only, and seemingly empty, pub, the Lion, and further up past Mouse's small Victorian school at the northern edge of the village. I felt alert and energised. The country air was rich and smoky as though every one of the Wychwooders had cooked their lunch by barbecue. That day Wychwood's roads, roofs, trees, sky all dripped with the same sealy glisten. After the snow it had rained for a week, and the elderly villagers, if any did dare leave their low cottages, scuttled beneath the shiny black shells of their umbrellas.

We did see a few children as we walked, raggedy kids who sniggered as they eyed us. No tractors, cattle lorries or feed tankers passed us by. What did people do in Wychwood? The European Union must demand they dig up their fields at midnight and be gone back to their burrows by morning. The black-and-white dog crossed our path again. I agreed that we could follow it a little further, though we had to return before the onset of evening because out there in the wintery Yorkshire countryside night came like a sudden spill of ink around 4 p.m., tipping everything instantly into darkness.

Still, Mouse and I casually wandered up a steep hill. Overhead a crow cawed. A rustle and a snap led to a gentle falling of dark twigs. In a moment we were walking on the edge of evening in hazy air. We were on a deserted farm track. We said nothing – rather a relief after Misty and Brian's endless chatter – but when I pressed my fingertips against a holly thorn I remembered the leaf in Hepsie's hair. And then a dream from the night before: Misty standing out

55

in the front garden in a patch of cerise stalks. She was slender and wan as a candle and the February cold seemed to have frosted her with an angelic glow. Wearing only her silken nightdress and drawing on a cigarette she kept a ghostly guard over our sleep.

Soon we rounded a corner from where, in the distance, we could see two women talking. The first of the females had a blaze of black hair. The second clutched to her chest a snake-print scarf, which squirmed against her large breasts. I recognised that way of looking down at the earth as if some serpent were slithering around her feet. Her cheeks were sore with the harsh slap of make-up. Her lips swollen to stings. My heart raced. Her eyes were heavy behind dark rings, which I first thought were sunglasses but then noticed were the natural shadows of sleeplessness. Was she weeping? From a distance she seemed spectacularly thin, like she'd not eaten this century. Her bones seemed on the outside like scaffolding. It was beauty, sure, but it was also like her face had been hit over and over with a wooden stick. The look stirred a feeling I'd had about Wychwood since we first arrived: a feeling half of fearful discontent and half of visceral intoxication.

'Freaky, Mummyman! That's Misty,' Mouse said. 'And Jewels.'

'Is she crying?'

'Is the lady taking her medication?' Mouse had asked me only that morning. I too had been troubled by Miss Moore's behaviour; again she seemed anxious and distracted, but most of all, sad. 'Or perhaps it's wearing off?'

I could not imagine why she was taking things so hard. Years later when I discovered a little more about women I imagined that they liked my emotional ignorance, for it allowed them to keep all their secrets. It's the reason why nowadays the papers are right: my romantic history is a lurid catalogue of liars, cheats, fantasists and basket cases, and I have no one to blame but myself.

'Look, Mummyman,' Mouse had said quietly, taking my fingers in his cold white palm, 'you have to make sure the lady takes her pills. She's not doing too great. She feels kinda frightened. I know.'

I understood what the boy meant. But I could pretend to Mouse and myself that Miss Moore was anxious about the malicious phone calls, or the hate mail. Or that the object of her unease was a well-known female journalist who had visited us the week before and then written a witty article about Miss Moore's diet, weight, hair and clothes. 'She's right, of course,' Miss Moore had smiled when she'd read the spiteful article that some 'fan' had posted to her. Miss Moore said some of the information used in the article, attributed to 'a close friend', could only have come from someone who knew her intimately.

'No,' I'd protested, shocked by the ease with which my boss accepted the ferocious insults. 'No, the journalist's just being unkind. She's jealous.'

'No, I agree with everything she says.'

'That's ridiculous.'

'But what she misses,' Miss Moore continued calmly, 'is the truth: I couldn't *do* anything else. Not everyone has the chances those smart, educated, well-loved women have.' And then she gave me and Jewels a steady stare.

Now Miss Moore was walking away from Mouse and me back along the lane. The raven-haired woman remained still. She swept a hand over her forehead as she watched Miss Moore depart. Then she turned and looked directly at us. And I saw the face that had transfixed me a month earlier. This was Hepsie.

And yet it was not Hepsie. This woman was older. Though she had the same ripe lips, the similar neat figure. The same fresh and slender flow as she moved – which commanded that I hung there, spellbound.

Then, the more I looked on the woman's hair, I realised it lacked that rubbed-plum black blush. Instead the colour was the dusty dark of a burnt match. Still I felt emboldened and ultra-alive (I believed then only in the rational and, I'm ashamed to admit, I thought everything shocking that happened to me in my life would be material I could one day use in my painting, writing or movie-making). We walked closer to where the woman waited. This woman seemed small. More imp than the great gazelle who had just escaped along the lane. Before she spoke the woman searched my face very closely as though listening simultaneously to another story my eyes told.

'I'm her mother,' the woman smiled. Then wiped at her cheek, flicking back those black tresses so I could see her striking face more clearly. Despite her obvious poverty and exhaustion her eyes retained an ember of her daughter's flame. 'She's still my little girl. And I miss her terribly.'

'No one told me!' I exclaimed.

The delight must have radiated from every pore, for the woman raised a heavily ringed finger to cork my over-exuberance.

'Just me, my mother and my other children live 'ere,' she said rather sternly. 'We don't even know when Hepsie'll be back. Or if she'll ever come back.'

We followed the woman when she turned and soon we were in a different place where my eyes ached in adjustment to the light. We could see a panorama of fields. There was the thick sizzled scent of smoke still in the air. A singed burn of sunlight on a blasted oak. Mouse trailed behind me beating at the raging nettles with his belt, prodding bubbling cowpats with a stick.

Not far from the boundary of the wood was a gate, behind which another, older woman rested. She too looked like a face from the international news – very poor, even her tears dried up in some recent drought. A row of bright washing danced wildly above, skirts hugged the lines and sleeves slapped at themselves madly. The woman grinned, leaning over the gateway to greet me. She was small too, for her wizened head rose only a short way above the gate. Touching her hand – so tiny, light and deadly dry – was like grasping an autumn leaf.

'Mum, this is John. He's the one down there looking after the baby.'

'Pleased to meet you,' I nodded. 'And this is Mr Mouse.'

'I'm not staying here long,' the boy whispered. 'My mom has a lawyer.'

'Now tell me, is it true she's going all minimalistic?'

'Pardon?'

'In the End. I heard she's having all steel but with ruby-studded bath plugs.'

'This is my mother-in-law, John,' the younger woman continued, 'another Mrs Vine.'

They both had similar freefall hairstyles, though the older woman's hair had died to a long wig of ash and her white cheeks had sunken softly in a poked crater of creases. I was repulsed by them, and surrendered to them simultaneously. They were the roughest women I'd ever been close to.

'Are they trailer trash?' Mouse said, widening his eyes at the sight.

Behind the gate there was a yard and two long modern caravans, which might more accurately be described as large mobile homes. They were oddly familiar, as though I'd recently dreamt this scene. The black-and-white sheepdog we had seen earlier stood sentinel by the door of the nearest caravan, smiling at us through fangs.

'Where's Miss Moore gone?' I asked politely. There was no reply. 'I just wondered what she was doing out here with the baby.'

'Oh just taking a walk,' the grandmother replied.

'That's odd. She doesn't usually like to go outside.'

'Is that right?' the younger Mrs Vine said sadly.

'What's happened?' I continued. 'Is she OK? She seemed upset.'

Chickens jabbed in the yard amidst the detritus of coils, tubing, plastic buckets, sacking, sunken bales of sodden straw, barrels and butts, and a mound of manure. Jumbled and chaotic, this was no thriving farm.

'What was wrong with her?' I asked again. 'Where's she gone?'

To the left of the caravans a hulk of heavy machinery rusted under a collapsing shed. In one corner of the yard, as though just flown in from distant graves, was a pile of blind beauties, freckled with lichen, gowns mossy as mountainsides, resting atop one another, breast to throat, cheek to toe.

'Do you still farm?' I asked politely, when I became uneasy with the pair staring pool-deep into my face.

'Nothing to farm,' the older Mrs Vine said. 'We look after the bairns and sell things.'

'Those garden angels, for example,' her daughter said, pointing at the pile of stone statues. 'Stuff like that.'

'We don't like what Hepsie's doing in London,' the grandmother said.

'She thinks she can handle herself, and that she's untouchable.'

'But all pretty girls think that, don't they? Really she's very impressionable.'

'Hepsie's caused our family no end of trouble, John, but we love her dearly. And we want her back.'

But nothing I knew about girls had prepared me for Hepsie Vine, or her mucky family, so I smiled and said nothing. Then as I looked at the caravans a little heart-leap reminded me why the place seemed so familiar: these long windows were the ones we looked up at from Long Meadow End, lit, blazing blue.

'Are they freako twins?' Mouse scowled. 'They're kinda dressed weird.' Indeed on her legs the older woman wore the kind of woollen stockings more often found hanging from mantelpieces on Christmas Eve. 'Tell me,' Mouse shouted, tugging at my sleeve, 'are they, like, you know, white trash?'

'Until today we've not seen her outdoors at all,' the grandmother smiled. 'I imagine she's shy.'

I smiled too, for the old woman seemed to know the story Brian had told me: that Misty Moore was legendary as the woman who once upon a time rode down Oxford Street on an open-top bus at midday in just high heels and a pair of bikini pants, to promote her album: *Topless*. And then complained to the police that she was being stared at.

'I imagine Hepsie told you all about Miss Moore,' I said. I was thrilled just to speak Hepsie's name aloud. 'She seemed very excited to be in London. She must have had an amazing time working for her.'

'Ha,' the mother Mrs Vine said with a little snort.

'Sssh,' the grandmother Mrs Vine replied. 'Yes, she's been very lucky.'

'Look, I'm rather embarrassed to ask this,' I said, stroking my hand over my forehead, 'but do you have an address for her? I'd love to write and . . .' But I stopped suddenly because the women had folded their arms and were pressing their lips in tightly and scowling. 'I'm sure she'll be excellent in the media,' I said instead. 'I thought she was very, very . . . driven. And she obviously wants it enormously. You're lucky to have . . .'

'Oh there's not just Hepsie, we have six of 'em. Hepsie's the eldest – and the most troublesome – then there's Celeste, Isolde, Betsie, Violet and Alice an' all.'

'Oh,' I gasped, and my thoughts fell upon the mound of garden ornaments piled in the yard.

There was nothing welcoming about the complex of caravans. No sweet smoke curled from chimney pots, no candles glowed cosily in the windows, no weary farmer folk tramped home through the distant fields for buttery sustenance. These were not traditional horse-drawn caravans dotted with rustic quilts, embroidered tea-towels, hand-painted furniture, enamelled teapots, yet I still longed to be invited inside. For now that the idea of sex was warm within me there was, I suddenly found, something oddly chic about the gypsyish arrangement of junk and caravans and the dazzling blow of Mrs and Mrs Vine.

'You look tired,' the older woman said.

'I am,' I said, because there was no disagreeing with Wychwood women; I knew that instantly.

'Is she not a good baby?' the younger Mrs Vine asked. 'Doesn't she sleep?'

'The baby wakes us – well, just me actually – three times a night,' I confessed without intending to.

'You probably need help,' the grandmother said consolingly. 'That house once had at least five staff.'

Mouse began to moan and rip at my arm, urging me desperately to leave.

'As soon as we've settled in we'll be having a big housewarming party. I'm sure that Misty'll be inviting everyone. She's an amazing hostess and is terribly keen to . . .' But I stopped speaking then for in my mind I saw that unfortunate alien – my boss, tall, heartbroken, pale and pneumatic, lost in a lane.

They knew what I'd been thinking, for the younger Mrs Vine said, 'Oh and better not to mention that you saw Miss Moore. You know how she is about her privacy.'

I knew then that night was coming because Mrs Vine's black hair had suddenly smoothed into the sky so just her face floated before me pale as a moon-lily. 'She was crying,' I said. 'Is that normal? I mean for someone who's just had a baby.'

Mouse's aching moan seemed not even to be registered by Mrs and Mrs Vine who continued to stare at me calmly; either that or they saw the noise as an appropriate soundtrack to the scene. 'Ah, sometimes,' the younger woman said with disinterest. 'And sometimes not. She has a cold.'

Ha! I wanted to exclaim. Everything was now explained! Your husbands both killed themselves in a field because of debts, your divine young daughter takes drugs to get into TV and interplanetary Misty Moore weeps on a farm track because she has a cold. Nothing more to report.

But my tremble must have translated to a sneer or a smirk because Hepsie's mother continued sternly, 'She has a cold because she was out in the garden last night only wearing her nightie.'

'We saw her,' the older woman said with a sad shake of the head. 'From the window of the caravan.'

'Poor woman,' Mrs Vine younger said. 'She's more unhappy than people realise.'

'She doesn't get any help from Jewels' father. And she has the abandoned Mouse to care for too,' I said. 'And she hardly eats anything. She doesn't seem to have any friends except Brian. No one ever calls us or cares to ask how she's doing.'

'From what I can see I don't think she's coping, John,' the Vine grandmother added gently.

And when I turned around it was true that from up here you could see the whole dismal village of Wychwood laid out as if in grey Lego. Particularly you could see the three elms and the weeping willow, which stood in our rear garden. You could run down to us barefoot in one ecstatic sweep. And yes, beyond the trees you could see the high window of the attic in which Misty Moore slept. Yes, you could see everything that happened down in Long Meadow End most clearly. Even the things that happened in our dreams.

'You were watching us?' I said quietly, turning to look back at the caravans, for I'd felt a prickle of many eyes on me.

Chapter Five

My first serious childcare disaster happened almost straight after I met Mrs and Mrs Vine. Early on into my contract. I remember the date exactly: Saturday 9 February, the time 4.16 p.m. It was almost dark. I was in the driveway of Long Meadow End. I was still pleased to be working for Miss Moore, delighted to have a front-row seat at her mysterious show, but I was also becoming increasingly anxious. I had that feeling constantly of being watched, as though there were faces in the tree trunks, whispers in the leaves. Was Miss Moore watching me sternly from a high dusty window? Was her pretty face mottled to a sinister frown by the dusty ancient glass? Yes, I had that familiar peeping feeling that never left me in Wychwood: I was being spied on. Eyes were on me. If I turned quickly I might catch them dashing back under the ferns.

I had just driven home from the supermarket and was standing with Mouse, close by the car. The boy was cold and I had to get him inside. I was tired, wrecked, from another night of sleeplessness, and a day of nerve-jangling childcare. Even at the weekends I did not get a day off.

There had been no news from Mouse's parents. Or Jewels' father. Our only friend was Brian.

Mouse was shivering in the wintery dark. Jewels was awake and alert in the back seat. The weather rocked at the low yellow car like a hooligan. The boot was stuffed with the slim blocks of ready meals, which now formed our entire diet. There was an icy wind, and a flurry of snow whirled in the darkening air.

Foggily I was thinking of how I had to get Mouse out of the cold, and how hard it would be to carry both the baby and the shopping into the house. I decided to take Mouse and the shopping in first, and then come back for the baby. She would be happier in her car seat than without me in the strange cold house. To protect her from the icy weather I closed the car door. I began to take the shopping bags from the boot. By the time the boot was closed and the shopping on the driveway, and shivering Mouse was at my side preparing to help carry the bags inside, Jewels was crying.

'What you gonna do, Mummyman?' Mouse asked, then looked at me and rolled his eyes, aiming for a comic lightness of touch.

I knew Mouse felt it was alarming that I was in charge of the baby. Though kindly he did not voice his concern often, perhaps hoping against hope that I was not the man I appeared to be.

Seeing Jewels weeping, I remembered Hepsie's look of sudden despair in the pink-bloomed living room that Christmassy day, when she had spoken of her career in TV. I saw again the slow seeping of tears begin to fall from her enchanting eyes and the tree lights blur her perfect ashen skin to a wet city at night: a haze of red, orange, yellow, blue.

'TV! I mean,' I'd stuttered as I gazed upon her, 'it's what . . .'

'Everyone wants to do?'

'Yes.'

'Hmm, it does seem to be, doesn't it?' she cried. 'And I want it too. Yes! If my life's to have any value I simply must make this work.' And then she began to sob.

I did not know what to do with the now screaming Jewels. Mouse was right: when the baby howled I felt helpless and exposed. Partly because I was a useless male and partly because I was feeling Jewels' sorrow more each day.

'I'll give her the keys to play with,' I said to Mouse, hoping I was not betraying to the boy my feelings of bleakness.

Decisively I opened the door and placed the keys on the child's lap. She quietened immediately as she began to stroke her fingers over the keys. She began a facial squirm that I could interpret as a smile. I closed the door. It continued to snow. I allowed myself a sigh of relief as I began to hurry Mouse along with the shopping.

'Uh oh, no,' Mouse said immediately. 'I think that was, like, a seriously not good idea.'

And when I turned I saw that Jewels had passed her tiny finger over the keypad's sensor and locked all doors from the inside.

'What you gonna do now, Mummyman?' Mouse said, giving me that quizzical look that was without malice but which was most annoying. 'She's like, trapped, inside now, right?'

Hepsie. What would she do?

'Remind me, why are you here?' Hepsie had said to me

suddenly that day we met in the twinkling living room. She was rubbing her fingers into her forehead in a gesture of complete exhaustion.

'To be the nanny,' I'd replied, bewildered.

'A nanny!' she'd said, turning to Brian with an incredulous laugh. 'I thought he was an *au pair*!'

'What's the difference between a nanny and an au pair, anyway?' I'd smiled.

'About fifty pounds a week. Though I imagine they're both slaves.'

'We must stick together then,' I'd winked at her. 'Form a union.'

Mouse and I tried for some time to encourage the baby to press the button herself and release the locks. But it was fruitless and I could no longer conceal my despair. I kicked the wheels, thumped the felty roof. I hurled insults at the iron clouds.

'I'm gonna smash a window,' I said to Mouse resolutely.

'Right, but you don't want to, like, scar her for life, do you?' Mouse replied. 'That might not go down too well with Mrs Big Tits.'

'Stay there, I'll call the fire brigade,' I replied, and was just dashing inside when a face appeared from the trees, and then another.

They were spectacularly shabby in their hotchpotch of cheap bright clothing. As soon as I saw them I felt certain they had both caused the disaster and would avert it. A stream of dark-haired young girls followed the two women out of the bushes. The girls were all hair and flesh and tinkled so magically with cheap jewellery, necklaces, rings, bangles, bracelets, trinkets, pendants, lockets, ear-hoops, from waists, wrists, necks, toes, fingers and belly buttons that I was sure just a wiggle would charm parrots and penguins from the Wychwood trees.

Once I had seen Celeste, Isolde, Betsie, Violet and Alice, I built a little room in my mind where they lived. I locked and unlocked the door as I wished. I glimpsed them in this sweet room in my psyche whenever I dreamed over the dark garden. I discovered that Celeste, aged fifteen, was well formed, robust and businesslike; Isolde, just thirteen, was serene and love-longing; Betsie, only nine, was a handful, being the one most tainted with her eldest sister's wild beauty; the twins, seven-year-old Violet and Alice – Malice and Violent as they were soon known to Mouse – were rotund, mischievous and boyish. I envied them all their busy, warm, girlish lives. I felt their puppy-soft skin when I touched the chill glass of the window and looked up towards their caravans. Soon I had the idea: women at work were so much stronger, muscular and purposeful than I had imagined and I decided that if I got the time I would make a few sketches of the girls. Perhaps develop the work into a series of paintings with a contemporary theme, for it was soothing to have real people around me, rather than the constant trotting after fripperies that I sometimes feared marked the daily lives of Brian and Miss Moore.

'She's locked in the car,' I said to the younger Mrs Vine. The woman, who, it was still extraordinary to know, was Hepsie's mother, tutted and sighed angrily.

I was suddenly very conscious in front of those women of what I was wearing: the old grey wool jacket that I wore every day during my first couple of months in Long Meadow End. It was an oversized men's suit jacket from the 1950s, bought during my first, and only, year at university from a charity shop. I imagined it gave me the shabby yet suave air of the hawk-eyed, non-materialistic, relaxed young artist. My mother hated it. My father laughed at it. In the mildewed pocket I kept rolled cigarettes in a vintage tobacco tin. Stains I liked, and the fact that it smelt of smoke and petrol. Of course now I see quite clearly what my father saw, that my comical attire was a clear marker that I was still just a boy. I was playing, ironically, with the outfit of an adult male, because I was still unwilling and unable to assume the true responsibilities of a well-fitted, newly bought jacket. Everyone saw that but me. Mrs and Mrs Vine knew I was nothing more than a child. The tatty jacket is of importance because I am now convinced that this item ensured that Brian, Misty and the Vines detected no threat in me. They had hired me, not, as Hepsie had pretended, because of my royal good looks, but simply because of my ridiculous jacket! No one could wear such a thing and be anything but a marshmallowhead. Yes, in 200 – I looked exactly like someone who could be easily duped.

'Call Wayne,' the grandmother said to her daughter-in-law. Neither woman addressed me directly that day, but as the seven Vine women peered into the cream leather interior I felt as if every crevice of my soul was being examined by those seven pairs of all-seeing, all-criticising female eyes. Again I remembered beautiful Hepsie Vine. Reclining in the living room of Chessington Vale on that very first day: the smoke, the ruby red. Perhaps all that was missing were horns and a bubble of sulphur.

Then, surely no more than a moment later, a scruffy long-haired teenage male lolloped into the driveway to join our group. Thin, slouched, wolf-like. 'Freaky! This looks like trouble,' I heard Mouse whisper to himself as Mrs and

Mrs Vine explained the situation to the sneering boy, who was shocking ugly and dressed in clothes so dirty and ill-fitting he could have just robbed them from a local scarecrow. This awful village lad who proceeded to fiddle around the door for some time, frowning.

I looked at our watching group. These were Hepsie's people. These were the crazy clan she had meant when she'd spoken last month of homesickness. 'Though I imagine the truth is Mouse's too homesick to eat. Have you ever been that way?' Hepsie had fixed me again with the rearing stare. 'So homesick you think you'll die?' I admitted that I had not, and she'd sighed and turned away again muttering something, which I think was, 'I have.'

Before me Wayne continued to pick at the closed door with his dirty fingernail. He took a handful of metal objects from his pockets and poked them into the lock.

Suddenly, and for the first time, my whole employment by Miss Misty Moore and my incarceration in Wychwood seemed like some hideous mistake. I should have asked someone who knew her before agreeing. There had in fact been the perfect opportunity (though I realise now I had been firmly discouraged the previous month from making any contact with anyone but Brian and Hepsie Vine). When I was leaving Chessington Vale that fantastical December day I had encountered a group of young people standing uneasily in the hall.

'Clare, Alex and Hugo. PA, PR and PT,' Brian said, as he led me through the corridors to the door. 'PT stands for Personal Trainer. I suppose in the olden days it would have been the butler, the housekeeper and the maid.'

'Should I go and say hello?' I'd asked, ever eager to please.

'I wouldn't bother,' Brian said with that annoying little laugh, 'they have all just been sacked.' And then he looked at me with genuine concern as if he needed urgently to see how I would take this news and then added, 'You're her only member of staff now.'

And yes, when I turned back I saw the group of young people had been transformed into weary travellers, suddenly standing by a heap of bulging grey suitcases draped with greyer blankets, their grey packing done hastily, even angrily.

Wayne grunted. To fill the womanly silence that was fattening all around me I turned directly to Mrs and Mrs Vine and said, 'Do you have Hepsie's address? I'd love to know how she's getting on.'

'She's working very hard,' the grandmother said. 'Too hard if you ask me.'

'And I don't think she'd want to be disturbed by you,' the mother added bluntly.

Wayne was nearly done. He bent down with his eye to the keyhole and with one twist he unlocked the golden door swiftly and easily with a piece of bent metal. The alarm on my beautiful yellow car didn't even ring.

'Well done, Wayne,' the grandmother clapped.

'I knew he'd come in useful one day,' her daughter laughed.

Then the creature pawed at his wet nose, was given a few notes from the pocket of the elderly Mrs Vine and was away, carried off, it seemed, on the wind.

'Give her to me,' the grandmother said sharply, as I reached inside the car for the baby.

Without a moment's hesitation at the command I handed little bewildered Jewels to the women. Mouse moved so he was close to my leg, hiding from Mrs and Mrs Vine. Then those veined old hands, streaked with blue like cheese, began to feel the child all over firmly and gently, with fingers obviously expert at handling human young.

'She's fine,' the woman said to her daughter-in-law, 'There's no harm come to her.'

For some time the Vine women passed our baby between them, kissing and nuzzling at her, like she-wolves over a cub. I was alarmed and so began to shower the women with thanks, garbled apologies. I made jokes and tried to laugh the accident off, but there was a burning edge to the women now, which spoke most simply of rage at my failure. And we're talking here about women who, it was quite obvious, had long ago stopped expecting much of men.

'It's amazing how quick they got there,' I said to Brian that night.

We had not expected Brian that day, but he'd popped out of the night like a sparkling meteorite, sliding his slim bronzed car to a halt on the driveway gravel with a skid. Something or someone had told him to get in his car and drive 200 miles to see us – and for some reason he did it, as easily as if he'd just had to drop next door for a chat.

'Just don't tell Misty,' Brian sighed. I was about to question him about this when he added, 'We don't want her to think you're incompetent, do we?' Then Brian's face contorted as though he'd just sipped a potion tinged with poison. 'And I don't think she'd like to think Mrs and Mrs had been near her family.'

But then he went on at some length about how women do not trust their own sex. I knew he was talking so much to stop me asking questions, but I didn't have the strength to protest. Brian chatted on about how women flaunt their sexuality, their youth and beauty not for men, but just to show their advantage over other women.

I pictured Hepsie. Her twisting curves. And how the more I'd stared on her that first day the more I felt sure she'd been sacked by Miss Moore. For she had beneath her burning ambition that druggy wariness, hopelessness and despair. And a heavy daze alternating between sleepiness and panic.

'Did Miss Moore get rid of Hepsie Vine?' I asked. 'What did she do wrong?'

But Brian was continuing, saying how women would all rather work for men, and have men work for them. This was the reason why Miss Moore wanted a male nanny. 'And of course why Hepsie wanted you too, John,' he laughed. 'Women scare women,' he said very seriously.

The way he looked at me made me uneasy. Though I understood that it must be humiliating to pass the days as little more than the stroker of a rich woman's ego, Brian seemed unnecessarily unkind. My parents would hate Brian, I knew that for certain. Not even because he was black and gay, but because he was rude and hungry. And he was one of the new sorts of people who relied on no one, and wanted nothing for the world but the fulfilment of their own desires, and who had no time for anything that did not propel them towards ultimate triumph.

'Whereas all the men I know will always put another man above a woman. Look at team sports, for example. What top-ranking female team sports are there? See! It would be impossible. And can you imagine forty thousand women cheering on a team of eleven women? Ha, I don't think so! No! Women neither like one another nor trust one another enough to be in a team. And if they were they definitely wouldn't have any supporters, would they?'

Brian was looking at me very seriously, as though there was a deeper meaning hidden in his words. It was not a reassuring look. He had carried on in this vein for a while, as we walked to and fro licked by those red-hot screams. Though it was a cliché to recognise it, I could not avoid the knowledge that, whatever the purpose of this tale, Brian was a woman-hater. Everything he said was brilliant misogyny and it made me fearful for Miss Moore.

Chapter Six

Hepsie Vine only ever telephoned me on four occasions at Long Meadow End and the first was Sunday 10 February, the time 6.08 a.m. I was sure that she did not intend to get me, but I was the one staggering through the icy farmhouse rocking a restless baby, so it was I who picked up the telephone.

'I'm so glad to speak to you,' Hepsie said quietly after we had stumbled through the usual nervous pleasantries.

She sounded flat and weary. I feared she was going to mention the disaster in the car. On Brian's advice I had told Miss Moore nothing about what happened, partly because I did not want to mention Mrs and Mrs Vine, but also because I feared exposing my ineptitude. I was pleased to discover that Mouse had not mentioned the odd crisis, and particularly its resolution, to anyone either. 'You're a numbskull, Mummyman, but you're all I've got,' he'd told me with a shrug. In turn I'd said nothing to Miss Moore about the boy's continuing bed-wetting and night-waking. 'If you tell them I'll have to go back to the doctor, and I don't want to take any more pills,' he'd told me calmly.

'I've been thinking about you and the kids endlessly,'

76

Hepsie whispered. 'I wanted to call yesterday but I've been locked in the studio all week. And I have another photo shoot for a magazine this morning. You've no idea how busy I am.'

'Wow, it's all taking off. What an incredible opportunity,' I said, aware of an unkind prickle of envy spiking my words.

'It's what I've always wanted,' she said quietly. 'Since I was a tiny girl.'

It was a freezing morning and the air sparkled with frost. Hepsie asked about the children in some detail. Rarely did I speak of my true feelings about the mothering duties. I'd realised that when I spoke truthfully about caring for the children I came over as dangerously depressed; I'd heard myself and it was all moaning and complaints, so early on I'd decided upon an enduring silence.

'So Jewels is happy?' she asked twice. 'And safe?'

'Oh absolutely,' I enthused, 'she's thriving. Though Miss Moore never mentions the baby's father, which is a shame, don't you think? I had assumed she and Mouse had the same father but Mouse tells me that's not the case.'

'That just means Jewels loves you even more, John. You're like a dad to her.'

'So, who is the kid's father?'

'Some loser, lost in the night.'

'Poor little girl, never to know her dad.'

'At least I knew my dad for fourteen years.'

'Yes. I remember what you told me. I'm so sorry.'

'Girls do need a man around. It's true. To me that was one of the advantages of choosing a male nanny for Jewels.'

'She does seem to like me. At least I hope she does.'

'And the poor little Mouse?' I could hear the suck and sigh of her furious smoking.

'He's coping. Though there's still no sign of his mother or father. I can't imagine why his mother's not coming back to get him. She must be worrying about where he is, surely.'

Then Hepsie asked about my welfare, about the weather, the journey, the car and what Miss Moore was eating (nothing, it turned out, for she had been advised by her manager to get back to her ideal weight by substituting cigarettes for food). Hepsie had not apologised for the early hour of her call, and I imagine now that she couldn't even tell midnight from noon.

'Oh help me, John, please help me,' Hepsie said midway through our conversation. The cry was followed by a moon-moving sob that caused Jewels to begin crying all over again. 'Oh that's Jewels,' Hepsie exclaimed. 'What a darling little sound.'

I had the babe on my aching shoulder. She slept better that way. The perfect weight of her is something I shall always remember. It is what began the bonding between us, that simple sandbaggy heaviness of her, firm and squeezably soft in my throbbing arms. That and the guilt I felt at having failed her already – I could afford to take no more chances. I had to be watchful every minute of the day.

'Do you always have her by you?' Hepsie asked.

I told her I rarely put Jewels down now, and instead carried her everywhere with me, Mouse trailing us both like a little bodyguard. I was sure then that Hepsie knew what had happened in the car, and was calling simply to check that such a calamity could not happen again. I explained I was beginning to feel a great concern for the baby. I had become sure that there was no one I would trust her with but myself. It was all true; I loved Jewels. I told Hepsie how I'd learnt how gently stroking Jewels' little finger could soothe her. The baby was growing fine cottony threads of dark hair, and I admitted this gave me a silly pride. I knew exactly what temperature she liked her milk and was elated almost to tears on the first occasion that I was sure she had smiled.

'Help me,' Hepsie said again.

'Why, that's the very reason I was put on this crazy planet,' I whispered. Outside the day was coming in a rise of purple.

'I used to think I'd do anything, anything! To not be a nobody.'

'Why didn't you tell me you lived round here?'

'To be truly me.'

'You should have said you were a Wychwood girl.'

'Oh John, it's not like I expected at all. I had such high hopes but everyone I meet these days is a donkey.'

'It'll get better. You'll get used to them. And if you don't like it you can always come home.'

'No I can't.'

'Of course you can. Your mum seemed pretty cool. A career in the media is not a life sentence.'

'Oh John, you've no idea how hard I'm going to find it if I fail in London and have to go back to my old life.'

Outside now in the iron-blue clouds I gazed dramatically on the drab, the endlessness, the avenue after avenue of afternoons, which linked up over years to form the unknown woman's unbearable life. My mother had told me from an early age that housework was the very worst thing a woman could find herself doing. We'd had a sequence of foreign cleaners throughout my childhood in order to allow my mother to pursue her career. I understood that there was no drudgery worse than being a stay-at-home wife and mother.

'Have you noticed the way no one listens to a word that pretty women say?' my twilit-eyed beauty said eventually.

'Well, it might be just because you're young,' I said, transfixed just by her sorrowful tone.

'I'm not just on about me,' she said sharply. 'Though young is the most important bit. In TV presenting you're finished by the time you're twenty-five. That's what Brian says.'

'I think that's a little cynical,' I laughed. She sounded dangerously fragile.

'Oh yeah, I bloody hate cynicism, don't you? That and *cool*. Why is everyone who is successful and from London and who lives in *apartments* so bloody cool and cynical? I think it's a smokescreen, don't you? I mean, so no one else believes their bloody amazing lives are possible, or desirable.'

'So if you're not living in an apartment where are you living?'

There was a pause. I looked down at Jewels and kissed her warm little nose. She smelt malty, as if she'd just rolled in biscuits. In the doorway Mouse appeared, hooded as always by his balaclava, to stand there still, silent, watching me. Often now he seemed to be waiting for me to give answers.

'Oh what shall I do?' Hepsie continued. It was the exact same tone of melodrama and gloom that I'd fallen for that first day in Chessington Vale – fifty per cent despair, fifty per cent gall.

'You must honour your gift,' I said softly, sparkly with solemnity, 'release your creative talent.'

'Yes,' she whispered, so her blue breath iced my ear. 'If I can't prove myself I'll die.'

To live in a hotel where there was a different family every day, to go abroad, to find a ridiculous job, to shimmer in sunlight where strangers were dazzled and content to see only your shell. Become a beautiful little witch who cared for no one but herself. I see now that this is what you had to do to protect your secrets.

'I'm sure you'll settle in soon, and you'll meet more people,' I whispered to Hepsie. 'It's a fantastic opportunity. You mustn't mess it up by worrying about it. Just enjoy it.'

'Somedays I have to pinch myself to check I'm not dreaming.'

'I'm jealous, actually. Imagine all the stars you're gonna meet.'

At the other side of the room Mouse banged his head against the doorframe repeatedly, perhaps mocking my obviously flirtatious chat. Or perhaps finally driven to madness by loneliness and the continued absence of his mother. Playfully I threw a bootie at him. He sank to the floor cross-legged and began drumming his fists on the rug.

'Don't you have any friends to go visit?' I'd asked him earlier when he'd complained of boredom.

'Schoolfriends? Like, local Wychwood kids? Hello! I think I'll stay in, Mummyman, thank you.'

'You could go for a walk,' I'd said, 'in the fields.'

'It's kinda a horrible village, don't you think? Kinda derelict. Kinda totally creepy. Kinda odd that we're here at all, right?'

I said nothing, but the truth was Wychwood was indeed ugly, but there was a beauty somewhere, just out of our reach. Just as there was when I was speaking to Hepsie.

Some deeply felt sureness was in Hepsie that I had glimpsed elsewhere in Wychwood – and which captivated me.

'But I've started to think that it's the people that make it terrible,' Hepsie replied eventually. She had been thinking hard. There was a high-pitched edge of agitation in her voice that made me think she'd not slept that night, or perhaps didn't even know that for the rest of earthbound England hours of quiet darkness had passed.

'We must stay in touch,' I said urgently, suddenly unable to imagine how I would ever live without her voice in my ear. 'We've no computers for emails, but I'll write to you. I'd love to do that.'

'Oh John, but that would take too long, just call me on this mobile number whenever you're able to talk. Or if anything's worrying you just call me.'

I wrote down the number she gave me. My hand was trembling and my throat was dry. Outside birds winged wild in the hedges.

'I miss my own family too much,' she whispered. She spoke to me so intimately. I imagined her resting her head on my shoulder and kissing my neck as she spoke. 'Brian thought I could do it, and of course I agreed because it was, as you said, such an incredible opportunity. But I think I've made a terrible mistake.' Then Hepsie said in a very small voice, 'I'm lonely.'

'Oh please! Of course everyone's lonely in London,' Miss Moore exploded when I told her of the conversation that evening. 'It's *London*!'

'But I never meet anyone,' Hepsie had said, when I too had tried to console her. 'All the other presenters are too busy to go out. Everyone's always working.'

'But really they're lonely too,' Miss Moore had said to me when she insisted I repeat the conversation word for word. That night Miss Moore was wearing a tight red dress in a darkly lit room. She was leaning forward as though urging the absent Hepsie to understand. 'It just feels more lonely because you're so successful. You're busy, so you're never lonely at the same time as the other lonely people.'

Her face was overcome with shadows. 'You see, darling, that's why loneliness is always worse for the winners. At least the losers have time to meet each other.'

I'm sure Miss Moore saw young Hepsie Vine sparkling there before her, and me, dull John, as nothing but the crazy glass-eyed medium. Mouse was at my side gazing on Miss Moore in his usual bewilderment. 'Hey, Mummyman, is the lady, like, sick?' he asked me later that night. 'Bizarro! Aren't you worried about her? Because if you're not, Mummyman, I think you, like, should be, yeah? Believe me, I've seen wacko women before. I have a mom, don't forget. I know what can happen to them when they're left all alone.'

'She's not alone. She's got me and Brian and you.'

'Hello! How freaky is that!'

'She'll cheer up,' Brian said brightly when I told him about my conversation with Hepsie. 'Is she on drugs?'

'Drugs! No, darling, no,' he'd laughed. 'Mouse is the only one round here who does drugs.'

'So neither of them is on illegal drugs.'

'Nope. Honestly, Misty don't do that no more. Didn't suit her. And Hepsie's the only woman I know who got depressed on Ecstasy. Don't worry, both the broads are fine.'

I'd told Brian the day before that I agreed with Mouse, and feared Miss Moore was unwell. I said that she seemed dangerously afraid in Wychwood but unable to confess what troubled her, and Brian said, 'Having a conversation with Karen Moore, and I say this as her *best friend*, is like burgling a house with bars on the windows and bolts on all the doors, John. I mean, for hell's sake, even I'm scared of the bitch.'

'She looks seriously, like, totally weird a lot of the time,' Mouse had said to me. I too had noticed how Miss Moore's fingers trembled when she drank her apple juice. How she held the glass tight as a tumbler of whisky. 'She seems so, kinda, unhappy, kinda worried,' Mouse continued. 'Why's everyone pretending it's great here?'

'It's all spin,' Brian laughed and I sensed Brian was somehow right. Though I now know pictures had been published that spring showing Miss Moore heavy-footed with her head hung low, she believed that, though people might see her as unhappy, they would never guess why she was unhappy. I still wonder how she found the loneliness of this bearable. 'I mean, don't get me wrong, I like Misty, I love her in fact, it's just an undisputed fact that she's got *LIAR* stamped in pink letters right through her rock-hard heart, and believe me, I say that as her *best friend*.'

'How long have you worked for her?' I asked Brian next.

'Oh about a hundred years, or at least it feels that long,' he laughed. 'But gee, it's been fun. I imagine half the time she don't even know she's lying,' Brian continued, 'because there's another thing not everyone knows about Misty Moore: sure she doesn't do drugs, but the poor lady takes so many pills that if you shake her she rattles.' Brian flung his head back and laughed. 'Yep, everything's going really well.'

I hated him. But faced with the daily fright of Miss Moore, the hot pink baby, the balaclavaed boy and the unsettling phone calls from Hepsie Vine, I couldn't help but be impressed by the man's optimism.

Chapter Seven

'Mummyman,' Mouse whispered to me in early March. 'Do you, like, hear anything in the night? Like sneaky footsteps? Like a woman walking?'

I laughed and said it was an old and decaying house. Prone to creaking. But it was true that during the many night hours that I lay awake I'd heard a thousand creaks and tip-taps. A hum that could just be electricity, a drip that was hopefully only a tap, a gurgle in a pipe, the rumble and whirl of probably just the new central-heating boiler. And the one time I'd thought I'd heard distinctive footsteps, adult and firmly climbing, I'd sprung from my room only to find myself alone in the chill seawater glow of the landing.

'Mouse thinks he's heard someone in the night,' I told Miss Moore. 'Have you ever had a similar feeling?'

'Oh golly, no,' she laughed breezily. 'I'm out like a light.'

'Mouse needs help. He's getting completely obsessed,' I said to Brian.

'Honey, just because he's paranoid doesn't mean they're not after him.'

* * *

Then, a few days later, around the end of February, Brian admitted that he too was worried about the house.

Worried that a minimal spacious look might not be possible in Long Meadow End. Minimalism, apparently, is a style more suited to warehouse apartments and other reclaimed industrial spaces. Brian was in charge of restyling the farmhouse. If there was a ghostly intruder in that house Brian had set about banishing it. He told me he had decided, though we were only staying in Wychwood for another four months, to proceed with the makeover because he hoped it would distract Miss Moore and take her mind off 'other things'.

First Brian had arranged for men to come with pellets, electrical currents, sprays, smoke bombs, nets, gasses, guns and kill the visitors with furry faces. Mouse was kept from the room as their tiny stiffened corpses were collected in a sack and burnt. Next Brian and the designers, architects, textile artists and security specialists made detailed plans for the transformation of Long Meadow End from rural slum to luxury abode. The design team, hired from an exclusive agency, were liberated by their bottomless budget, for during our entire time in Wychwood we lived as though money had no meaning. And despite all the things I could say to the contrary, and my artist's heart did retain some ideological distaste at the excess, our endless freedom to spend lightened our darkest days.

It was decided, as cost was irrelevant, to illuminate the classic features of Long Meadow End within a modern minimal setting. Misty protested, but was ignored. Brian and the architects loved the idea. This meant much glass, wood, chrome and white paint. The placing of antiques alongside twenty-first-century modern-art details. Much discussion was given over to lighting. We had gold uplights and silver downlights. Flickering chandeliers with impossibly real flames. We lost our shadowy dark corners to exciting design concepts. A Perspex cello collection arrived and was screwed as an artwork to the wall. A bearded London artist who chewed constantly on a wooden lolly stick came to recommend abstract paintings and sculptures. The long, dark, narrow passageway, which led from the kitchen to the laundry room, was given a glass roof and the damp walls replaced with a maroon mosaic. Another unsmiling London woman insisted we knock down one entire internal wall and replace it with Sicilian glass bricks.

The designers, architects and artists that Brian had chosen seemed gaudy and gaunt. But it was exciting to watch the transformation take place and fun to see the personalities clash and regroup. I felt relaxed and relieved by their presence. I was foolish and young then, and believed adults of wealth, power and influence were less dangerous than the poor, the unknown or the unexplained. And Miss Moore and Brian had recently presented me with a wardrobe of fashionable clothes. That morning I'd spent considerable time sculpting a modish hairstyle. And my first ever attempt at a fake tan was a subtle success. Yes, I was embarrassed by myself initially, but I soon convinced myself that being sniffed at incredulously by strangers was a positive rather than a negative experience. And as the designers and stylists swarmed around our house I smiled and moved so my new hair bounced. It was beneficial to be good-looking, and wealthy and happy; it made others happy too. It kept the show on the road, so it was socially important, particularly in those days of obesity, depression and debt.

Still, Mouse seemed no closer to being collected by his mother. Our phone never rang. Mobile phones could not find a signal out there in the spring countryside. Brian said we just had to wait and see if the boy's mother got in touch.

In turn the boy gazed in horror at the furnishings and asked me many times if we were joking. 'It's kinda, like, weirder here every day,' he said. 'Does she want this to happen? Or is she, like, so far gone she can't make her own decisions any more?'

I didn't want to tell Mouse but the truth was that if I asked Miss Moore any questions often she ignored me. I was no more than a member of the audience, paid to watch and clap, not interact and question. Still, Mouse had alerted me to a problem. Was Brian laughing at us, or was he serious? I couldn't tell.

'It's important to have somewhere nice to live,' I replied inanely.

'But don't you think she's got, like, more important things to worry about, Mummyman? Like those footsteps in the night, for a start?'

Fifteen workmen used pulleys to lift a leather sofa, the size of a saloon car, up the stairs to create a reception room on the square first-floor landing. The ground level was covered with thick Chinese handmade rugs. The house no longer creaked. Upstairs each oak plank was polished to a sunny glisten. It was a ridiculous environment for small children and Mouse was forever crashing into the 'stunningly lit' alcoves and smashing the tiny fat figures and porcelain vases on display.

Misty offered no suggestions, and continued to answer no questions about the design. Her only concern was that all the locks in Long Meadow End were changed and additional security electrified every window. No sly foot-steps could come up the staircase now. In those early days she just laughed a lot and sighed and hugged herself wildly and stared at the ceiling and laughed some more. Though she sniffed and swallowed repeatedly I still found her appealing. Often she chewed hard on her thumbnail and was silent: hours passed during which she said nothing at all – perfect for me to stuff her with my bathroom fantasies. I was watching her breasts keenly, for that day they seemed to have been newly inflated with a foot pump. Then she looked to the left, gazing through a narrowed eye at the very corner point of the room. And there she concentrated hard, as though listening to faint music, or waiting to spot a familiar spider. I thought of all the dirty things I would do to her if I were a different man, and she would let me. *Saved from lunacy! Misty Moore reveals the love secrets of the sex god who pleasured her back to bliss.*

At other times she was livelier than the smartest, cutest small child, and talked happily of what she had bought, and would buy, and where she could go on holidays. I liked her happy almost as much as I liked her sad. The one constant during those days was an enduring fascina-tion with the distortion of her own face in a chrome splashback the builder was fitting. She could stare at herself reflected there for many minutes, turning left and right and pulling a series of comic faces to her own amusement.

'Why does she do that?' Mouse asked me one day, when we'd caught her at it in the kitchen. 'It's kinda freaky. Like she's bullying herself.'

'Do you want me to get her to talk to you?' I said to Mouse, wondering if such a meeting might calm both of them. 'I know you're missing your mum. Perhaps Miss Moore could reassure you.'

'My mom will be coming real soon.'

'Perhaps you and Miss Moore could sit down together and talk about your feelings?'

'Hello! Talk to her! Are you crazy? I'd rather eat bees.'

'I'm sure I heard something again last night,' Mouse said to me the next morning. 'There's another person in the house.'

'No way. We've better security than Alcatraz,' I laughed.

Every night Miss Moore ensured every door was locked, bolted and then checked in an elaborate ritual. But there was something more happening that I didn't mention to Mouse. A feeling in the night that had not disappeared with the disguising of our home. As if unseen life made startled movements in the shadows. It was full spring and from the earth rose up a moist groan of growing as the night soil cooked. I'd asked Miss Moore if she'd been into my room as I slept. The reason was a certainty that warm breath had drifted over me in the few odd hours I slumbered there. And more than once I'd imagined – the consequence of some intense sexual frustration, I quickly assumed – that I'd glimpsed a beautiful female face. Looming over me.

Sticky and dry-mouthed, I woke again and again to the sound of a door gently closing.

Chapter Eight

M isty, Mouse, Brian and I continued to be lonely. Though it was not true to say that we were alone. We had company. I began to believe that the visitors left it until our third month so that we had time to establish an uneasy security – before they started to crawl towards us from all the moist cracks in the village. I assumed at first that they came because their lives were poor and bleak and we were rich and brilliant – so to see our beautifully redesigned abode gave them great pleasure. I sensed nothing unpleasant about the villagers' interest in my boss. Mainly because my new proximity to beauty, success and riches had pumped up my own ego: I expected people to be interested in us and I took Miss Moore's anxiety to be just the guilty paranoia of the famous when faced with the ordinary.

'Everyone seems to be being very friendly,' I remarked cheerfully to Mouse one morning when two local ladies had just left. I was still content to be in Long Meadow End, though I noticed more regularly how oddly the house came alive as I slept.

'Yes,' Mouse replied very seriously, 'so are those big dogs when they sniff at your crotch.'

Another night, following a visit by a curious and obese Wychwood villager, Miss Moore made her thumbnail bleed. 'I don't know why it is, John,' she smiled sadly, 'but I have to be aware that some people really hate me.'

I blushed and pressed Jewels tighter to me. I wished Mouse would appear to distract us with some excessively mad or bad behaviour. The boy spent most of his time in his bedroom playing with the unusual insects he kept with salad leaves in a sandwich box. I made sure he had his medication each morning, a single tablet taken from a high locked cupboard and swallowed before me with a cup of water. Doped, he was much easier to handle – if only because he asked less penetrating questions.

Initially, when she realised she had no choice but to entertain, Miss Moore behaved well during the visits by the strangers. She silked flat her golden hair, which under Brian's expert hand had acquired a yellowed ultra blonde, a spun fairy-tale shine, so now even at a distance the million-dollar hair was the first thing you noticed, before even the breasts. She wore tight-fitting fashion outfits. Often in dazzling white, as was the fashion that season. Zips pulled halfway open down the front to reveal that nutty-brown, toffee-soft torso.

'Freaky! Is she, like, serious?' Mouse had exclaimed when he'd walked into the room unexpectedly. 'Jesus, Mummyman, get the lady a mirror.'

But I used the opportunity of the visits for my own ends. To flirt. I found a great relief in forgetting myself this way. Though it was coming up close to the fans that showed me the dark truth of their love for Miss Moore.

'Oh that's her! I do so wish I could afford tits like that,' a young female villager exclaimed one day as I led her into the drawing room to meet Miss Moore.

'That's one area where you can definitely save your money,' I said, hooking an arm around her fleshy waist and leading her into the drawing room.

This kind of wolfish confidence didn't come easy to me. But I was learning. Around Brian and Miss Moore anything seemed acceptable and possible. Hoping to trade secrets for favours, I went on to explain to the visitor that Miss Moore had confessed to me that she was under quite considerable strain living in Wychwood, looking after the baby and trying to get her career back on track. I was surprised by the rage of the young woman's reply.

'Ha!' she exclaimed. 'Saying you are very rich and very busy, and are tired out from redecorating your big house in the country, and exhausted from having a new baby to care for, is not called confessing, it's called *boasting*.'

Miss Moore was right: the fans often seemed to loathe her. And Mouse had noticed it too. 'Gee, being a Mrs Big Tits is worse than being on death row,' he said to me once as we watched another trio of plump high-heeled ladies coming up the gravel drive. 'At least the public can't get at you there.'

'Anyway, she's coping alone quite well,' I said to the fan, hoping to end the topic.

'Coping! Come off it, she's going crazy. I read last year that it's only the world pharmaceutical industry that's keeping her upright. I can't wait to meet her.'

It was a lesson for me that the visitors, though they professed to love Miss Moore, were keen to see her exposed and ruined. They came to her because she was rumoured to be rich and beautiful. Then, like teen vandals, trashed what they found. Yet Miss Moore's post-pregnancy figure was impressive, and she appeared keen as a streaker to reveal herself. She needed people to listen. She entertained her guests with energetic anecdotes about her life in America, her early adventures in showbiz, and particularly, and here she would widen her eyes and sigh, confessions about her newfound joy as a mother. And I know now – ten years on, and exposing myself daily to millions in my TV soap – yes, from my very own experience, that it's not just vanity, it's worse: a terrible need for the smiles of strangers in this silver-backed world where your closest friend is the mirror.

Sometimes the visitors asked to be shown around the newly styled farmhouse. Knowing her private room to be locked Miss Moore didn't care where the visitors went and waved them away to explore the house for themselves. Thrilled, they would dance from room to room, hating Misty more and more with every skip. Racing along as though the house were on fire. Pulling ornaments off shelves and fingering through drawers, screaming, 'Oh look at this!' or, 'Oh my God, I can't believe she has this!' or, 'This is so *not* fashionable!'

Often Misty spoke to the visitors about the men she had known and the affairs she had had. Later I realised that to survive as a glamorous woman in this world you had to dramatise every moment. But then I believed – fantasised, imagined – that Miss Moore had lived boldly and wildly. She had undertaken an odyssey in the sexual underworld. She was a woman who knew more about violet romance than I could dream of, so when she spoke her confessions I nodded as though I had just learnt a great lesson about love.

The visitors listened politely to these tales. But I began to notice the slow seep of delighted pity in their faces. I too felt a sweet sadness on those long afternoons. It was a pleasant feeling. We knew Miss Moore had got trapped in a place where there was nothing she could do but smile. Prowling around her pretty cage we offered buns through the bars. On and on she laboured to disguise her emotions with her own more elaborate stories and detailed remembrances. Lurid confessions. It came close to an embarrassing egotism. When she could speak no more she bounced around the room with Jewels, who at three months was pretty and plump, fragrant and healthy. When holding Jewels, Miss Moore laughed and cooed and sang. 'I do so love being a mummy,' she cried, and the visitors smiled back and clutched their hands together in encouraging agreement. I realised Miss Moore was always aware of being watched. And as she laughed and we smiled we were all sprinkled with a refreshing silvered sorrow.

We liked it best when she told us secrets. Though often the confessions were not exactly geared to the target market. 'You know, my second husband once said to me, "Why don't you tell me when you have an orgasm?" and I'd say, "Honey, I would do but you're never there."' Then visitors tipped towards the edge of their seats and watched her carefully. I too was transfixed by the stories, staring without blinking. Several guests smirked, others smiled weakly. Most memorably, several emitted little groans, sounds akin to pleasure, at Miss Moore's humiliating performance. I pressed my hands to Jewels' little ears to prevent her hearing her mother exposed this way.

Some of the more elderly visitors let their jaws drop slightly, but they did not protest, gazing instead on Misty forlornly, as a grandparent on a hurt child. The younger country guests smirked, some sighed or scoffed, others laughed. One clapped, I remember. I think now that if anyone was shocked it was not because Miss Moore spoke of sex like a man, but because she was unabashed. And because they sensed, as I had sensed with Brian, that being sexually brazen carried with it the potential for great ruthlessness. For hers, it seemed on those occasions, was the blatant shamelessness of a naughty child as she threw her bright confidences around like confetti.

'I had no boobs at all when I was a teenager,' Misty told her audience of two middle-aged men on another occasion. Grunts greeted this astonishing news. 'I know that's incredible to think of now. But true! And everyone would tease me mercilessly about it. "I don't know why you bother wearing a bra," the boys would say, and what do you think I'd yell at them? I'd yell, "Well, you wear underpants, don't you?"'

If there was even a small splattering of encouraging, embarrassed applause Misty went on to confess all sorts of intimate stuff about her marriages. I realised that Miss Moore talked most dirty – and so became the woman the visitors most eagerly wanted to shame – when she was most desperate. I now know all about shame: you feel it only when you have failed yourself. It is guilt when you have failed others. Shame is worse.

Perhaps that's the story: how in the company of Miss Moore I went from being a boy guilty at his lack of achievement to a man ashamed of his success.

So, self-revelation was, Miss Moore believed, the most powerful way of deflecting attention away from her true self. And, more importantly, away from Jewels. It had certainly not been an easy week for Miss Moore. Six pornographic letters had been delivered. All were written in the same hand but signed with different names. Annette Curtain was the least obscene of the pseudonyms, and I did manage to make her see the funny side of Emma Roydes – but she wasn't soothed by my insistence that the hate mail was just the work of bored country teenagers.

Over the coming months her sexual confessions, most of which, I assumed, were pure fantasy, would preoccupy her interrogators and satiate their need for true intimacy. But running underneath everything Miss Moore said in public was another dialogue that you only heard by watching closely the cool sapphire in her eyes: 'I've never committed to anything or anyone but myself, John. I have kept myself at a distance from everyone who ever wanted to be close to me so I could be free to be successful. I value nothing other than what I achieve alone. Love has never meant that much to me because it has to be shared. In truth I don't care terribly for sex, because I don't like the idea of being that close to other people.'

Sometimes I couldn't bear it and took Jewels away from the horror of her mother, up to my room where we sat with Mouse and played games in imitation of happy families. I needed Mouse and Jewels on those occasions in exactly the same way as Miss Moore needed the children, to distract me from the cruelty of adults.

But Mouse was still no better. The boy had received no news from either his mother or his father. He had been extremely frightened for the last few nights. He had barricaded his door with chairs and stayed awake all night shining a torch under his porcelain chin. I also had woken again only last night to the familiar bang-click of a door closing. I almost mentioned the fact to Miss Moore but feared, just like telling the truth about childcare, it would make me appear a depressed, possibly paranoid, lunatic.

Occasionally our guests did ask provocative questions. 'Does Miss Moore sleep with her eyes shut?' a Mrs Parker enquired of me when Misty had left the room. When I responded with some puzzlement the woman whispered in all seriousness, 'Oh it's just that we heard she'd had so much messing done to her face by doctors in London that now she had to sleep with her eyes open.' A high-pitched excitable giggle followed this spiteful comment.

'Does she really have a terrible temper?' a studious-looking girl with glasses asked on another occasion. 'I heard she slapped a photographer.'

'Slapped!' her brute of a father exclaimed. 'Not slapped, stabbed! She stabbed a photographer who tried to take a picture of little Jewels! I read it in the paper.'

On the first Thursday in February I made polite conversation as I was showing a gossipy elderly villager to the door. 'Oh we do love the house,' I chattered. 'We often wonder who lived here before we arrived, it's so character-ful!'

The woman paused and looked down at the floor of the hallway in some puzzlement. 'Who lived here before?' she repeated. I rattled on about the wonders of the house. The magical garden. Until she said, 'Mr and Mrs Vine lived here, with his parents, and their girls, of course.'

'What? Here?'

'They were such a happy family.'

'The Vines lived here in Long Meadow End?'

'Daughters, all of them. Isn't that strange? No, this was their house for years and years. They were very much an extended family, as we used to say. They really looked after one another. And Long Meadow End, well, it was the centre of the village really. Didn't you know that, John?'

'Oh didn't you know, John,' Misty said vaguely when I told her later of the conversation.

The look on her face transformed me instantly to a fool. Didn't I understand the game? Poor me. Had I taken everything said to me as the truth? Had I no imagination? No sense of mystery and fun? I'd probably taken her anecdotes as truth too, stupid me! Or was I so vain, so self-important that I expected to be told all the details of the family's private domestic arrangements? Had I begun to think of myself as more than a servant? I was a vain foolish egotistical young man. I should question no more the glittering lives of the successful and famous. Theirs was a world I quite obviously did not understand.

'The Vines!' I'd exclaimed to the villager after she'd revealed more family information about the happy Vines. 'But they never told me that. Why did they move out? When?'

The elderly woman put her gnarled fists in her pockets and shrugged. 'They got poor,' she said, her eyes firmly fixed on mine. 'Couldn't afford a place this big any more. Money's tight round here for some people. Debt can have a devastating impact on families.'

I pictured the cold underwear I'd found in the rusty washing tub. The tiny shoes. Those big soft beds sagged in the middle from generations of sleeping Vines. 'So it's Mrs and Mrs Vine who are renting the house to Miss Moore?' I asked the old woman. 'That's incredible.'

'I've no idea,' she replied indignantly. 'You'd need to ask Miss Moore about that.'

'Yes, it was the Vines who used to live here. Hmm. That's how we found the place. Hmm.'

'You know, I just wish someone would be straight with me,' I cried.

Miss Moore flinched as though I'd just pulled a knife. There was something she really didn't want me to know. 'Oh John, honestly, don't take it all so personally. We'll be out of this hell-hole in a few months and then I'll tell you it all.'

Then she inhaled and wandered off, giving me the cool practised look of hazy inattention that she reserved for reminding me that I was nothing more than a domestic employee. I was not paid to be privy to any private family information. When she got to the door she turned and gave me a simple smile that was ninety-nine per cent panic. It was familiar because it was the way she looked at the children.

Chapter Nine

Hepsie contacted me again in early March. This time her call came not during the night hours but on a crisp spring morning while Miss Moore was at the gym and Mouse at school. The calm weather, and the gently sleeping baby in my arms, the warmed patisserie Brian had brought me on a china plate beside my chair, Radio 4 chortling smugly in the background made the conversation radiating from glamorous London seem all the stranger.

Again our chat moved quickly through the usual pleasantries. Then I asked Hepsie about her work. She said little other than that she was tired. She asked me about my nannying, about which I was dishonestly cheery and upbeat. I loved the children but they still exhausted me. I often felt frustrated and bleak.

'I'm so glad you're as good as we thought you'd be,' she said.

'Why didn't you say you used to live in this house?'

'I knew you'd be fab.'

'I feel a fool. I've been living in your family home all along and I didn't even know.'

'At babysitting, I mean.'

'Ah, so I've gone from nanny, to au pair, to babysitter. Quite a demotion,' I flirted, giving up on the interrogation. It might not come as a surprise to know that I was the kind of person who could quickly ignore the mysteries of the world and turn quite happily, every time, to sex.

'You're a natural,' she said. 'It's not something you can train for, anyway.'

'So how did you get the job as Miss Moore's nanny?'

'I lied, of course,' she replied.

'What about?' I asked. I see now that I was scared of her dishonesty, but I interpreted my nervousness as excitement and passion. Then I heard a sudden burst of female laughter in the background. I assumed it was because Hepsie was calling me from some chic café.

'Oh stuff. Told her I had professional experience. With kids.'

'And she believed you?'

'Oh yes, she needs to believe everything I say. She hardly wants to believe I'm a crook, does she? She probably convinced herself I'm the sweetest person she's ever met in her life.'

'Aren't you?'

'No. As every woman realises nowadays, there's no money in sweet.'

It still amazes me how quickly I was able to delete anything troubling from my remembrance. Live only with memories that were new and shiny and pleasurable. Every time the tired, smoky faces of Brian and Hepsie, grinning on that first day in Chessington Vale, popped into my head I deleted the image. I replaced it with a picture of pale, innocent Hepsie smiling, alone, single, available, gazing lovingly up at me from a soft riverbank repose. Hepsie pale and pure as spring blossom.

Even the fact that Hepsie had concealed both her family's presence in the village and Long Meadow End as her birthplace didn't trouble me terribly. Later, hurt and stunned – when Hepsie had come and gone, and before I'd got my first acting job in TV – I thought differently, that perhaps Brian was right and women were just like that, liars, cheats and deceivers, and you might as well get used to it.

'Well, it's opened some doors for you anyway,' I said, hoping to soothe her. She didn't reply immediately and in the pause I heard more background chat, muttering, whispering, distinctly female and high-pitched.

'What do you mean by that?' she said.

'In London.'

'Oh, yeah, doors flying open in my face every minute of the day.'

'Contacts. People.'

'Oh John, I do still want to be famous and rich, but some days I just wish I'd never even met Miss Moore. But what choice did I have but to go to her? Though she didn't seem as bad then as she does now. Yesterday she looked completely wrecked.'

'Yesterday!' I exclaimed. 'What do you mean? How come you saw her yesterday?'

'Oh I mean in the papers. I mean I saw a picture of her in a magazine yesterday.'

I didn't believe her. For some time I pressed her to tell me if she had been to Wychwood to visit her family.

But Hepsie Vine would not answer any of my questions directly. 'All I'm saying, John, is that she looks ill,' she cried. 'Now leave it at that, please.'

Then at that moment someone called out Hepsie's name. With a shock I recognised the sturdy voice of the elder Mrs Vine. 'That's your gran,' I said. 'Where are you?'

'This isn't about me, John. I'm just telling you that I'm worried about Miss Moore. You have to keep a special eye on Jewels.'

'Where are you?'

'Because she's not well. She's not capable of being in charge of a child.'

Of course Hepsie was right and it was not only because of the ghosts Miss Moore saw all around her in spring 200 – that her eyebrows were arched in permanent alarm. Brian had suggested Miss Moore make weekly visits to a far-off beauty salon for treatment to nails, face, hair and other more hidden parts. The most visible effects were that Miss Moore's lips had been re-plumped, and her cheeks newly de-creased. Dissolving her entire expression into something simpler. The more often she went to the beauty salon, and the more regularly she was restyled, the more eerie she looked. It was like gloom preserved in a hard jelly.

I should have helped Miss Moore, I see that now. If, that March, I'd asked a few questions and listened to the answers I could have changed everything. And I would have done if I'd not been so tired out from looking after the children – and if, ultimately, I had not cared so utterly for myself. Even Mouse had suggested I call her a doctor, but I'd laughed off the suggestion and said that she just needed a rest.

'How did you meet Miss Moore?' I asked Hepsie when I feared she was tiring of our conversation and about to vanish. Leaving me hanging on the line, gazing on the garden and longing for more. I suddenly felt sure all of us at Long Meadow End were at the mercy of strange country people and the ways they did things here.

'Do you love her?'

'No,' I muttered, 'but I'm a bloke and so obviously I can't help finding her kind of attractive.'

'Not her! Jewels, you idiot!'

'Oh yes, sorry, yes I do. Of course. I adore her.'

'I'm so glad,' she said softly. 'I knew you would, the first time I saw you. It's so important to be loved, don't you think?'

I sensed that Hepsie wanted me to ask her something. I tried to read the subtext of our conversation, but it was hard suddenly to switch my attitude dial from blissful ignorance to wily insight. 'Please tell me how you and Miss Moore met,' I said.

'We have to trust them and their mysterious powers to make our tomorrows better than our todays. We live solely by rubbing up against their lives. It's totally nineteenth century.'

'Tell me.'

'I've been nothing more than a scullery maid all along, hoping for a spray of her ladyship's eau de toilette.'

'So why did you choose to be a nanny?'

'*Choose!*' she shrieked, in that angry Northern rasp.

It was still sunny. Birds still flew in the glassy blue spring sky. I noticed Brian waving at me from the garden where he was exercising, jogging on the spot.

'Sorry, I didn't mean to annoy you.'

'Oh, that's so typical of you handsome London guys! Everything you do you *choose* to do.'

'Sorry.'

Suddenly I heard a burst of arguing in the background. It

was the smaller of the Vine sisters. Then suddenly Hepsie was crying, raging, a terrible sound that I had to control by holding the receiver at some distance to my ear. On and on Hepsie sobbed. I hated it when women did that. I had no idea what to do. It stopped me in my tracks, which, it took me a while to realise, was the very idea: she was trying to conceal the sounds of her family.

'What's wrong? Is it where you're living?'

'What on earth do you mean?'

'Your accommodation, is it OK? Perhaps you'd cheer up if you found somewhere better to live.'

'It's more than OK, John. It's heaven. It's like living on a film set.'

'Oh. Where is it?'

'Chessington Vale, of course. Miss Moore's house. She's letting me stay until I'm established enough in the business to get my own place.'

'But I had no idea! That's so generous of her. You lucky thing.'

'Actually, I'm doing her a favour too. Without me here the place'd be empty while she's up there with you.'

'It must be like a dream come true. I wish I was down there rather than up here,' I said, betraying a flash of envy that Hespie had exchanged this for that.

'It is. But it's a big house and apart from a few staff I'm completely alone, which can be a bit scary at night.'

'I wouldn't complain,' I said a little frostily. 'Nights here are not great either. It sounds to me like choosing to work for Miss Moore was the best decision you ever made.'

Suddenly she began to cry again. The noise shattered eventually into long slow sighs, followed then by sniffs and coughs. Jewels, awoken by Hepsie's cries, began to whimper too.

'What have I done?' I asked helplessly.

'I didn't *choose*, you fucking idiot! Of course not. Why do you keep saying *choose*?'

'OK, I'm sorry.'

'Who'd choose to do the work that a woman should do herself, but doesn't because she's sure she's made for better things.'

'So you didn't choose to do the job,' I said, 'but you did choose to lie about it.' I was hoping for a touch of paternal authority, but instantly knew that I'd sounded sharp and mean. 'I just think that you've not been straight with me, and that makes me angry.'

There was a long pause. What was Hepsie thinking as I watched Brian exercising – swollen arms sinking his black chest rapidly into the cold green grass? When he stood up and began to jog again, I grinned at him and waved. His athleticism impressed me; he had so much energy, so much focus and determination despite his flaky job. He was incredibly masculine. Good to look at. A bit scary perhaps, a bit menacing, but compelling. It was some time before Hepsie spoke.

'Often, John, it's the people who have *no choice* who lie,' she said quietly, and then hung up.

Chapter Ten

As the verges came up thick and soft we had our second, more serious nannying crisis. Jewels got sick. It came on suddenly one morning, soon after Miss Moore had left for the gym. In addition to her daily workout Miss Moore was now also running several miles each morning and evening. Jogging didn't quite describe it, for she ran like a criminal, supernaturally fast and with a look of terror on her face, as though she were caught on CCTV fleeing the scene of a crime.

'Is she, like, dying?' Mouse asked anxiously as the baby began to puke repeatedly. We were dining at the chrome kitchen table, which always made me imagine we were eating our food off a morgue trolley. 'She could die, huh, Mummyman?'

'No,' I laughed uneasily, 'it's quite natural for babies to be sick.'

'Is it? How would you know, Mummyman?'

At first I was professional and calm. I found the childcare book and tried to take the baby's temperature, but found it impossible to keep the stick under her thrashing arm. I called Miss Moore and when her ansaphone greeted me I called Brian, because he was the only friend I had. 'She's sick!' I yelled. 'And I don't know what to do. She's vomiting and she's gone vague and blotchy.'

'It's a hangover,' he sighed languidly. 'Make her some strong coffee, give her a few pills and she'll pick up after lunch.' I groaned and began to whimper desperately. 'Hell, man,' Brian howled back, 'you've gotta learn to hide your feelings!'

At this point I should say that many times that year Brian teased me for not being manly enough. For lack of courage and, later that year, for my fears about the Vines. 'Do all people who are different to you scare you, John?' he asked.

The sick came more fiercely so within the hour Jewels was throwing mouthloads of vomit right across the sitting room. Mouse began to cry in sympathy. Both children needed their mothers, and this was the one thing they could not have. My shirt was soon covered with sticky fluids. It wasn't true that men were as capable with babies as women. It just wasn't true. I tried to call Hepsie, but another ansaphone mocked me. I tried to call the gym where Miss Moore exercised, finding the number from directory enquiries, and though the 'luxury palace', the Primrose Path Health Spa, did indeed exist they told me that they had not seen Miss Moore that day. Another fucking mystery.

'Well,' I said desperately to Mouse, as though the crazy boy might be able to instruct me, 'what next?'

'Medicine,' he said helpfully.

I measured out a teaspoon but the baby's head-tossing refusal flicked it back over my face. Mouse tried to hold her arms but she fought us violently. We gave up. For a moment it did occur to me that it could be my powerful new scent that was affecting the baby. That week Miss Moore had presented me with some aftershave ('No, you berk!' Brian cried. '*Cologne*'), which she suggested I wear every day. And Brian had given me several pairs of tighter designer jeans in a range of expertly faded colours – which, to my surprise, I looked good in. Brian had also, to my initial embarrassment, suggested a deeper fake tan ('It's nearly summer, sweetie, you can't trot around like a stick of chalk'). Messily, alone in my bedroom, I applied the stronger tanning cream till I glowed, at first like a Dutch cheese, then, as summer came on, like a varnished pine. By the terrible climax of our time in Wychwood I was the hue of aged oak.

The baby was getting worse. My crooning became more strained. I could feel the baby's pain and it agonised me. I suggested Mouse play in the garden while I called more people for advice. I tried my mother but the office said she was in Paris at a meeting and could not be contacted, even in an emergency. An angry rash began to dapple the baby's neck and cheeks purple. I called Miss Moore again, and Hepsie, but their phones were still switched off. Jewels was heating up. She'd turned from pink to red to scarlet. I ran a cool bath but as soon as I dipped the child in the water she began to writhe and scream more ferociously.

I called Brian again, my trembling fingertips slipping on the keys. 'I need you to find someone. Some woman.'

'We pay you to be the woman, toots.'

'Find Hepsie. Or her mother. It's getting worse.'

'Hepsie? Why Hepsie? What will she know about it?' he laughed. In the background I could hear the busy hum of a pub or restaurant, men calling out and clapping.

'She's female. She did the job. She knows the routine.'

'Are you kidding? She's a model, sweetie. She couldn't keep a houseplant alive. Call Misty, she's the mother.'

I knew Brian was acting, but what was he acting, and why?

'It's her fortieth soon,' Brian said, and then shuddered. 'Poor cow.'

'I thought she was thirty-eight.'

'Oh sure! It's just not the first time she's been thirty-eight.' He began to laugh. 'Look, take the kid to the doctor's.'

The irritation had now spread over Jewels' chest and had turned to the white lumps of nettle rash. I returned to the bathroom and splashed water over the baby's tiny body to cool her, so soon we were paddling around the bathroom floor. Mouse looked at me doubtfully, saying nothing but communicating all the same that I had failed some test. I was not a good Mummyman. I was not able to protect the children in a time of crisis. Worse would come. The dark house stank of the hot red baby. Jewels screamed on and continued to retch, so soon the water over the floor was swimming with strings of mucus. I ran into the garden to look for help but there was no one around. Just that shining aluminium sky above, a misty drizzle pressing down over us.

All the time I was wrestling with the feverish child, Mouse was following me anxiously. His gaze was swivelled upwards, never leaving my face. 'If my mom was here . . .' he repeated, nibbling on the corner of his woolly mouth holes and clenching each thumb in the fingers of each hand.

Jewels was now depositing yellowed bubbling bile, first in a pot plant and then over the back of the expensive sofa. When the diarrhoea began dribbling down her leg like strong tea I hurried to call the emergency numbers and had an interminably lengthy consultation with a nurse, which included me pressing various glass objects to the baby's chest to check the rash disappeared under pressure. It was suggested I take her to the local surgery, open in a neighbouring village that very afternoon. The nurse diagnosed an allergic reaction to something Jewels had eaten.

'So she's not, like, dying,' Mouse asked urgently, again and again, tugging on my trouser pocket. 'Is she?'

'How the hell do I know,' I shouted, and the boy, shocked, turned and began to thump the expensive walls with his little fists, crying and calling for his mother.

I felt terrible. Then suddenly envious of Hepsie, living alone far away from all this in easy luxury. I too wanted to be rich and free to explore my talents and to live for myself, not other people. The urgent pained cries of the two desperate children echoed back around the lonely farmhouse. I began to taste disaster prowling in the silvered air. This is how tragedy comes: unexpectedly then irreversibly.

I had an hour to wait until I could reasonably leave for the surgery and in that time I tried to feed Jewels some cooled boiled water as the nurse had suggested. Every wall in the house felt hot to the touch. The air was flushed and sickly. If things got any worse, I could call an ambulance. The baby seemed paler now and her lips were sea-grey. Almost alone in Long Meadow End I had that familiar feeling of being watched, judged and found lacking. The red rugs pulsed. Around me I could see wet towels flung, sweaty sleep suits, open bottles of medicine, and dirty nappies unfurled. The bathroom smelt like a muddy sty. From the extensive chaos it looked like we had entertained a hundred sick babies in the last hour. Leaving Mouse watching over Jewels in the crib I went to call Miss Moore again.

When I returned, having failed once more to contact the mother, the boy was kissing Jewels robotically on her flushed forehead and saying, 'Sorry, baby, sorry, sorry.'

'Why you apologising?' I asked, but Mouse ignored me and continued with the strange repetitive action, as though he'd not registered me at all. The light bulbs seemed to be swinging, and I swayed dizzily. 'Tell me, Mouse, why are you saying sorry to Jewels?' I shook his woollen head to urge a confession.

'I, like, gave her a little bit of a pill? To, like, calm her down? She was sad. But I don't think she liked it.'

'What pill?'

'My pills. They are to relax you. She's kinda, like, unhappy, don't you think?'

I rushed downstairs and, almost without thinking, tried Hepsie again. I think I just wanted to hear her ansaphone voice, and was quite shocked when she answered.

'What is it?' she said anxiously. But it was as if she already knew. 'Tell me, what's happened to her?'

'She's sick. And now –' Before I could finish the sentence, she stopped me.

'Wait there,' she said, and hung up.

I dialled the emergency nurse again. An ambulance was called. But when I had collected hats and coats for the children and raced back upstairs the room hung with a humming calm. Silent, spacey, there was no sign of Mouse or Jewels. The room was empty. I called their names. The only reply was the ghostly chug of our expensive appliances. The children were gone. Immediately I sniffed for that too-sweet smell of Mrs and Mrs Vine. And I listened.

And remembered that first strange day at Chessington Vale, the arguments overhead and the little nymph twisting on the sofa before me, and how I'd once wanted mystery more than anything in my life. But a screaming dash around the house and out into the garden, wailing to the treetops, and thumping my head with my fist provided no further clues to the whereabouts of the two sick children. Like water into a sponge, the sky felty and grey ate up my cries.

I ran back inside, upstairs, paused on the landing, that night-time square of squeaks and sounds, then ran on, up to the very top of the house. It was no surprise that the door to Miss Moore's room was locked. Thumping the wood and rattling the handle made no difference. It felt eerie to be up there alone. Danker, smellier, shiftier, it was not an easy place to be. There was no sign of life. Wolves, I remembered, had raised children in many parts of the world, not just in mythology, but in truth, in England, in not too distant times. Dingoes had taken newborns from their cribs. Foxes had dashed through nursery windows and given tiny noses fatal nips. Malevolent country people had raised princes as paupers. I could hear that distant Wychwood groan, the chaotic push of the real world cracking open our gloss.

Then I dashed outside to search those Vine outbuildings. It must be my fault that Mouse had found a tablet to give to Jewels. I should resign. The medication should be kept high up in a locked cupboard. I wandered through the sheds panting with despair. The pile of tiny shoes, the soft beds indented by shapes of sleeping girls. Before I even looked through the ivy-shaded window I had the picture of a large green cattle truck rumbling furiously along the lanes. I've seen bullets leave guns more slowly than that van coming towards me that day. I ran out to meet it. With a screeching lurch it turned into the gravel driveway of Long Meadow End, came to a rattling stop and out of each passenger door jumped a Mrs Vine.

'I can't find the children,' I cried. 'They were here a minute ago but they seem to have disappeared.' Behind Mrs and Mrs Vine the girls poured like treacle, sweet and sticky and so strong they were all over me inside and out. The seven women of the family stopped to look at me and I was held there by their gaze for a decade, until the girls began to hunt around. The mother Vine glared a moment longer with a special murderous look.

Yes, garish – that was the way I saw the world; no longer was anything ordinary to me, no desire not corrupted, no love not doomed, no romance not damned. No suitcase not a valise, no perfume not a cologne, every woman a lunatic or a crook.

'We'll spread out,' the grandmother shouted, and without pausing to discuss the matter the family began a quick military operation. 'You go into the house,' Mrs Vine junior ordered her two elder daughters, 'and you go into the sheds,' she said to the twins, 'and you come with me,' she said to Betsie.

Already the grandmother could be seen up ahead racing through the trees like a hound. I can still see the five Vine girls running around in the green with sunlight cloaked around them, and they are still bouncing on smiles, sweet and sparkly as though they had been dipped in sugar. It was like the Vine women had never left Long Meadow End, now that they were back where they so obviously belonged.

'Hi, John,' a voice said. 'How are things?' It was Miss Moore. She was outside the house in the sunshine and she

116

was carrying Jewels, gently, a tender hand on the baby's forehead. Miss Moore was wearing a tight white T-shirt that revealed her midriff and a short silver skirt, an outfit Brian must have suggested to make her look utterly helpless. Beside her stood Mouse, his arms hanging limply by his side, his expression concealed beneath his woolly headgear. The baby looked better. She was no longer vomiting, and her rash had almost gone. 'I gave her some antihistamine, John.' My smile of shock, relief, anger, love and confusion spoke for me. 'You know that's what you should do if a baby has a bad reaction like that.'

'I thought you were at the gym,' I said.

She looked at me as if she had no idea of the meaning of the word. 'I found them sitting on the stairs,' Miss Moore said quietly, stroking a hand over Mouse's head. 'She's all right now. I was upstairs. You should have called me.' Her voice had the odd singsong lilt of a maniac in a dream.

Mouse looked at me and shrugged. 'Freaky, Mummyman. All the time you're watching us, she's watching you, and they're watching her, right?' He would tell me later he believed Miss Moore had taken him and Jewels to her room when she saw Mrs and Mrs Vine approaching Long Meadow End from their hill. 'A long arm appeared, just like in a spooky movie, and just plucked us clean away, Mummyman.'

'I came to your room,' I said.

'Only when I looked out the window . . .' Miss Moore said, gazing beyond me at Mrs and Mrs Vine and not even caring to complete the sentence. Behind me the Vines had come to a halt in the driveway. All seven of the strange women were looking keenly at Miss Moore, the baby and the boy. 'Look,' Miss Moore continued suddenly, 'we're doing our best in very difficult circumstances.'

'So, aren't you going to invite us all inside for a glass of champagne?' Isolde Vine said insolently, and behind her the smaller sisters giggled.

'Or a line of cocaine,' Celeste added, and was promptly slapped by her grandmother.

'You know we miss Hepsie terribly,' the mother said. 'This isn't easy for us either. The last two years since Hepsie's been in London have been dreadful. Not a day has passed without me expecting a visit from the police.'

There were tears in the mother Vine's eyes. 'They genuinely love her,' Miss Moore would say to me later that night, 'and we can never compete with that.'

'I think we are doing pretty well out here,' Miss Moore said to the Vines quietly. 'Why don't you just go back up there and leave us alone?'

'So, how come the baby came to be poisoned?' the grandmother said harshly.

'It doesn't need to be this difficult,' Hepsie's mother said softly. 'We could help you out. Look at poor John, he's exhausted. No wonder things are going wrong. I mean, we'd be happy to take the baby for a few hours a day, just to give him a break.'

'Oh yes, how kind! I bet you would be more than happy to do that!' Miss Moore exclaimed with a sharp laugh.

'I'm sorry,' Mouse said suddenly, as if sensing the conversation could descend any minute into violence, 'it was me. I gave her the pill.'

'That boy needs his mother,' the grandmother said quietly. 'And soon.'

'Excuse me, here comes the ambulance. I'd better go with Jewels to the hospital,' Miss Moore said, pulling herself up authoritatively in front of the women. 'I refuse to take any chances with my baby.'

'We can take her in the ambulance, if you like,' Mrs Vine said, her stare transfixed by the interplanetary eyes before her. 'We're not as busy as you. We've got all day to spend with the children.'

The two Vine women narrowed their eyes at us.

'No, thank you,' Miss Moore replied. 'I know what my priorities are.'

'Look, you musn't let her lie on her back in case she's sick again,' the grandmother said brusquely. 'Hold her like this.' And the old woman reached those dry twiggy fingers towards our plump fresh baby.

'Get off her!' Miss Moore shouted, wrenching the baby away from Mrs and Mrs Vine. 'I know that!'

'Well, do it then!' Isolde said angrily.

Miss Moore held Jewels upright, very stiffly, and clutched at her. Like the child was a precious statuette, a long-coveted award she'd won for a glittering performance. A few minutes later Miss Moore escaped with the ambulance crew, leaving me alone in the outdoors with the seven strange women from the caravans.

'You need a cleaner,' was all that the grandmother said eventually. I knew something had changed: Mrs and Mrs Vine no longer trusted me with the baby. 'Just a few hours every day. To give you a break. And make sure nothing like this happens again.' I could hear a dissenting grumbling begin amongst the girls. 'Celeste and Isolde will help you. Alternate days.'

I could hear groaning and loud swears, culminating in a united drone of 'Muuuuuuuuuuum!'

'I actually don't think Miss Moore would agree,' I said

politely, though the thought of the girls in the house delighted me. 'She's a very private person. She prefers for us to keep ourselves to ourselves.'

'Though I guess we, like, totally don't have any choice, right?' Mouse said, gazing at the females.

They had gathered in a tight ring around us. We couldn't even make a run for it.

Mouse was correct. Though my objections continued politely, they were greeted with a smiling silence, and no more was said on the matter as the women climbed back into their dusty vehicle.

'Celeste will start tomorrow morning,' the grandmother said as she waved to me slowly from the window of the departing truck.

Chapter Eleven

B rian decided the best way to deal with Miss Moore's fears, Mouse's nightmares and particularly the increasingly intrusive and intimate visits of the Wychwood villagers was to grasp hard the nettle. We should welcome 'the ordinary people' into our life. Sling open every cupboard, throw open every drawer, and allow the poor damned serfs a little familiarity, in the hope that they would release us from the awful intensity of their watery gaze. Brian later also insisted, rather contrary to the initial aim, that by parading the international calibre of Miss Moore's most superior friends we could intimidate the dowdy peasants into a retreat.

All proceeds were to go to charity.

Long Meadow End had been cleaned to perfection by Isolde and Celeste and then themed by professionals with a hundred golden metre-high rabbits. In every room a ceiling shower of silver eggs hailed. Hung throughout the house, from floor to ceiling, were illuminated rows of bunnies. Ladies came in the most surprising bonnets, and fine gentlemen wore them too. The holly wreaths were long gone from the cottage doors and our chrome kitchen was fully fitted. It was April and Brian had decreed our house-warming party the Wychwood Easter Bonnet Ball 200 –. By midnight the house was too hot and we had to fling wide the windows and doors and spill out into the winter garden, and further into the fields. Dance into the cold Wychwood lanes to let the icy air cool us.

Though I knew my focus should be on Miss Moore and the children it was hard not to be swept up in the hot glamour of the incredible party. All around the village sporty London men chased slender London women who fled on screams of delight as the Wychwood wind moaned like lost laughter. All the men were big and handsome as cattle, and all the women wore hard diamonds in their precious cold eyes.

Brian was using the party to distract us.

There was no sign of Hepsie Vine, or her dark sisters, though I estimated at least a hundred partygoers. Drunken silhouettes could be seen leaning into one another, at such a tilt that sure desire looked like deep sorrow. Some guests stood head to head sighing in far-off outhouses, or laughing in farm buildings where the tips of cannabis cigarettes jigged like ruby flies through abandoned barns.

(I took as many snaps as I could manage before I became too drunk to focus.)

Misty Moore, just by staying young and keeping pretty and getting rich, had given us all of this. And just by being *her* nanny I was part of this wonderful glittering world. I smiled at every face I saw. That night because we were all so rich and beautiful we could make anything happen just by wanting it to be so. As I looked at the sky, endless icy stars appeared, as though nature had decided to crash the party as our special guests.

'He said I was an improbable Lady Macbeth,' a high voice sang as it twirled past me. 'I mean, what on earth did he mean by that?'

'Improbably good, probably,' I called after the babe as she flickered away through the sleek and silky crowd.

'Oh yes,' she cried back, delighted, 'probably. And isn't this place hilarious! Trust Misty Moore.'

'On top of everything she has her own dark castle,' the chasing critic agreed. 'What a girl!'

'But won't it just be perfect for photo-shoots,' the woman laughed back. Then vanished with the critic through a hole in a hedge.

'At least this isn't quite as tasteless as that weird Chessington place,' a woman whispered, retching out an amazing indigo tongue. 'God, that place is awful.'

'Give it a few months,' her young companion smiled.

'S'a miracle she has a baby at all.'

'I know! According to Emily she's been infertile for years.'

'Don't make me laugh!' said a man with a tiny sparse designer beard, grown on just his under-chin and his upper lip. 'She's had at least four abortions since I've known her.'

'Do you think she's breast-feeding?' a thin glistening woman mused to her fat perspiring companion.

'Get real,' he panted, 'she'd be lucky to suckle Tiny Tears with those tits.'

I heard all of this and more. Yet so impressed must I have been by the quality of our guests that night that I can still remember who I photographed at the Wychwood Easter Bonnet Ball and where they ranked in public importance.

The crowd was doubtless most impressed by newly busty Katie McMasters, just back from filming a guest appearance in a sitcom in New York and fabulously arm in arm with a tall sardonic script editor called 'spelt with an x' Jaxon. They took a great picture. There was surprise too at the appearance of positively drug-tested former Olympic swimmer Unity Etienne. Nina Stone, who read the news that year on Channel Five, came, though speaking, everyone commented, in a very different voice to the one she used on TV. The richest guest was certainly Honor Wilkes, whose father steered unitedmeatpackers.com through a hostile takeover. Dulcie Bleu came, the groundbreaking erotic actress and controversial performance artiste, who was taking that year her X-rated new show to the Edinburgh Festival. She insisted on sticking her tongue out for the picture. All wore the most ridiculous hats.

I could go on and on because just remembering these names still excites me. Surely the English were the finest, most handsome people on this earth. If we could do nothing else we could still do youth and beauty most perfectly. Never in my life had I talked so passionately about that multitude of human things that mattered not a jot. By midnight I'd forgotten I'd trapped then poisoned the baby and had crazy thoughts about Miss Moore, Isolde and Celeste. I decided to devote my entire life to making frosty women smile. Even our army of hired caterers were beautiful enough to make you want to sign over your kidneys with nothing but a wink and a spring roll in return.

Did some young women really arrive from Edinburgh by helicopter? Did they wear transparent bonnets with tiny glass propellers? I think so, for I remember six young passengers in tiny tight evening dresses jumping the last few feet to earth in their bare feet. Before being borne over the dark wet grasses to our wide door on a riot of cheers. Behind them, in the black field, the furious blades still slew the country air. A web of moonlight catching the glass machine as it hits the ground gently. Did Misty twirl in through the door on the light embrace of the pilot? Did she catch me by the buffet table and, giving me that hard lunar smile, say, 'It's going to be all right! Everyone's come, John, oh everyone I've ever loved is here. And still there's no sign of *them*.' Yes, I think so, and I congratulated her again on her popularity, which had made the event such a success. She kissed and congratulated me too. I felt a fizz of pleasure when the glamorous guests marvelled at our Sicilian glass bricks, Perspex cellos, abstract sculptures and camel-hair rugs. I felt pride at the way they melted as they sipped on our finest pink champagnes, giggled when they swallowed our colourful cocktails. Everything was new and bright. Misty nodded as I praised her, but did not look in my eye.

I didn't like to picture too closely how he had achieved it, but that night of the Easter Bonnet Ball Brian was definitely a man of the moment. He wore a bonnet in the shape of a peacock's plume. With real feathers. Just looking at him unnerved me. Made me fear that there was something grotesque about the event: everyone had come like puppets, to perform. 'So what? What did you expect? They're mostly actors, they're trained to pretend,' Hepsie had remarked when months later I confessed my thoughts.

And for a gay guy Brian displayed an enviable ability to make pretty women laugh. And something so unsettling happened when he gazed at you – did he want to punch you or possess you? Either way it was a challenge that ripped you out of complacency and made you reassess everything you'd ever thought about the world. Brian had mixed up desire, loathing, servitude and mastery into a combination that was uniquely, frighteningly, he. (Over the last ten years Brian has gone on to be a rich and successful guy, running his own music-management firm. He takes pretty girls and makes them household names. He has friends, contacts and business the world over.)

No one old or ugly was celebrated at our party. That night we triumphed over the natural world. The villagers and their shabby hats were kept in the shadows in the manner of a studio audience, only there to encourage and applaud the young and fresh. No one saw anything about our lives in Long Meadow End, other than what we wanted to show them.

Every so often I could see Misty sweep through her party like a flame. I assumed that she was having as much fun as I was. To announce the return of her pre-pregnancy figure (she now went to the gym for up to six hours every day and ran so many miles that she would surely soon qualify for the Olympics), her dress was no more than a breath of grey smoke.

She'd lit the touch paper of the evening by descending the wide stairs of Long Meadow End alone. Step by step. Slow as honey down a spoon. The silk dress stroked her hips and breasts in a dawdling caress. Her bonnet, a spray of primroses and snowdrops, scenting her so fragrantly. And the whooshing intake of breath her entrance provoked was as fast and physical as when a smooth city train hurtles through a silent country field.

We were all utterly sure that if we gazed upon that smoky dress hard enough we would witness the exact moment it evaporated into air. Because her shoes were so high she gazed down on her guests as though from a balloon over-head. Then she swept forward and was clutched by arm after arm. Cooed over, adored as a child. Thunderstruck, we were all touched. Everyone wanted to fall in love instantly. I was not alone in my blindness. We all wanted to find meaning in that complicated dumbness. We gazed at her harder and harder to try and catch a ghostly whisper of that foreign meaning in her smile, her wiggle. For that night her gestures, that body's wordless manipulation, seemed not a mark of gross irrelevance, but rather evidence of a true tenderness capable of changing the world.

Sometime after midnight I saw Mouse pass by in the arms of an unfamiliar man. Mouse had refused to wear the expensive silly clothes that Brian had bought him. All he would say was, 'Mummyman, I, like, don't wanna draw attention to myself. You dress up as a clown if you want to, but if my mom turns up I want her to be able to recognise me.' He was quiet and dopy, his head heavy beneath his balaclava, his eyes half closed, his lips lolled slightly open. In the last couple of weeks I'd discovered that since the poisoning Mouse kept, in addition to the insects, a vole under a glass cheese dome in his bedroom. It was late; perhaps the boy was tired. But I wondered. If they would ever . . . ever just slightly increase his medication to ensure good behaviour – perhaps just once, on this most important of nights?

Misty passed by, wearing Jewels tight on her chest like a brooch. The baby had its tiny pink hands up over its face as though desperately embarrassed by us all. Misty nuzzled her daughter over and over, drinking her innocence in. Each minute she seemed to love the child more. 'They've not come,' Miss Moore whispered, clutching me by the arm, a moment later, 'the Vines. It's such a relief. Honestly, John, I do think we're going to be all right after all.'

'Oh yes,' I replied. 'We're going to have the most wonderful summer.'

'And I do so love seeing you driving your little yellow car,' she beamed. 'You look so gorgeous and happy. It's so you.' Secrets: that concealment, an edgy mystery that lies so close to charm. That cold self-serving dagger of dark light in her eye.

'Yes, I think I truly love that car. I'm ecstatic.'

'I am too! I'm over the moon in seventh heaven floating on cloud nine.'

Would she kiss me too then? Long and deep. Again and again. I guess it was the hope of it that prevented me questioning her more. Take me upstairs and tie me to her bedposts, thrash me with her golden hair? There was something about our life that spring, lonely and isolated as animals, the Vines pawing around us spreading their scent, that made me unable to lose the thought that mating seemed our most likely occupation. I flirted wordlessly, running my tongue slowly, drunkenly, around my upper lip, snorting slightly down my nose, letting one hand rest heavily on my belt buckle, the other stroke lightly against my inner thigh.

'We just have to ensure that the Vines stay away, especially Hepsie,' she whispered, as her smiles shattered to the more familiar haunted stare.

'Why, when she's living in luxury in your magnificent London house, would Hepsie ever come back here?'

'It's safer for it to be lived in,' she said flatly. Then she touched my cheek – touched me truly and tenderly for the first time – and gave me an apologetic smile, to say she was aware Hepsie's London location was another thing she had concealed from me.

'Anyway,' I said sadly, 'she ran away from Wychwood, so I doubt she'll be in any hurry to return.'

'Did she really?' Miss Moore said, as though she'd never heard that before, and for once I believed her. 'There's really nothing that girl wouldn't do to be famous.'

'What's the problem between you and Hepsie?'

'Though I'm glad she ran away. You're right, it makes it less likely that she'd choose to come back.'

'After her father and grandfather shot themselves, she ran off to London.'

'Oh yes,' Miss Moore giggled, 'the suicides! Do you believe that?' And she wandered off, laughing at the high ceiling.

Dizzied with the mention of the young Vine beauties, I wandered outside into the lane. To the right I could see three limousines, two with their curtains firmly drawn, one occupied by a glossy couple, wide-mouthed with gluey ecstasy. I went round to the back garden again where I could see our weeping willow, our high elms. For a long time I watched the trees creaking above, down at the dark grass alive with insects. I listened to the hedgerows rustling with chirps scuttled through with rats and mice. Misty had refused to allow bright lights to be twisted through the branches of her trees, or orange flares to mark the borders of her land, or fairy lights to loop above her black pool of lawn. It had been agreed that the party designers could do anything inside the house as long as they preserved the garden.

'Sweetie,' a man cried, 'what *on earth* are you *doing* living out *here*?'

I fancied I saw a silver hare soar through the darkness aglow with moonlight. I lay down on the icy ground, so blades of frosted grass pricked my skin. I closed my eyes. I could smell the bloody juices of animals simmering in the ground. Occasionally I fancied I heard a far-off dog whine from the Vinery. Right now perhaps a slender girl was unlatching the caravan door, tiptoeing away from the crones, treading softly down the three steel steps, slipping quietly past a sleeping dog, inching out the gate, running though the forest and skipping down the long hill towards our house. I had checked from the drawing-room window earlier and the low bar of cerulean blue still flickered far across the meadow, on the top of the dark hill.

Just when my mood was sinking into a pit of lovesickness and I was in danger of losing faith with the beauty and affluence around me I saw in my mind's eye a line of faces looming through the shadows. Some fuzz sparked and bounced around them like curls of ash up from a flame. But they carried no torches, and flickered no tall candles before them. Yet they came forwards into our party illuminated in the dark countryside in a way that the London folk were not. And when I struggled to my feet, yes, it was they. Mrs and Mrs Vine! Coming through black fields towards the twinkling manor. Down they came. Upon us they descended. Behind them, darkly, silent, single file, like a row of devilish ducklings, came Celeste, Isolde, Betsie, Violet and Alice. And their dog.

I should say something about what the Vines wore – those outfits that made such an impression on the London guests. Or rather what they didn't wear. Shorts, which could not have been tighter if they'd been brushed on with denim paint, miniskirts, bikini tops – and that was just the mother. And the grandmother, whose nut-brown wrinkled tits were like two apples, fallen in September and discovered in December, and hanging there shockingly visible. It seemed the whole family had dressed, not to come to the chicest party of their sorry lives, but to sit in the window of a bordello.

Sometime later that night a man with a camera would catch Hepsie's mother by the arm and swing her round like a ballerina and then lower her to the ground. With a low bow he'd tell the younger Mrs Vine (whose startling outfit had immediately been condemned by several whispering women as inappropriately tight, cheap and sexy and ex-alted by others as the very latest thing in White Trash Chic) that he was an art director working that summer for a Parisian style magazine. Would she mind him taking her number and a few Polaroids of her smoking and scowling, for him to show to his colleagues in London, Paris, New York and Moscow?

'Is, she . . .?'

'I'm afraid not, lad,' the grandmother said with a frown to acknowledge my disappointment. In the presence of such youth and riches old Mrs Vine seemed like she'd been just dug from a grave. I knew they were still angry with me for allowing Jewels to be poisoned.

'But she's fine fine fine,' Hepsie's mother said instantly, waving her rough hand in my face, as though to conjure away my mad interest in her daughter. 'Everything's getting sorted out. I think she might be back soon.'

'Did you tell Hepsie about Jewels and the tablets?' I asked.

'Didn't want to worry her,' the older Mrs replied. 'She's got enough to bother about.'

Having realised Hepsie was not with them, I was disappointed by the presence of Mrs and Mrs Vine at our party. 'Did Miss Moore invite you?'

'No. But we thought we'd come anyway,' the grandmother replied.

'I know this used to be your house. And that Hepsie's swapped it for Miss Moore's.'

'We miss it,' the mother said. 'Just like we miss our Hepsie.'

'Why did you leave?'

'When my husband and son died we didn't have any choice. No money,' the grandmother said bluntly. 'We put it up for sale and moved to the caravans. We miss it dreadfully but the girls miss it more.'

'Just like they all miss Hepsie. Isolde especially.'

I'm ashamed to say I understood what Brian meant when he commented later that the attendance of the Vine women was 'like a few specks of grit in a bowl of perfect cream'. They were old and poor, and we were young and rich. Isolde and Celeste were our *cleaners*, for heaven's sake, and while the girls were indeed quite stunning in their trashy near-nudity, they were not Hepsie. Not yet quite pretty *enough*, slender and sexy *enough*, to justify a prime position at our party.

Meanwhile the Vine dog sniffed noisily up the skirts of the most fashionable women and dribbled bubbling fluid on the polished shoes of their men. The five Vine girls were crowded around the buffet table giggling obscenely. All had Hepsie's dark hair and eyebrows, all were so ripe and fruity they could have just been plucked from a tree.

'You look exhausted,' the elder Vine said to me. I nodded and sighed. No matter how much money we had we couldn't ignore the fact that Mrs and Mrs Vine and their daughters had something we couldn't buy – it was quite infuriating. 'Even with help with the cleaning it's too much for you. You need more assistance. You need a cook maybe, or some time off from the kids.'

'Would you bring Jewels up to us one afternoon?' the mother Mrs Vine asked.

'You don't have to tell *her*,' the grandmother added.

'You can have a rest and our girls can take care of Jewels.'

In the distance I saw Celeste, Isolde, Betsie, Violet and Alice slinking through the crowd like dusky snakes. Their midnight eyes tipping between the floor and the ceiling slowly. And soon came the giggles and gasps, the songs and screeches, of the party reaching its height; love and dancing spilling through all the Wychwood lanes easy as blown bubbles. This was the crucial hour, before it dragged, sank, and popped on the hedgerows leaving nothing but a pet-rolled party-mist in the morning air.

I found Jewels in my arms and a moment later a thin woman stopped me and said, 'Huh, so that's the kid.' I nodded, and for some time praised the baby like I was her personal PR agent. 'I can see what they mean though,' the woman said with a quizzical frown. I said nothing. I no longer asked for information, but she continued. 'Those who say it's not hers. It looks nothing like her.'

I saw Brian speaking urgently on his mobile phone, and then Miss Moore alone at the edge of the garden. She was looking not to where the party was raging, blaring in all its golden triumph, but away up the hill to the light that shone from the caravans. She had folded her arms and rubbed at her shivers so her thin body moved in a rocking motion. I wanted to go and speak to Miss Moore but could think of nothing to say that would be cheering and exuberant enough. Instead I slunk through the party to where the white limousine had its door flung wide. A stream of stooped and giggling guests was pressing inside.

Since the Vines had arrived I was finding it hard to sustain my pleasure in the champagne party. Cider, sweet and strong. This was the smell the Vine women brought into their old house, and soon I was smashed on it, quickly hungover and nauseous. I couldn't forget the younger Mrs Vine's hands. They were gnarled and manly. I might be naive and self-centred but I was not entirely blind to the world around me. Now the preening party chat ached at my ears. The louche poses of the beautiful women were suddenly as grotesque to me as the kisses of drunken mannequins. They were thin and long-limbed, but cruel and controlled. All the beautiful outfits were no more than ornate disguises. I saw Brian sitting with a leering beauty on the boot of the black limousine. He was pitching forward and clapping his hands, delirious with mirth, as though he'd just met the sexiest, funniest woman in the entire planetary system, and had forgotten me entirely.

Then I felt a tap on my back and I turned to see strange Isolde Vine staring at me. Her bonnet was no more than a baseball cap speared with a daffodil. 'The thing is,' Isolde said, raising her girlish voice to a shout to be heard above the noise of the party, 'they don't seem in the least guilty about what they've done! I can't believe they're having this ridiculous posh party. It's obvious they're just rubbing it in.'

'Guilty about what exactly?'

'Oh nowt!' she cried. Then, as though deciding she had to continue, she said, 'Having a girl cleaning up after 'em.'

'I think you'll find employing staff is not a crime. And if you're really angry because Miss Moore bought your old house, well, I'm sorry, and I can see that it could be upsetting, but I'm afraid that's just the way the market works.'

'And leaving the children all day long in the care of one teenage bloke.'

'Brian helps me,' I said defensively. 'And I do my best. Pretty well, actually.'

'Brian! Oh I hate him. I hated him as soon as . . . He's got a lot to answer for. He's just as responsible.'

'What should we be guilty for?' I laughed.

At university I'd seen the wacko political cults into which middle-class guilt had pushed some students. I refused to hate and destroy myself just because I had more than someone else. My mother and father had their faults, sure, but they'd worked for everything they had. They couldn't expect to be blamed for the random unfairness of the world, or the laziness and ineptitude of others.

'I just mean they should do their dirty work themselves . . .' Isolde was almost crying now, red sobs that reminded me again of a beautiful girl one day six months ago in a millionairess's house in London. It seemed more and more likely to me that Miss Moore had sacked Hepsie for a serious reason I had not yet discovered.

'And they should cook proper food! No wonder poor Mouse is crazy, he only eats crisps! I hate to see him so ill and unhappy. Why don't you cook him something nice?'

'We employ you as a cleaner,' I said nastily, 'not to comment on our diet.'

'You don't know what it's like scrapping around on someone else's carpet all day,' she said, twisting a fist into her tired eyes. 'And having to go poking around in their toilet bowl and picking hairs and phlegm from plugholes and finding all kinds of stuff at the bottom of the bed in the morning.'

But before I could blush the bad-tempered girl vanished in the crowd, leaving just a trace of sulphur behind her.

Several hours passed and I had not seen Miss Moore. Our guests began to ask after her. So I went up to her room and I knocked. I was not alarmed by her disappearance: she preferred dazzlingly to appear then vanish. Perhaps she was down in the bathroom. Miss Moore and I both had our own bathrooms. I had no idea what went on in hers, except she stayed in there for a long time and came out looking very different to how she went in. I continued to knock. I thought I heard a movement. She must have retreated to her room, exhausted by her public performance. I'd come to understand my boss's unease about the general public. On the one occasion I'd walked the streets freely with Miss Moore, three young men, around my own age though from a rather different social sphere, flew past us on bicycles yelling, 'Slag, slag, slag.' She'd not responded to the screaming insult, though a familiar shade of sadness clouded those unnatural eyes.

I knew she was in the room because I could hear a shuffling. I called to her and offered Jewels, food, a stiff drink, and nothing worked, until the most shocking thing happened. Perhaps I pressed too hard, or perhaps she flicked the key, or perhaps the magical door just dissolved at my touch, for the next thing I knew I was inside Miss Moore's private room: the attic room, at the top of Long Meadow End. I'd never stepped a single toe inside before. Perhaps I could have ignored the sight before me – I certainly tried, keeping my eyes high and ahead and gazing at the tall body of my employer with a butler's cold attention – but then my curiosity betrayed me and my shocked eyes were roving wildly.

The room into which I had just crashed had a murky haze. As though gauze of endless dreams still hung milkily in the air. It was a smoky yellow radiance as over city rooftops towards the end of a stinky summer's day. Elsewhere, in corners, there was a blue-black bruise to the light – a boundary of terror. In other places the ache of disorder as clothes were strewn over the floor, glasses, cups and plates littered the furniture. Piles of newspapers were overhung with underwear. A bin liner squatted and fermented by the window. I saw now that of all the many rooms in Long Meadow End this was the only one that had not been redesigned.

Miss Moore saw me. She opened her mouth wide – then spoke. 'I'm such a slut,' she sighed, perhaps hoping for a jaunty tone.

'Is it Mrs and Mrs Vine? Are you afraid of them?' I said, because, just as their arrival had ruined the party for me, I sensed it was they Miss Moore was hiding from.

'I should live in a dusty motel with room service.'

The room was no accident. Miss Moore had chosen to live like this. The carpet was still threadbare and floral, the walls were still chipped and purple. The furnishings, which were all at least fifty years old, were cheap, dark, heavy wood. The curtain at the window, by which Miss Moore shivered, was still a tattered rag. But most overpowering of all was the smell. It was the sweet drift I had smelt a million times taken to sickening strength. 'It's goat's rue,' she said when she saw me sniffing. Her eyes had doubled in size. I was staring then at the enormous pile of moth-eaten blankets heaped like a nest on the floor, and pressed into the centre a human imprint, as if someone had recently slept there, curled up, foetal. 'It's a galactagogue,' Miss Moore said brightly.

At first it was hard for me to believe the woman who lived in this room had once been a model, and maybe a minor porn star – then it was obvious, Brian was to blame: her secret slovenliness was a desperate reply to the constant public prinking. And the Vines too, I knew that for certain, the way their eyes were torches with far-reaching rays. They caught us in their radiant beam, showing both the stark yellow dazzle of our lives and the terrible everlasting darkness on all sides. But I could not believe that Brian, Celeste or Isolde had not told me about the state of her room. And it made me instantly, self-servingly fearful of what else they might not have told me about Miss Moore.

'Are you all right in here? Didn't you want them to update the room for you?'

'But I like it! It's my very favourite room in the whole house. In fact, I'd go so far as to say, sweet John, that I absolutely hate every single other room in this deeply detestable farmhouse except this one. Now go back to the party.'

'But . . .'

'Go! Leave me to sleep.'

*　　*　　*

I did go, and because I was in shock and needed instant distraction I quickly found a woman. She worked in television and was, beneath all her taut cherry-red smiles, very unhappy. As we talked about her future I touched her frequently. I told her I was a photographer for a magazine. I gasped as though struck by lightning whenever she spoke. She told me her name was Jane. I told her mine was Juan. She kept tight and calculated. The way she straightened her skirt, the quick one-fingered swish of her fringe, the tight interlacing of fingers into a hard fist – all her gestures seemed premediated to achieve an objective without wasting energy. We came eventually to a shaded patch of dry grass under a spreading maple tree. I threw down my coat. We lay across it. Together to chase away the cold we drank and at one point the woman had an itchy toe and she stood up to remove her shoe. The unbalancing caused her to stumble and fall over on top of me. At last! A woman on top of me! When I kissed her it was like we both might cry with relief. Then some time later she was too hot and so peeling off her silver dress and shivering in under the bedding of coats we had made on the leafy ground. We were both a little drunk. Then very. I told her about my career in magazines and memorable shoots in New York and Tokyo. I spent a lifetime listening to tales of her trips to Cannes. She should have been tossed immediately into an icy bath. Yet . . . Yet it was soon to be summer and another exhausting day was coming, and Misty's unhappiness singed me too and I couldn't stop remembering the way Hepsie Vine had lain over that sofa. If I closed my eyes I could imagine that this country bower was my expensively furnished London bedroom, my soft hand-made mattress, duckling-feather pillows, crisp Egyptian cotton sheets. I'd slept with far too few women, and we were deep in the ancient countryside, its fields of rolling green roaring. Surely things were different here, in Wychwood, where no tom cat could be condemned, kicked and slung, simply for catching the dozy mouse.

Chapter Twelve

M rs and Mrs Vine had provided their sulky elder daughters with traditional cleaners' smocks. Those checked polyester working tunics most commonly worn by ashen ladies yawning when boarding the dawn bus. This effective protection from dirt, dust and any other substances thrown up by their work had the downside of totally concealing the girls' bodies.

Still, Isolde and Celeste had settled into a pattern with their cleaning. I was fascinated by them both. Like birds settling on a branch they were both there and untouchable, present, eerie even in their strange chirping and preening, but if you turned your head too quickly to see them, gone. They both excited and alarmed me, particularly as I'd realised pretty quickly that Isolde and Celeste had been told to keep an eye on Jewels. They insisted on seeing the baby when they arrived and when they left. It was not enough for me to tell them she was fine; like government inspectors they had actually to check her. Twice a day a Vine sister monitored Jewels. She was five months now and gorgeous. I had her on a range of expensive organic solids from the supermarket. Each day the sisters interrogated;

they asked me how Jewels had slept, if she had had a dirty nappy, if she had eaten a full pot of food. They unpopped her sleep suits to rub her chest and caress her skin. They sniffed her and stroked her hair, and on one occasion I am certain that they licked her.

Celeste came before school, often arriving at Long Meadow End around 6 a.m., and Isolde came the next day on her way home from school. Consequently it was Isolde I saw the most of. I made sure I was waiting at 4 p.m., my hair brushed, my shirt cleaned of sick and mush, for her arrival. I tried to conceal my excitement by busying myself with my own domestic tasks. Mouse too was delighted by the presence in our lives of the girls, and would wake early to greet Celeste, and as soon as he came home from school would trail around Isolde, asking for any jobs he could do to help. A woman was what he had needed all along.

Sometimes the girls arrived with warm tins of fresh cakes and biscuits that Mrs and Mrs Vine had baked. Mouse loved to eat those glistening tarts: red jam, pink jam, yellow jam, each smooth as satin. After they had eaten, Isolde would supply Mouse with a cloth and a tin of polish and the boy would work calmly by her side. They were like mother and child. I rather envied him the ease with which he had slipped into her affections. I heard the pair talking together, gently and at length and in a way that Mouse rarely spoke to me. Theirs were strange chats about the fields and the trees and when alone with Isolde, Mouse seemed gifted to the point of poetry when he spoke of the natural world.

'Tell me what you've seen in the forest, Mouse,' Isolde asked him one day.

'Ruby pools. Dark as wine. This is where fallen leaves cook up red over ages.'

'Bogs,' she said.

'Bubble into these deep bottomless puddles of blood.'

'Exactly.'

'Some stretch on, like, wider than trucks. And it really stinks in there, yeah? And is all coldy-warm? Like that funny wet tan witch cake?'

'Malt loaf?'

'Like there's all these varieties of shit and then far below the dung-juice, both meaty and ice-chilled, like a turkey roast left to ooze its trickledrip, its scarlet goo, its sap, till midnight.'

In contrast to their affection for Mouse both girls seemed reluctant to speak to me. If I asked Isolde any questions about how Hepsie was faring in London she would shake her head and shrug without saying a word then move away with her duster. Dislike seemed too gentle a word for her feelings towards me: both too gentle and too misleading, for she was rather like that bird on the branch – she had no idea why I could be stumbling, tiptoeing, towards that space that was airborne and only hers. It was as if they knew exactly how I pictured them whenever I took a bath. (I'd not yet had time to begin work on my sketches, but I planned to soon.)

I was longing for information about Hepsie. Brian would tell me nothing either.

'I've been looking out for Hepsie on TV,' I'd said to Brian brightly one morning, 'but I've not seen anything yet.'

'Oh I don't think you'll see her during the day,' he replied. There was a pause before he burst out like a nasty girl. 'I mean it's probably the kind of stuff that's on during the night.' I was confused. 'In Holland!' Brian shrieked.

Miss Moore never mentioned Hepsie. She continued to

gaze most days over our humming garden. Rather than speak to Isolde she left little notes: 'Please could you make sure you concentrate on the downstairs toilet today,' she might write, or 'Hall carpet needs attention.' Isolde seemed to take no offence; she worked calmly. Though both were industrious in their work, Isolde and Celeste had different ways of cleaning. Celeste, the older, more developed and rebellious of the pair, wore a constant scowl. She took frequent rests, during which she leant slumped against the wall with her hands on her curvy hips or twiddled the trashy silver love-heart pendant she wore on her chest, while gazing into the distance. She chewed gum that surely tasted, from the intoxicated way she was masticating, of pure nectar. It was an annoyingly ugly look. Abandoning her task she would take a moment to rifle through our cupboards, removing for closer examination anything that interested her, perhaps stealing a biscuit or helping herself to a glass of chilled champagne (for by early summer that was Misty and Brian's daily beverage of choice). On several occasions, when Celeste believed she was unseen, I would catch her breaking out into a sudden dance, as though helplessly possessed with some inner musical hope. Pursing her lips, wiggling her head from side to side and pumping her arms in furious circles. Sometimes she put the radio on to a pop station as she worked. Washing up caused her to frown as though the job concerned her deeply. It was with a look of disgust that she wiped the inside of the fridge, as Miss Moore had suggested she do on a daily basis.

Watching Celeste gave me the idea I should not paint or draw, but photograph the girls. As a project. As a matter of public record. I had already taken some pictures with my camera but my misty landscapes had proved not so much moody as dull and out of focus. Brian had mockingly condemned them as 'evidence for a planning application' or 'an undergraduate study of drizzle'. He bought me an expensive new camera and advised me to get some people in on the action. The initial idea was to watch Celeste so that I could preserve her glum adolescence on film. If Brian had wanted me preoccupied that spring, then with that gift he'd succeeded.

I discovered Isolde was quieter and more diligent than Celeste. Chairs were lifted off the floor when she vacuumed. To wipe away our breakfast crumbs she would lean right over the chrome kitchen table till she was balanced balletically on just one sturdy leg. Concentration would push the pointy tip of her pink tongue up till it almost touched the end of her stubby nose. She was also the angrier of the two. 'You probably think I like doing this,' she yelled at me. 'I've seen those programmes about cleaning. You probably think housework is so unfashionable that it must be the next big thing!' She wore her hair pulled back in a tight ponytail, whereas Celeste would leave her hair free, pushing it irritably away from her face when she worked. Isolde enjoyed polishing, and seemed to have arranged with her sister that this would be her special duty, for I never saw the elder girl attempt it. I liked to watch Isolde holding the yellow cloth, moving it tenderly, not rubbing but stroking over the woodwork as one washing the back of a much-loved man.

Mouse's friendship with Isolde deepened every day. She would refer to him as 'big man'. 'Hey, big man, do you want to help me do the windows.' Mouse loved to help. When he came home from school he would race to sit outside on the step waiting for Isolde to arrive.

The girls began to bring more elaborate food for Mouse. 'He won't ever get well if he doesn't get a proper diet, will he?' Isolde scowled as she unpacked a huge fluted meat pie from a tin. It was baked to a golden glint and grand as the forest fungi Mouse so adored. Isolde sat at the chrome table and polished cutlery while Mouse ate the pie. On another occasion Celeste arrived with a hunk of ruby ham sequinned with a million peppercorns. 'Eat some yourself, if you like,' Celeste said, 'but really my gran did it especially for Mouse. And she's mushed some up in this jar for Jewels.'

The ham perfumed the house with warm juice for days. After Mouse had eaten the food Mrs and Mrs Vine had prepared for him I would hear him giggling in the kitchen and come in to discover him strikingly without his balaclava, innocent and fresh as a daisy. Some days he did his own baking with Isolde, and I found him with flour in his hair and his arms in a bowl of batter. I felt envious of their closeness. Now that Mouse had left my company and I was no longer a main Mummyman I was more abandoned to the strange light of the fields.

One day I found Mouse cleaning the windows with a crumple of newspaper and a jar of vinegar. Seeing that he had newsprint staining his cheek I went to wipe him with a facecloth. 'Issy, Issy,' he moaned as I approached him. Instantly the girl appeared behind us, swooping, rushing forward and sweeping the boy up into her arms and back safely into the nest of her love. 'It's all right, big man,' she said soothingly, 'it's all right, I'm here now.' And the boy nuzzled into her shoulder. His little arm firmly around her sturdy back, clutching her like he would never let her go. 'I won't let them take you,' Isolde scowled. Mouse was straddling her waist. Then he crossed his legs at the ankles like a toddler, and placed one hand above her left breast. Cuddled together that way the girl and the boy eyed me suspiciously. (Whenever I saw the girls kissing Mouse or Jewels I felt bad about the other things I had pictured them doing, and vowed to stop it for that moment on – until the next time.)

'He's told me he wants to go back to America, back to his mother,' Isolde told me one morning. Mouse was in the room so we spoke in harsh whispers, like bitter parents.

'Can't you tell how lonely he is?'

'Well, no one's stopping him,' I replied frostily.

'Are you sure? How come you've not even tried to find his mother and father? How come no one seems to care that he's living here with you two lunatics?'

'It seems to me he's been abandoned. His mother thinks he's with his dad, and his dad has pissed off somewhere. How's that our fault?'

'You don't think maybe they're looking for him frantically, but they can't find him?'

'Why would we stop them finding him?' I exclaimed, too loudly, so Mouse looked round sadly. 'We're only here so Misty can get over the birth of the baby then we're off back to London.'

'You're such an idiot. Do you know that? Do you really think anyone would come here to get over anything?'

'Mouse's family, whoever they are, should be very grateful Misty's done all she has. Anyone else would have handed him over to social workers. His parents only have to come looking and they'll find him.'

'It's hardly an obvious place for him to be, is it? How

would they find him here? Isn't that precisely why you're all here, so that no one finds you?'

The conversation had become a sequence of hot hisses. 'It's his mother who doesn't want him, and his father. Why are you and your family so determined to make us feel guilty? Are you maybe all a little jealous, perhaps?'

'You really believe Mouse is here voluntarily. You don't think maybe that Miss Moore snatched him.'

'Why on earth . . .?'

But tears were bulging over the reddened rims of her eyes and Isolde dashed away into a far corner of the house. Flying upstairs in her pale smock like some frightened angel. After that Isolde and Mouse fell into a conspiratorial silence whenever I appeared. They ate their delicious home-cooked feasts with the kitchen door firmly closed. If they spoke of Hepsie, Mouse would tell me nothing about it, for though I probed him he would reveal nothing of what passed between him and Isolde.

One morning Celeste arrived with her three younger sisters, Violet, Alice and Betsie, and two yellow sponge cakes, so light they seemed to hover like spacecraft above their white china plates. 'Mum's gone to London with my gran,' she informed me, 'so I had to bring this lot along. Where's Jewels?'

'London?' I asked. 'To see Hepsie? Is she all right? What's happened?'

'Where's Jewels? I need to check that she's OK.'

'So your mum and gran are seeing Hepsie? Is something wrong?'

'Hmm,' she nodded, 'she's miserable,' but would say nothing further on the matter.

There was no time to question her more keenly, for there

was considerable chaos in the house, as after they had eaten the sponge cake the girls chased poor Mouse up and down the stairs, shrieking. Celeste insisted later that day that I let the girls play with Jewels. The three littlest sisters spent several hours cooing over the baby adoringly.

'It's a great idea to have a cleaner,' I said to Miss Moore one evening when we were sitting gazing over the black garden, sipping a glass of wine, bored beyond sanity by our endless attempts at sunniness. Before us lay a plate of fresh baking delivered that day by Isolde: two frosted choux fingers rippled with cream, and six misted pink buns.

'Oh yes, doesn't cleaning look relaxing! I do wish I had time to do some cleaning. I'm sure I'd find it really spiritually calming. And baking!'

'They both seem to be doing a really good job.'

'Hmm, I've been watching them both.'

'You have?'

'Hmm, though they don't know of course that I'm watching them, that might put them off and freak them out, but I am.'

'Are you?' I said, deeply embarrassed that I was not alone in my voycurism.

'I thought I'd better.'

'You did?'

'Yes, I'm very, very quiet,' she said breathlessly. So she was as alarmed and amazed by them both as I. 'Sometimes I just look down from the top banisters as she's scuttling around in the hall. Once I spied from the laundry cupboard while she was wandering around on the stairs with the broom.'

'Oh,' I said with a thrill.

'And if you hide beneath that big coat stand, it's amazing how totally you are concealed! Have you ever hidden there?'

The vision was so comic that immediately I bubbled into laughter. Miss Moore laughed too, dirty, deeply and entirely falsely. That laugh that had bolstered her bank account for the last two decades. 'No,' I chuckled, 'I've never hidden there.'

Though it was true that I had, while waiting for photographic inspiration, occasionally spied on Isolde and Celeste from other dark corners of the house. I needed to, for I was increasingly afraid of them both. It seemed all of us now understood the pleasure of watching those who believe they are unseen – particularly those whose delicious darkness cannot be absorbed in public.

'Oh, I thoroughly recommend it. You see people in their true light only when they don't know you're watching. It's the only way I could make sure that they weren't getting up to anything dangerous with Jewels.'

Or to put it another way, our polished deception was the only shield we had against their raw candour.

'You're a peeping Tom,' I said jovially, but was then worried. What secrets had Miss Moore seen in me? What had I done not knowing that I was being observed? Like Miss Moore, from now on I would have to learn always to be prepared for unexpected sightings. Never to let my guard drop in public. Just create one place, a bedroom, a cupboard, a hole, where I could ensure I was unwatched. And learn only ever to be unguarded in that one space.

Chapter Thirteen

'You know I was once jealous of her, can you believe that!' Hepsie shouted when I picked up the phone later that week. Despite what Brian had told me, drugs were the first thought I had. Crack, heroin, amphetamines, for she raved on as though she didn't even know she had me, a listener.

'I discovered how once she ate mouthfuls of food at mealtimes rather than platefuls. How she had truck-loads of cellulite sucked out of her thighs every month by a team of Harley Street fat experts. I knew where exactly they injected the freezing poison to ensure that her brow stayed as smooth as a china tea-plate. And you see, it worked. Even when she was in her mid-thirties she looked like a teenager. My mother could have been her *mother*. Though you know in fact they are the same age.'

'Hi, Hepsie,' I said, 'hello, it's John here. Are you OK?'

'I read that every time she had an interview for a magazine she agreed to meet up with every journalist in a lap-dancing joint. At first I was amazed, I couldn't believe that.' It was obvious that Hepsie had once studied Miss Moore as keenly as a scholar over a classic text.

'How you doing, Hepsie? It's me, John. How was it when your mum and gran came down to see you?'

'The magazine said she was enjoying the naked dancers sliding up and down the slimy pole as she swigged a cold beer from a bottle at the bar. That's what she did every Friday night, according to the magazines.'

Later I realised that this conversation was not an aberration; Hepsie preferred to talk to me when she couldn't see me. This way I was just like Miss Moore's visitors to Long Meadow End, a spectator in the crowd, watching and listening and later giving a standing ovation, but no more worth gazing on than the spotlight operator.

'I wanted to be empowered like that. She said she wasn't a victim, not when she danced before men like that. She was not the prey but the hunter. She gave me the idea that I might be able to do that myself, you know . . .'

'What's wrong?' I asked, for Hepsie's voice was tearful. 'Darling, tell me.'

'. . . just take control of my life by playing them at their own game. It felt really daring at first. It changed everything for me.'

As Hepsie sobbed I was reminded of how Brian had raved on nastily about how of all the people who hated Miss Moore, and there were many, the worst were other women. 'Sure, women throughout the world have at various times bought magazines just because Misty Moore is splattered around inside, but only so they can *examine the wreckage*. Little girls like her for a while, because the ridiculous tits and hair and lips remind them of their grotesque plastic fashion dolls, but that's the problem with little girls – *they grow up*. And, unlike men, once they become women they don't have pure honest friendships any more – not like us, not like you and me, Johnny-boy, we'll be friends for life. But women! They put men, boys, babies first – high above their own sex. Once you understand that about women you understand everything.'

'I imagine Miss Moore's a role model to lots of girls,' I said to Hepsie.

'Until then I thought of acting in a sexy way as simply pleasing men, and so ending up like my mother, fucked basically, but no, there was another way to look at it entirely. And though it can be seriously crap, at other times it's fun.'

But Hepsie's relationship with Miss Moore was forged by more than jealousy – it was desperation. Longing. That's what Miss Moore created in us all. Desire we could never satiate. She reached out to us, and she snatched back. She offered and she withheld. Over and over and it made us want her, and anything she sold, all the more. Yes, I was sure I understood it all.

'That's what I've fucking learnt about this hell-hole called life,' Hepsie shouted, then laughed, sounding more thrillingly vulgar than any girl I'd ever known.

I could feel her slipping away into the deep waters of her youth, pulled on by both the teenager's timeless right to irresponsibility and the new century's mood of righteous self-interest. I had just one year of teenagedom left: yes, I would dive in and join her.

'Can we meet?' I pleaded. 'I want to see you. Soon.'

'There's no point waiting for other people to change it for you. She taught us that. You either shoot a hole in your head or you grab what you want when you want it. I know what I'm going to do.'

Unseen Hepsie raved on, confessing that when she first

used to read about Miss Moore most of all she was jealous that often in interviews Miss Moore said how she 'loved sex' and 'felt totally at one with her beautiful body' and 'enjoyed naked pretty girls'. That she was not only a model but had starred in blue movies and centrefolds. Was free and liberated and wild. 'You know, when I met her,' she laughed, 'I weighed three times what she did. And I looked like her ugly little sister, when in truth she could have been my *mother*.'

'I think Hepsie wants to be Misty,' I said to Brian later. 'In fact I think she'd give anything to be her.'

'Perhaps Misty'd give anything to be Hepsie,' Brian replied. 'Envy. Jealousy. Suspicion. Resentment. Spite. Greed. Basically that's a woman in a nutshell. The overriding purpose of any female life is to obtain exactly what another woman has or wants, and then flash it in her face triumphantly.'

'That's pretty cynical,' I said.

'Not really. Not if you think of it as an opportunity,' he smiled.

Chapter Fourteen

There is the thud again.

Walking, I call out the boy's name. Then wander out on to the moonlit landing of Long Meadow End. There the milky little insomniac is, odd-looking without his balaclava. He is silent, pale as a grave. Holding, in a potentially humorous martial arts pose, a chair. I inhale, shocked, then want to laugh. Then rush and hold the lonely motherless boy. Who says nothing but just stares straight ahead. 'There's nothing there, Mouse.' But the truth was earlier that night I'd woken to the sound of walking. I hoped it was the pacing overhead of my boss. As she walked the night away with those small heartbroken footsteps.

Mouse's pale face is white in the black night like a single dot on a domino. He begins thumping his left foot hard against the polished oak floorboard and moaning. I glance round, and round. There is no transparent woman walking amongst us, breathing those odd sighs over our skin. I wonder if Mouse is asleep for, though his eyes are open, his face is rigid as porcelain. His eyes unblinking as blue stones. His lips trembled to the bloodless milk of dreamers. I look over the banisters at nothing but air. But when I sniff it is to inhale a heady perfume – part home-cooking, part pollen. Together Mouse and I raise our tired, scared eyes and listen. No doors closing, no footsteps, but our unconscious is giving us a woman – we feel her presence.

So many things I was first fascinated by I now feared. Several days earlier I'd heard a loud scratching in the night. The scrabbling had been accompanied by deep moans and an incessant high-pitched whine. It was not human, and to my disbelief I had later discovered that Mouse had been keeping a large brown rabbit locked within his designer wardrobe.

I reached out to hold his cold hand. I wondered if Mouse had taken too many pills. Provinciality, Hepsie would later imply, had squatted on any seeds of my spiritual self.

'What is it?' I say, bending to Mouse-level and smiling anxiously in his stricken face. 'Tell me what's wrong.'

Perhaps the sight before me came from a nightmare. But when I touched Mouse's newly revealed forehead it was hot, though his shoulders were shocked with an Arctic chill. He had been standing sentinel outside my room for some time.

'Mummyman, there's someone in Jewels' room.'

'No, Mouse,' I said. 'The baby's in with me.'

Mouse's eyes were aglow with excitement; the poor boy was so lonely he'd fallen in love with a ghost.

'Go look, Mummyman.'

So I go across the hallway. Open the door to the luxury unused nursery. Where teddies and toys have been put down under a butchering moonlight. The cherrywood cot is iced with frills, filled with a frosty lace. Above, a mobile of pearly seashells are falling from the ceiling. I feel worse than nervous. From a silver rail pastel dresses are hovering in tiny clouds of pink and yellow chiffon. Three balloons are bloating by the window. On several occasions I'd wondered about this excessively deluxe fairy-tale nursery. Surely only a princess or a doll could ever need such a room. The reason I'd not yet laid Jewels down in there was because it was a flamboyantly inappropriate place for a baby. Designed, it seemed, by a man and a woman who knew nothing about babies. Or love. On the far wall a specially illustrated mural shows a snarling lion weaving through a thick khaki jungle. A salmon-pink cloud of flamingos in flight overhead. A hoary rhino galloping along in the rear. I go right up to the cot and look down. There, breathing safely on soft rasps of sleep, is indeed our baby, Jewels.

'The ghost moved Jewels from your room, Mummyman,' Mouse whispered. I looked at the peaceful child. My heart beat in my throat. The boy said, 'See, he's starting to get real mischievous. Isolde said this would happen. Isolde said there was a ghost and that he would come and visit me.'

'It was probably just Misty, wanting to get her out of my room and settled in here.' I felt a dizzying nausea.

'Hello! Mummyman, you know she's afraid of this house, and the baby, and never comes out here at night.'

'Did you see anyone?'

'Nope. But the ghost is very friendly, Isolde says. I shouldn't be frightened if I hear footsteps in the night or creaking on the stairs.'

I said nothing to anyone about the incident. I decided to assume, just as with the poisoning, that Mouse had played a dangerous trick with baby Jewels to get my attention. He was desperate. It would not help his unhappiness if Miss

Moore chastised him. The poisoning had alerted us all to Mouse's dangerous behaviour and now I assumed everyone wanted an excuse to get rid of Mouse. All that kept him with us was the fact that he had nowhere else to go. Though I never saw my boss act unkindly towards the boy because only occasionally did she seem to notice him at all. Only when he got under her feet, like some kitten she'd got for Christmas one year and since forgotten she owned, did Miss Moore look at Mouse at all. It was impossible to think that she had snatched him away from his family. Mainly because when she did look it was not with joy or annoyance or displeasure. Just complete bafflement. How had it happened that she was living with a balaclavaed little boy in a huge farmhouse in Yorkshire? Of all the things men had left her with over the years Mouse was surely the strangest. If, of course, I believed what I had been told, and that that was how Miss Moore had really acquired Mouse.

So, alarmed and insomniac, I let the incident pass. But the next day Mouse was discovered hiding not only another big dusty rabbit in his wardrobe, but also a black bird in the drawer of his desk. He'd swivelled the balaclava round so that his face was completely covered by black wool and tufts of white hair sprang from the eye and mouth holes at the back of his head.

And that night when he woke me at 3.30 a.m. I rose with a shout. And to find myself sweating. I felt hacked up, as one attacked by some terrible dream, though I was also sure I'd not slept a wink. Mouse loomed above me, his pale fingers pressed to his woollen mouth, and widened his eyes to shsh me. 'It's the first time I've had proof,' he drawled excitedly in the half-light. 'You've gotta come see, Mummy-man. Isolde's right.' I stumbled out of my bed. I was dry-mouthed, aching. I followed to where the little balaclava boy stood trembling in front of a square of white dust spread over the landing. 'Look,' the boy said, 'at the sneaky footprints.'

I saw a row of faint steps. Like paws through faint frost. They led from the start of the stairs across the wide landing and into my room. 'Something's landed on the landing, Mummyman,' he said and pointed at four prints in the dust. Three were smudged and rather indistinct but one was a perfect bare print of a round heel, a bony out-step and five small toes. The print was unmistakably human.

'What's this?' I cried.

I had assumed an odd position: crouched, as if ready to pounce. I moved around quickly as if I held a knife within a ring of attackers. They were, I guessed, a little bigger than a child's step. Not quite the size of an adult foot. On closer examination of the footprints I saw that alongside the line heading towards my room was another fainter line of four prints upside down – exiting. I dashed then, stumbling, half asleep and weak, back into my room. Jewels was there, asleep in her usual crib, safe.

'She's still there,' I said breathlessly, returning to the boy who stood calmly in the gloom.

'No one's taken her.'

'Whose do you think they are? I can't wait to tell Issy,' Mouse said.

I sank to the floor and rubbed my fingers in the white dust and sniffed. I wanted to cry. It smelt of lavender, a gentle purple tang.

'It's Misty's talcum powder,' the boy said. 'I put it down to get proof of the ghost.'

I reached up and switched the overhead light on. The prints

faded. All around us our expensive furnishings, ornaments and artworks were illuminated starkly. Wanting to run, I tried to smile. Mouse bit his lip excitedly. He was delighted just to have been noticed, even if it was by a ghoul.

'Mouse isn't coping,' I said to Brian.

'It's a weird environment for all of us, not just the kid.'

We were alone at the dining-room table at night, illuminated only by firelight.

'Do you think the Vines are all right?' I asked.

'They really are lovely trousers, John,' he replied.

'Oh thanks,' I murmured. 'Miss Moore bought them for me.'

'Very expensive,' he said, stroking my thigh.

Brian had on white leather trousers and a black T-shirt with the words *Porn Star* written in red glitter. Sometimes Brian even seemed to make himself snigger. I almost giggled weepily, but then composed myself and thought of uniforms, and my thesis about how they concealed the truth. Uniforms gave an impression of a person that was not necessarily correct. They pandered to our prejudices.

'You don't think the Vines are up to something, do you?'

'They do look such a perfect fit. Tight without being lurid.'

'Seriously. Perhaps they are here in our house for sinister reasons.'

'Yummy. Milky white baby flesh to use in midnight rituals. Oh I do hope I get an invite. It'll be the party of the year.'

'I know it sounds wacko but at night I hear footsteps. I'm afraid.'

'I really can't take my eyes off your trousers, John.'

'But I can't help thinking about it. I'm getting obsessed with the idea that everything is not all it seems.'

'They look so beautiful on you.'

'I really think Mrs and Mrs Vine might be up to something,' I whispered. 'Or Miss Moore. Or Isolde. Or Hepsie. Or all of them.'

'But they'd look even nicer on my bedroom floor.'

I decided to approach Isolde when she arrived for her duties that afternoon, to see if she had any clues to the boy's strange behaviour. She arrived a little late, and carrying a huge roast turkey, which she'd dashed up to the caravans after school to collect. Her grandmother had just taken it out of the oven. Hot and golden, it seemed three times the size of any earthly bird.

'Has Mouse said anything to you?' I asked her as we stood together in the expensive kitchen. Behind us on the chrome table Mouse ate his turkey eagerly.

'All Hepsie's ever wanted in her life is to be an actress, or a dancer or a singer. Anything up on a stage. Though the kind of dancing she ended up doing wasn't what she'd intended.' Only much later would I understand what Isolde was telling me: her sister simply saw lying as the most wonderful training for acting. 'I think she'd do anything for a part in a film,' Isolde continued.

'Anything?'

'Yes. That's why she left us and went down to London. She'd always been obsessed with London. Even as a real little lass she had this big picture of Buckingham Palace on her bedroom wall. And then as she got older she added all these other pictures from magazines, of places like Big Ben and the River Thames.'

I should have taken this chance to ask Isolde more about Hepsie and her early fascination with London, but instead, embarrassed by my passion, I repeated my previous question about Mouse, to which Isolde replied, 'Wouldn't tell you if he had.' She spoke softly, wrapping her stocky arms tight around her chest and pouting. Was she flirting?

'He thinks he's seen a ghost,' I whispered. 'He says you told him there was a ghost.'

'That's called imagination,' she smiled, and raised her eyebrows with the insolence that the young confuse with cleverness. 'It's quite common. Like Hepsie always imagining she could be a model or a superstar. Imagination is what got her down to London in the first place. People often use their imagination to get out of hopeless situations. That's why Mouse invents things.'

'Yes, he's very creative,' I said, making sure I was focusing on her face, not her little pointy breasts, hard and stubby beneath her thin cotton T-shirt. Or her too-wide hips. Or the inch of white belly that tipped over the unbuttoned waistband of her cheap jeans like a roll of putty.

'But no matter how much wholesome food we give him, the little lad's still drugged up to the eyeballs, poor bugger. He probably thinks we're all zombies,' she said sadly. 'And why does he still wear this awful balaclava?'

'He likes to wear it!'

'Oh yes, you probably think it's so mad, so *distinctive*, it must be terribly fashionable.'

Her rage alarmed me, for it had a power that suggested she only had to click her fingers and her family would pop up at the window. I'd already noticed how in the presence of Isolde and Celeste our artworks shrivelled in embarrassment, the handmade rugs rolled back to dust. The chic paint flaked, and the throws, cushions, quilts, carpets all shrank to fluff as the Wychwood women crept their family's old mould back over Long Meadow End.

'And he might have moved the baby from my room into the nursery, to pretend that she was taken by a ghost.'

'You let the baby out of your sight!' she exclaimed furiously, her thick neck flushing crimson. 'You've already locked her in a car and nearly poisoned her, and had us all out looking for her. What else have you done that we don't know about? That baby's safety is your responsibility, God help us all.'

'It wasn't me, it was Mouse,' I said petulantly, but was angry and so flashed a look over her entire body to let her know that I saw her exactly as she was, and didn't find it too appealing. We glared at one another; I imagined little puffs of mist coming down her dragon's nostrils. An inferno to accompany the very next word she spoke. 'He seems terrified,' I muttered.

'Jesus, I bet there's all kinds of disasters happening every day of the week that are hidden from us. I'm surprised poor Jewels is even still alive.'

'Don't talk to me about secrets!' I hissed, and caught my own look in the chrome splash-back: distorted, discernibly aghast. 'I've hardly been kept well informed. I've only just discovered that you are all related to Hepsie and that you all used to live in this house.'

A silence fattened around us. Then I heard Mouse's knife scrape on the plate, and more thick meaty chewing. He was totally absorbed in eating.

'That's not all you don't know, city boy,' Isolde said with a smirk. Then, as if surprised by her own cruelty, she wiped her hand over her forehead and said softly, 'Look, there are things people are not telling you, John.'

On the silvered worktop, where I had just slammed and clutched at the chrome surface, I saw my fingertips slowly evaporate. 'Well, I think it's about time you all explained, if only for Mouse's sake.'

'Hepsie is a complete law unto herself, you know. She only told us she was off to London once she'd arrived and found a place to live. She could have ended up sleeping on the streets. She was that desperate to get away from here and get famous.'

'Mouse is terrified.'

'How could he be anything but, living here with you pack of nutters?' she cried with a laugh. 'I always knew Miss Moore would be completely crazy once Hepsie got to know her. I warned them. You only have to take one look at her! It's a disaster. But even as a little girl Hepsie used to keep all these pictures of different famous beautiful women, and buy the magazines with stories about them in.' Then, thrusting the mop she was working with into my hand, Isolde marched off. 'Come on, big man,' I heard her calling to Mouse, 'come and help me clean the cooker.'

'I think we should address the issue of Mouse's unhappiness,' I said to Miss Moore that evening.

'He's just attention-seeking.'

'No, he's homesick. We have to find his mother. Where is she?'

'You know, I was so homesick when I went to dance with the Kirov. Did I ever show you my first photograph? I'm sure I still have it somewhere. I look so miserable, it's really rather hilarious. But oh, what a ballet is the Kirov Ballet!'

'The Kirov Ballet!' I exclaimed.

'Yes, John,' she said blankly, 'I danced with them.'

'But I thought you danced with the Bolshoi.'

'Oh sorry, yes, I meant the Bolshoi. I'm getting all muddled up.'

Very gently I said, 'I've often wondered why Hepsie Vine stopped working for you. I mean, if perhaps you fell out, maybe.'

'Oh no, John, nothing like that. She was wonderful, really.' Miss Moore had that sour look, like one being asked to act a part against her will. A part she no longer even knew the lines for.

'I wondered if perhaps that's why . . .'

'Nope.'

'. . . why you feel concerned . . .'

'Nope.'

'. . . about her family. She seems like such a sweet, innocent girl.'

'Ha!' Was Brian right: did women dislike other members of their own sex so fiercely that just to talk about another, younger, prettier specimen caused instant denial and wide-eyed anxiety? 'Hmmm, sure, Hepsie was the most wonderful employee.'

'Right. Isolde told me Hepsie'd do anything for a part in a film. Anything.'

'I loved, simply loved, having sweet little Hepsie Vine working for me.'

'Oh good. We should invite her to stay longer when she next comes to visit her parents.'

'Oh no!' Miss Moore exclaimed. 'The thing is, John, I really don't want the Vines coming anywhere near my family. Is that clear? Really clear? I can just about cope with Isolde and Celeste here, because they're young enough, and so almost harmless. But not the others. You know, if I lost Jewels for any reason, I'd die.'

'Why would you lose her?'

But at that moment Mouse stepped into the room with his small white hands folded into a trembling nest. 'Hey, you freaks, look what I've got,' he said.

Quietly Miss Moore and I moved close. Bending, we gazed into where, through the cage of fingers, we saw a ferocious beak, and deeper in, a tiny scarlet tongue flickered by a beat of silver feathers. And all around the room rang the wild chirping spellbound pleading, high and angry like a hundred hungry babies, trapped.

Chapter Fifteen

Anyone who has worked as a nanny will agree that you are always troubled by the one who has gone before, fearing she was more loved, more efficient, more privy to the deep heart of the family. You are ever aware of the wisps of her influence. Her face in photos, her name in tales of remembered fun. Though these comparisons, of course, were only my imaginings. In fact what was really odd, I realised in May, was that Misty, Brian or Mouse never recalled Hepsic, ever. Her face only arose in Long Meadow End if I woke in the night seeing it and I only heard it on anyone's lips if I whispered it to myself.

In early June I journeyed to London. Miss Moore had agreed I needed my first weekend off alone: the secrets and the seclusion of Long Meadow End were making me moody and bleak. Isolde agreed to skip school to care for Jewels while I was away. She immediately suggested taking the baby up to the caravans for the afternoon, but Miss Moore would not allow it. I think now that Miss Moore agreed to my time off because she feared that I might quit – taking the terrible truth of her life with me. So she booked me into an expensive central hotel.

As soon as I was alone in the busy London street I realised that I had nowhere to go. And nothing to do. I feared I might slip from the kerb and find myself suddenly living my old life. But I no longer had friends to visit in London. I had no hobbies, interests or direction. In just six months my life had become feverish fantasies by dark, and by daylight caring for Mouse, Jewels and Miss Misty Moore. Any free time was given to peeping upon the Vine girls as they dipped in and out of their uniforms.

Dejected and alone I shopped, gazed at my gaunt ghost in boutique windows, and then bought three ridiculously expensive shirts, a pair of shoes, a jacket and a bottle of newly launched aftershave. Then I went to sit inside a café in Covent Garden. But even indoors I felt uneasy and exposed, too close to the seething mass of the general public. Outside in the square fire-eaters breathed the morning air smoky. Paving stones were ringing with the steel click of busy footsteps. No one looked in at me. I thought back over the people I had met in the last six months. My so-called friends and family. The Covent Garden café was warm. Why was I trembling? It was more than my lonely friendless state. I thought seriously for a moment about my tan, and decided to move outside of the café on to the sunlit terrace and watch the entertainers. The smoke from the burning batons made the air thick and oily. I had nothing to do, nowhere to go and no one to see. Glossy thin women strode past in a busy blur. I missed Mouse and Jewels. Particularly Mouse, for having the anxious boy to calm stopped my own dark imaginings. Or allowed me to blame them on the wild mind of the poor boy. I understood what a useful distracting purpose Mouse's illness had served for us all that year, allowing us to ignore our own paranoia – for what had we to fear, when we had *everything*?

I'd been sitting outside the café in Covent Garden a few minutes when I caught a glimpse from the corner of my eye of a man watching me. Between the shadowed bodies his silver stare flashed like a torch. I looked away and down at my table. Mouse was right, they were everywhere sniffing at your crotch. Poor Misty, the only people that were interested in her were the ones that didn't know her. And yet that lonely sunny day all I had to offer as balm against my friendlessness was my body. Served up to be looked at by strangers. My greatest fear was that my watcher would be gone, lost in the busy crowd. What was the inner life of a person whose body was the only thing anyone noticed? Suddenly I realised that being a famous man was as close as I could ever come to being a woman. Hepsie was right, all women had were their bodies – and now this was all I had – and all Brian had too. And Misty. It was terrible. I'd fallen into the company of corpses. I did not want to think further upon such miseries. But I had no one to talk to, and if there was one worse thing than being stalked in the dark countryside I saw now that it was being ignored in the sunny crowd.

How had I become so lonely in just a few months? I couldn't help but think it had to do with Brian, Hepsie, Miss Moore and the Vines. They spun mystery around me like a web and where there was a sprinkle of cold dew I saw diamonds. I missed Jewels. I actually ached for her innocent body to warm my cold heart up.

Now, shouts and sirens decreased, fell away to a distant chirp, as my own thoughts filled the smoky square. Since I had begun to work for Miss Moore I had gradually taken to thinking that everyone knew who I was, and everyone wanted to chat to me. It did not therefore surprise me as much as it might another young man that the unfamiliar person was still gazing at me keenly. I now believed myself a parrot in a flock of pigeons. When I looked up again the man was still staring at me. I felt a tiny crumb of comfort. Despite my aloneness I had an almost-companion. The more I thought of my body and the man who was looking at my body, the less I thought of all the things that troubled me. The man was handsome and he gave a little smile and a nod. I took out my newspaper and started a crossword. I moved around casually so the sunshine hit my face at a more appealing angle. My observer changed his position, surely, I decided, so that he could see my face more clearly. Through the glare I noticed that he was slightly older than I, mid-twenties, maybe. Handsome and tall with a muscular body. I wondered if this was just regular London flirtation, or if he knew me from somewhere. Perhaps he had seen me photographed in the Easter Bonnet Ball Exclusive. Yes, surely this was it! I felt a rush of excitement. (It would be many more years before I learnt that the greatest impediment to my becoming a successful artist of any kind had always been my susceptibility to flattery. A quality that, as you may have guessed, has made me, both as a boy and a man, a very poor judge of character.)

The man was still smiling at me. A surge of glee shot through me. Is this the day when it occurred? The moment when I moved from a man who wanted to love and be loved to a man who wanted to see and be seen? Perhaps. I certainly felt enormous pride that he was watching me. And then fear. I was being watched. Who was this man? What horrors was he capable of? What did he want with me? What fantasies had he drawn me into in the lunacy of his lonely mind? That year my paranoia moved swiftly from fear of a ghost in the night to alarm at strangers in daylight. It was all the consequence of living amongst so many secrets.

I had been rather pleased with the pictures of myself at the party. I glowed. They seemed to have added a filter to the lens. It gave me a deeper tan, and a healthier, more confident aura. My teeth were whiter. In several of the shots pretty women seemed to be looking at me longingly. My smile was wider. In other photographs people were laughing all around me, like I'd just cracked a clever joke.

What could the photographs in the magazine tell me about myself? I seemed tall and strong. But what if this made me not so much an icon as a target? Yes, definitely. The stranger who watched me so keenly must have seen these pictures. I wondered how the man had felt when he looked at me. Did looking at me make him happy, desirous, envious, needy, elated, deflated? What could he tell me about me?

There were lunatics everywhere! Ha! I was thinking like a woman! It was exhilarating to be so transformed! I looked up from my crossword and smiled briefly. To influence the mood of strangers simply by how you looked suddenly seemed a heady and important power. I felt I was discovering something about my potential for the first time. My watcher smiled back. A few metres away the fire-eater threw and threw the fiery batons. Soon he had all six up and blazing. All falling through the air towards him. I pretended to answer more clues in my crossword (though in fact I wrote my name and Hepsie's over and over in the little squares) and then smiled up at the man again. I wondered if I looked like the same guy, there in ordinary morning café light, as I did in the magazine. Then felt a quick flash of despondency when I realised that I probably did not. I needed lights and make-up and hair gels and instruction, and crucially lots of time, to be truly the new John Parks. Studiously I nibbled on the tip of my pen. Then filled in a few more clues. But then again, the café stranger had noticed me, had he not? And therefore the resemblance between my better image and the real me was obviously there to be made.

'Hi,' the man said, coming over to me. 'Don't I recognise you?'

'Urgh?' I smiled, feigning a gesture of being disturbed in deep thought.

'Yes, I'm sure it's you, now I see you close up.'

'Huh?'

'I thought it was you soon as I saw you.'

'Er, sorry,' I said casually, taking a moment carefully to fold my paper before glancing up lazily at the man. And smiling a wide handsome grin. Despite the unnatural smokiness of the sunny air, the poor guy stank out a heavy floral musk – as though he had a bouquet rotting in every pocket.

'We met at Misty Moore's house last year.'

'Oh,' I said idly, as though such intrusions happened to me every day of the week.

'Yeah, you were coming for an interview as her nanny and we were all getting sacked. Wow, what a day that was. So how's it going? You still with her?'

I was more than a little disappointed. In fact, I was devastated. He knew me, but only as a nanny. A servant! I was as eclipsed by Miss Moore as I had been all through the year. Though I longed to slink away to sulk and glower I forced my better self to welcome the man, whose name was Alex. For some time I struggled to recount breezily the lighter details of the last six months in Wychwood.

'I guess the baby's cheered her up. It's all she's wanted for years,' he said.

'Is it?'

'Oh yeah. Then suddenly, wham, she had a kid.'

'Any idea about the father?'

'All very hush hush.'

'I wonder sometimes if I live up to Miss Moore's last nanny,' I confessed with a smile.

'I don't think she ever had a nanny before,' the man said casually, sipping on a beer. Alex said the word 'she' with a slow joky slur. The way someone would perhaps refer to a family pet as 'she' to highlight the animal's amusing grandiose self-importance. 'Why would she have needed one?'

'Oh yes, she did,' I replied. 'For Mouse.'

'Mouse? But he'd only been there a few weeks.'

'She had Hepsie Vine,' I said. His terrible aftershave made me sneeze. I turned away and studied the thrown torchlight until it made my eyes ache, and the rumble and rush of busy Londoners dizzied me.

'Who?'

'Hepsie. The young girl with the black curly hair, who did the job before me.'

'No, no. I don't know anyone of that name and I'd worked for her for the last three years. I did her PR.'

'You know, Hepsie Vine. Young, pretty, from Yorkshire. She was there on that day I came for my interview. She was . . . strange.'

Alex looked at me curiously for quite a long time. Then he said, shaking his head, 'You know, John, I remember that happening to me. Eventually thinking that everyone else – all the civilians – were suddenly really odd.'

'Huh?'

'Only I realised later it was because all the people I was hanging out with were like alien beanpoles! – models and actors and TV tarts – and all the beauties I was aspiring to be like were really tall as fuck and really weird. And yet I thought they were the normal ones, and everyone else was really small, or fat, or just odd. It's a kind of mindfuck. The world outside your immediate circle starts to seem really frightening?'

'You must remember Hepsie Vine,' I said, deliberately ignoring him. 'She was very pretty and had a sprig of holly in her black curled hair.'

'Had holly in her hair, yeah? Oh yeah, I think I remember her. You mean that girl with the pretty pale face? Quite a cutie. Came with that jerk Brian.' I looked away from Alex. Quite a crowd had gathered around the fire-eater's show now, so I saw just a ring of backs and those glowing clubs tumbling down. 'I assumed she was just another poor tart trying to get into the business. Why do you mention her?'

'Oh, Miss Moore's rented a farmhouse from Hepsie's family. That's where we're staying while Hepsie's staying at Misty's London place.'

'Farmhouse! Misty in a farmhouse,' he cried and then roared off into laughter. 'Now I really have heard it all! Hey, look at this,' and Alex shook from his wallet a thick strip of spider which fluttered on to the table, horribly. There was a burst of shrieks and laughter from the audience, then applause. 'It's an eyelash. False. Like everything else about her. No idea why I keep it, but I do.'

Alex was not famous. He was not handsome. He looked

tired and ill and smelt like a funeral parlour. His unbearable truth was that, though he had always despised her, nothing exciting had happened to him since he worked for Misty Moore. Alex and I had another cup of coffee and I listened as he detailed his times with Misty Moore. My throat remained dry despite several beers. In the square the fire-eater was replaced by a unicyclist dressed as a clown.

When I asked Alex a question he said, 'Look, mate, I went all over Europe with her for sixteen months and I don't know any more about her than I do about you, John.'

'But you know Brian, right?' I asked.

The unicyclist's performance had turned into a mock chase. The clown's mouth stretched, eyes widened, shrieking, arms pumping, in imitation of fear and fleeing. I looked down at the table and blew at the eyelash.

'Sure, Brian, the rather unlikely fashion adviser.'

'How did he strike you?'

'Same as most of the guys drawn to her, greedy, ambitious and dishonest.'

Laughter in the square greeted the clown-unicyclist's furious parody of falling.

'Hey, what about your aftershave, eh?' Alex laughed. 'It's the same one she gave me. I should stop wearing it, everyone says it stinks like cat piss, but I guess I need the memories.'

I left the café and walked in some distraction through Leicester Square. I wanted sweet soft smiling Jewels. I paused for a while and watched the sickening lurch and rise, lurch and rise of fairground riders screaming in terror into the midday sky. There was no doubt that Hepsie had spoken of herself as the former nanny of Miss Moore – she had told me she had been in London for a long time, as long as Big Ben and St Paul's Cathedral. Mrs and Mrs Vine had both mentioned that the girl had once worked for Misty Moore, but was now changing to a media career. Miss Moore herself had said that she had been delighted with Hepsie in all the time she'd worked for her.

I did more shopping, which helped slightly. Of course my fears could be nothing other than the fact that the Vines were poor. Everyone who came into contact with them noticed it. Perhaps I'd end up like Alex. With only an eyelash for company.

The over-breeding, the calloused hands, the home-baking, those bright 1980s garments. And the light of Miss Moore's wealth faded the Vines into an even more displeasing shade, but still the Vine family sprinkled over us the strange sparkling texture of real life – it was a wild truth, and one we, with our vanities and insatiable desires and flimsy shimmering surfaces, didn't wish to know, but longed to possess.

I walked on, thinking, my arms aching with the weight of shopping bags and boxes. My heart heavy with the coming truth.

Chapter Sixteen

'Hello,' a faint creamy voice said.

All night in my expensive hotel bed I'd not slept, but writhed with hot fantasies and agonised about making that call. But I could dream no longer, I now had to do what I should have done months ago. I wanted no more mystery.

'It's John,' I said, 'I'm in London, do you want me?' I had intended, of course, to say, 'Do you want to meet me,' but fear concertinaed the request into something more truthful.

'Is it Jewels? Is she OK?'

I reassured Hepsie that the child was well.

'I'm on a shoot,' she said, with a strange laugh, and I smelt Hepsie's weary misery spun to the laconic cool of the teen model. 'But I could, this afternoon.'

And later, in a McDonald's close to Waterloo, as the afternoon sun hung low like a great fallen yolk, a finger poked me on the back. When I turned it was with bewilderment. There was a girl behind me with sharp black hair and a clean white face, milk instead of blood in her cheeks. She wore her red lipstick in the sticky slash that was the fashion that year. She was taller than Hepsie and tottered when she moved.

'Sorry to keep you,' she said. 'They had to do loads of retakes because the bloody fire kept going out. We're down in the underground pretending to be rats. Tell me, how is Jewels?'

I'd seen this woman walk in a moment earlier. Simply because of the awkward way she moved and the rocking slam of the door behind her, I'd turned away. I assumed she was one of that army of London girls who go shrouded in shivers on even the hottest days, female casualties who look at the pavement aghast, as if hurrying always from some shocking trouble.

'I didn't recognise you.' I had not seen Hepsie since that first December day and now she was utterly altered.

'I had lots of my hair cut off.'

'It's been six months since I saw you.'

'They dyed it too and made me wear these clothes. I've been restyled.'

'I've missed you. Terribly.'

'Oh, I have to walk around on these stilts too.'

I looked down: on her feet she wore a pair of gold-strapped shoes so high she seemed to be walking on tiptoes. I looked up slowly from her toes, as though my eyes inhaled her. Though Hepsie wore expensive designer clothes, her waif's body managed to make the garments look outrageously cheap, which, Misty would tell me later, is the allure of indigent people for such industries.

She sat down at the white plastic table. I sniffed, but only caught the thick oil of frying, and a tiny note of that wild fresh fleshiness now overlain with a glossy mask of make-up.

'They tell me you ran away from Wychwood. Want to tell me why?'

'Ach, don't get me started on that one,' she flirted, swatting a hand before her face then returning it to rest provocatively on her hip.

'OK, what is it between you and Miss Moore? Why's she living in your old house, while you live here in hers? Or perhaps you'd like to explain why your family watches our every move? Or maybe why you lied about working for Miss Moore? Because the thing is, Hepsie, I'm starting to have my own rather alarming ideas about what happened.'

She shook her head so her raven hair flew wildly. The new style worked, for it was still thick and cut to just above her shoulder. Voluptuous and careless and black as midnight, it was more woman than girl. She was not what I expected at all.

'Do you want a burger?'

'Too much fat.'

'A Fillet O' Fish?'

'Nope, mayonnaise,' she smiled.

'One French fry?'

I leant across and kissed her then. I know it was the despair brought on by the coming truth, the memory of her little sister half naked, tired and stepping carefully out of her school skirt, the recent gaudy luxury – all this fuelled my confidence, but I loved her too. And that close I could smell the old Hepsie still, her and all the lovelies of her village. She fought me at first, wrestled her gummy lips away. I held her wrists and then a hank of her new hair, and in that manner I pressed into her with all the love I had.

'Just a milkshake, please, John,' she said, quickly licking my kisses from her lips.

I wondered if in Hepsie Miss Moore had discovered her own girlish self. Not in the hard sheen of a tight body, nor in the eager energy of slim limbs. No, for Miss Moore had worked to ensure she had retained these outward manifestations of youthful femininity. But rather in the light, fearless beauty of Hepsie's face: hope, the one quality Miss Moore had long ago lost. Hope. Trust. Expectation. There was not yet an injection that could ensure the return of these qualities to an ageing woman's face.

'You don't seem very happy,' I said again, 'for a beautiful London fashion model.'

'I've told you. I think happiness is for the smug or stupid.'

'Oh I agree,' I said coolly. 'Bring on the bleakness.'

When Hephzibah Vine smiled, though, she was still my slinking beauty. Lips had still been invented by her alone. Her eyes were still twilight. She was just thinner and harsher. Her breasts were much smaller, and her bottom less plump.

'What's wrong?' I said, stroking her tiny grey hand, which was laid like a dead dove on the smeared white tabletop. 'Isolde told me you'd always wanted to live in London and be famous. And that you adored Miss Moore before you even met her. You should be very happy.'

'Oh don't listen to Isolde. She's just jealous because she has no ambitions.'

'She's a good cleaner.'

'Exactly.'

I could tell Hepsie was about to cry and for a long time she did not say anything, though her mouth opened and closed, like she was struggling to find words underwater. The tinkling fast-food silence, ripped with whining and the clank of cutlery, went on and on like our mad tune. I bristled with irritation. So accustomed had I become in the last six months to the company of those who are quick at being insincere, I found Hepsie's slow quest for authenticity tiring.

'Oh, I'm all right. It's just exhausting. It's not what I expected at all. And in the media you have to use every drop of your female charm, all the time,' she said at last. 'They want your mind as well as your body. It's much harder than what I was doing before.'

'Surely you don't wish you were back at home?' I said, stroking her. I wanted intimacy and to know someone deeply and truly.

'Well, if I was in Wychwood at least I could get rid of it all,' she said angrily. 'All my female charm'd just get eaten up by other people in an endless life of cleaning and cooking.'

'Isn't that why you left for London in the first place?'

She snorted furiously. I feared I was developing an old guy's gift for annoying young women. That way loneliness lay. She gazed over the street thoughtfully. I, putting on a similar look of moody concentration, ate the last of my fries.

'I know that you didn't work for Miss Moore as a nanny,' I said eventually. 'What is the deal with you and her?'

'I never said I did,' she sighed, blowing her cigarette smoke up in a hard horn. A gesture that was simultaneously aggressive and flirtatious.

'Yes, you did,' I said gently. 'You said you were an au pair.'

'No, I said I thought *you* were the au pair.'

'So what did you do?'

She looked at me coldly for a moment. She was so rude, so badly behaved that I was sure she'd someday be a star.

'Who are you, Hepsie Vine?' I whispered dramatically. She lit another cigarette and stared down at the tabletop as she smoked it. 'Tell me,' I urged. 'Who are you and what have you done?'

'Isolde's a complete mother hen. She's really worried about Mouse. She thinks perhaps he's been abducted by them, and they won't let him go back to his real mother.'

'Look, will you please tell me what's going on? Because what I'm thinking is really awful.'

Then she sighed and said, 'If she'd been a boy Misty agreed to call her John. That's why I was so pleased when I heard that you were called John. Though I'd still have picked you even if you'd been called Sebastian or Hugo or Oliver or Oscar or Rupert or Harrison.'

I moved seats until I was by her side. Reaching out I pulled her in and held her tight against me. She was light as a bird. Boyish rather than the curvy dreamboat I'd met months earlier in Chessington Vale. Now I had to remember not to squeeze too hard for fear I would crush to powder her lovely bones.

Just when I was about to kiss her, her mobile phone rang in the back pocket of her jeans. She answered it lazily. '. . . I've told you, I'm tired . . . I told you before . . . up to you . . . don't mind . . . take it or leave it.' Her neck smelt of wood smoke, her earlobes were melting marshmallows. 'I've got to be getting back,' she said, collecting her cigarettes, lighter and purse from the table and pushing them quickly into the handbag on her knee. 'Thanks for calling me. I'll come and see you when I'm next in Wychwood.'

'When will it be?' I asked, but she didn't answer.

Instead she said, 'Look after Jewels, won't you.'

'Of course.'

'I'm so glad we got you. I'd not trust *her* alone with the baby. She's not cut out for it.'

'She's not well. Clutching on to all these secrets and lies has driven her crazy. And I imagine, if it's what I'm thinking it is, that she's feeling guilty.'

'Oh, I wonder why! You know, there's a reason for guilt. You feel it when you've done something wrong.'

'Her fans hate her. She's forty and alone. And she's forbidden to eat pasta, potatoes or bread.'

'She could be just hungry,' Hepsie said with that wicked smile that made me want to know every naughty inch of her.

'Absolutely. I might have to contact the Red Cross. She's practically starving to death.'

Then before she could laugh Hepsie's phone rang again, and she opened it with an angry flick, 'Forget it then . . . yeah, fuck you too.' Then she slammed shut the phone and said to me, 'And you're surprised I don't want Jewels to be just a pretty face?'

'Do you want to tell me the truth,' I said in a little scared voice. Again she ignored me. 'It would be best for Jewels if we were all honest with one another.'

'I chose that name,' she said, gazing at me fiercely. I shot back quickly in my seat, scorched by the fury on her face. 'If you really want to know the truth, I chose the name Jewels. In fact I wanted to call her Julie. Yes, plain old simple fat old Julie. I bloody 'ate unusual names. I guess it comes from being called Hephzibah. My mother gave all of us stupid names. I always longed to be called something ordinary, like Sarah or Mary. But Misty wanted to call the baby something wild. She suggested Consuela or Sapphire or Cassandra, or even Anoushka! Poor little bugger. Do you love her?'

'I've told you I adore her.'

'I'd forgotten how intensely adorable babies are. Especially when they're sleeping. In the middle of the night.'

'I'm missing her like mad.'

'Good. All the Julies I've ever known were plain and simple and expected nothing from life but to find a man to love them and have a few kids. Just like Isolde, who in a few years will be very fat and married to a local farmer with about twenty kids.'

'Right.'

'Anyway, in the end Misty agreed to compromise and go for Jewels, which, of course, is how it should be, and anyway it will always mean Julie to me.'

Her eyelids were swelling, her cheeks purpling. The white blossom opening and falling, and change coming.

'Tell me,' I said. 'Admit it.' But she just shuffled around looking under the table for the high gold shoe, which she had slipped off while we had been talking. 'Come on, the truth. I know already. Just say it.'

'God, I hate wearing these,' she sniffed, rubbing at her nose. 'They're not me at all. They are so bloody uncomfortable, but everyone says I'm too small and insists I wear at least five-inch heels, and if I don't it's absolutely guaranteed that my career will go up in smoke faster than that subway fire.'

She was crying again and I couldn't bear to watch.

I bent down under the table to help locate the shoe. Her ankles were slimmer than wrists. Her calves carved to petals both hard and supple. Her thighs just fleshy enough to slightly strain the denim. And the zip of her jeans was pulled open an inch so that . . .

'Did I tell you that's what I have?' she said, tapping my

melting shoulder. 'A career? I'm not just a fashion model for ironic, cool photographers, oh no, I don't just have a crumby job any more: I now have a proper career. Not like the mummy Julies.'

And then I saw that bare foot. And it was a small, slender foot. It was pale with a pinker underside, rather like the whitest, freshest mushrooms we'd seen in the woods. Her nails were not painted but pure mint-pink orbs like summer moons. Her sweet tiny toes would have melted to warm sugar on your lips. I wanted to hold the foot, kiss it, worship it, but I feared I would startle her. And anyway now I was certain. This was the final proof. I closed my eyes in relief and a flashbulb boomed out pure moonlight. I saw stairs. Footprints. Powder. Feet going in and coming out. Yes, I knew immediately, it was the exact same size – the exact same foot – for I quickly measured it from my wrist to the tip of my little finger, as the mysterious light footprint Mouse has discovered (creeping up to see Jewels at midnight) in the lavender-scented talcum powder.

Chapter Seventeen

T he next day I returned to Wychwood.

'She's just left, Mummyman,' Mouse shouted, running along the hall to meet me. It was mid-morning and I had not immediately entered the farmhouse. Instead I had been out in the garden stumbling through the farm buildings smoking, stroking my hair. I'd been walking, muttering, for over an hour beneath a morning sky still hazy lemon with now a burning blue coming through. It was confirmed that my circle of friends contained the country's biggest liars, swindlers, fantasists and chancers. But what could be better material for an artist? And, of course, the appalling conduct of those into whose sphere I had stumbled liberated me to behave badly myself. Rather than weep I could grin and enjoy myself. If I had the courage to see adventure where others saw only anguish.

'Though she's been here for ages. I've been talking to her. She's, like, real pretty. After all those months trying to trap her, and she's not, like, spooky at all really. And she's quite cool. She held my rat.'

Mouse looked elated: at last he understood the situation. His balaclava was askew so only one of his eyes was visible and his words were a wild woollen muffle. In one hand he held the yellow cloth and in the other a can of polishing spray, which he pulled close to his chest as he spoke to me. In the chrome kitchen Jewels sat in her high chair chewing on a piece of toast. She was drumming her tiny toes furiously beneath her tray. Steaming on the chrome worktop I saw three freshly cooked chickens, bronzed as bells.

'Who brought Jewels down?' I said. 'Where's Misty?' Sunlight shot a gloss over the baby's thick black curls. There was no sign of Brian. Perhaps now that I no longer believed in him, or the ridiculous story he'd spun for me, he'd evaporated in a milky haze.

'And you know what, Mummyman? You know why she haunts this place?'

'Who fed Jewels?'

'She did. Listen to me! You know why she haunts this place?'

Already our modern furnishings looked dated, our artworks like the gaudiest student tat. One of the Perspex cellos hung lopsided from the wall. Even the chrome kitchen seemed embarrassed by its own flashiness. A soily dust, a mould perhaps, was reclaiming the whole place. There was the familiar aroma, unavoidable now as the scent of the old Vines, who were seeped deep in the walls through generations.

'Tell me, Mouse.'

'Because she used to live here herself! Isolde told me that and she's right! The ghost has confirmed it. Isn't that, like, totally wicked? Why didn't we think of that? It's, like, so obvious, yeah? I mean, that's how she knows how to get in without anyone seeing her. She comes up through the coal cellar. There's a window out of there on to a little yard, and a few steps up into the garden. She told me.'

'Really.'

'Sure. It's so cool. But it's a secret window. No one even knows about that window down in the coal cellar. How totally cool is that, Mummyman?'

'You'd better have some breakfast, Mouse,' I said.

'Her feet were so neat! Totally tiny. And she's so young and pretty and slim it's no wonder we never heard her,' Mouse said, pointing out of the doorway and imploring me to see where the quiet cool ghost had gone. I could hear the scratch and whistle of morning birds. 'And she's gonna get me a hedgepig to look after. That's so cool. To have my own hedgepig in my room. Go ask her if I can take it with me.' I stared, perhaps shook my head and refused to look despite the boy's pleading. 'Go after her, you idiot,' he cried, 'go after her, you freak. She'll tell you it's all true.'

Miss Moore came down into the room then. Her appearance startled me so fiercely that I'd jumped back from the table as I looked at her. The sudden accumulation of neglect indicated that she'd been thumped hard from the inside of her face. Something had pushed her a sorrow too far. She wore sunglasses. And I knew instantly that she would not yet tell me the truth, she was still so firmly closed against intrusion that she might as well have had a *Do not disturb* sign hanging from the tip of her nose.

'I know about Hepsie and Jewels,' I said. Then in case I'd not really spoken, I said again, 'I know everything.'

'Let's not do anything hasty, John,' Miss Moore said quietly. *I'm not giving up yet.* What shone out from her was a look of such extreme unhappiness that she was the perfect cover girl for *Sorrow*. And as she walked towards me I saw that she was so thin: slimmed on a diet of lies.

'You'd better tell me,' I said, 'the whole appalling story.'

'Make them go after the ghost, Mummyman,' Mouse raged, crying too. 'It was the ghost who has been coming every night. The ghost who used to live here!'

Miss Moore inhaled and gave me her model look, that doll's stare of dumb innocence. An expression that only a blowtorch could melt.

'I might be the only sincere man around, but I'm not a complete idiot,' I said loudly. 'I think it's appalling.'

'That's why she comes,' Mouse continued, 'because she used to *freaking live here*.'

I looked at little Jewels and she smiled. Her dark eyes and hair shone and already her incredible beauty mocked me for my ignorance. From beauty to decay and back, I moved my gaze between Miss Moore and the baby.

'Calm down,' I said quietly to Mouse.

Miss Moore was staring past me, looking upon the garden with a grave frown. Now that the truth was here the fantastic ladies and lords had gone, leaving just summer fields 200 miles from London. She could no longer distract herself with visions of beauty in ugliness.

'This is the reason why I haven't helped much with Jewels,' she said quietly. 'Why I left it all to you, John. I decided if this did happen, and Hepsie demanded the baby back, then the fact that I'd kept a distance would make it easier. I was wrong.'

I'd come to assume that the fast and famous life had become Miss Moore's addiction and this is what had almost driven her crazy. But watching her now made me reconsider: what if being an obsessive and an addict is what had attracted her to such a lifestyle in the first place? Who would believe in Misty Moore now that she no longer even believed in herself?

'I tried to tell you,' she smiled, then aimed for high drama by sighing melodramatically. 'But I'm like a fridge that's not been cleaned for months, John. Horrible, cold and dirty, if you look inside.'

'Oh shut up!' I cried. But her interplanetary stare gave me a cool clarity of thinking, like a glass of clear water after months of drinking only gin. I could tell, just from the way she sighed and smiled and played her tongue quickly over her upper teeth – *incredible! I'm a different woman entirely* – she was changed. She had the frightening abandon of a woman who no longer needed to use her beauty and her body to distract others from the truth of the world. Now anything could happen.

'Look,' Mouse screamed, ripping at my arm. 'Look!'

'If only we knew what would change her mind!' Miss Moore exclaimed.

'She's not happy being a presenter in London at all,' I said, as though I knew all the wild beauty's most intimate secrets.

'A presenter! Ah well, at least she doesn't have to live like she used to,' Miss Moore cried, reaching to steady her dark glasses as she raved. 'No one's expecting her to go back to that!'

'To what?' Mouse said curiously. He was listening to us keenly now. 'What's a presenter, Mummyman?' Mouse looked up at me, his mouth fallen a little open with that heartbreaking innocent stare. Isolde was right: he was a very imaginative boy, and his short life had taught him to expect shock after shock, but there was no way that even he could imagine the plan that Miss Moore and Hepsie Vine had devised – with a little help from Brian.

'To all the terrible things she used to have to do,' Miss Moore said, giving me that look that added, *You god-damned fool!* to the end of every sentence. Again she was pleading with me with those plump, silent lips.

'What's a presenter?' Mouse pleaded. 'Tell me. I'm old enough to know.'

'Someone who presents things,' I said quietly.

'What things?'

'Things people want to buy, or look at,' Miss Moore said, and gave me a weary smile.

'Look, quick, before she disappears!' Mouse cried, and I went to the window as Mouse demanded, where the tiny phantom was, of course, vanished into the blue morning. But when I turned to pick up Jewels I saw that the witch had already left her dark mark. Woven into the baby's thick curls was a single little leaf of holly, two dark berries and an emerald stalk.

'If you see Hepsie, offer her more money,' Miss Moore said to me as I stormed down the stairs with my suitcase.

I was packed and ready to go. Miss Moore was holding the baby tight to her, a look of ghastly passion on her face. If, as I suspected, she had never loved anyone before, then it had been so that she would never have had to face this moment of losing everything. Since I'd accepted that Jewels was Hepsie's child I too had been afflicted with a heart-thumping panic about losing the baby. I didn't know what I would do without Jewels in my life. I would miss her dreadfully. But for Miss Moore it would be worse: for ever she would wander unstable as one who has lost a limb.

'I'm not intending to see anyone,' I lied, gazing over the darkening garden. 'I'm leaving.'

'That's not to say you won't see her, though,' Miss Moore replied mysteriously, her glare adding the booming *she's everywhere* to the end of the sentence.

'It's over for me. I want nothing more to do with any of you.'

'Just one last favour, John,' she whispered. 'Go offer them more money.'

'Has she already had money?' I asked of the darkness. 'Are you telling me you *bought* Jewels?'

'Oh bizarro!' Mouse whispered, appearing in the kitchen doorway. 'You folk just get freakier and freakier.'

'Expenses, though God knows how much cocaine, champagne and caviar she and Brian must have craved to get through those expenses. Offer her as much as she wants.'

'I'd rather not be the one to ask her to sell her daughter.'

'Then go to the caravans and offer money to the grandmother,' Miss Moore said. She looked anguished and afraid as she spoke the words, and I realised, with some surprise, that she cared what I thought of her.

'It's sickening. It's nothing to do with me. I'm out of here.'

'I didn't intend it to happen like this, you know.'

'What on earth must they have thought when Hepsie told them she was selling their *granddaughter*?'

'She didn't tell them. Not until the very last minute. She went to London and didn't have a lot to do with them for the last couple of years. They didn't even know she was pregnant until the whole thing was arranged.'

I strode to the front door of Long Meadow End and with a firm hand I opened it very wide.

'Please ask them,' she said, softly but more desperately than I had ever heard a woman speak. 'They're poor.'

'You're asking them to put a price on their baby,' I said.

Her wide wet eyes indicated that she had no one in the world to help her but me.

'Desperate people will put a price on anything, John.'

Chapter Eighteen

'I thought you'd come to ask for my milky white hand in marriage,' Hepsie smiled from the door of her caravan. Her lips were chapped and her eyes tired to pink.

Summer nights, that scent of fragrant smoke, as if a mile away on an orange bonfire a million pink roses smouldered. I'd driven quickly and recklessly through the lanes and when I stopped outside the caravans my heart was still rolling with the lurches and curves of the road. The twilight was shot with such hot magic that I had not been surprised when Hepsie Vine emerged through the indigo haze outside the front door rolling like a ball of thistledown.

'I know,' I said. It was hard not to sound sulky and bitter – the ruthless brilliance of modern girls often made me feel that way. Duped, hoodwinked, swindled, conned, basically. How could we men love in such an atmosphere?

'Bravo! At last,' Hepsie said sharply. 'I thought you were never going to get it.'

'Why didn't you tell me about Jewels?'

'Because I was told not to, and you're too innocent to have realised.'

'I can't believe it. It's too ridiculous.'

'John, I told you before: that's because you're *well off*. Not much happens to you, so you imagine nothing happens to other people.'

There was a moment then, as if we'd just stepped from some fierce fairground ride, when we just breathed at one another, until I whispered, 'You're sad. I can hear the clank bang thump of your broken heart,' and she responded with a little dramatic cry.

You see, Hepsie and I expected our lives to be mosaiced by these shining sequences of tiny dramatic twists – which brought forth to our lives action, danger, wit, adventure, sociability – we could live with nothing less. It would lead to faithlessness, indifference and pain, but we'd have it no other way. We'd watched too much high-spirited American TV. The everyday would always disappoint us. We would forever expect quick little thrills, however disastrously they came to us.

She was quite a sight. Newly out of the bath, and still washing her dark hair. The white foam was piled in soft ice-creamy swirls. Around her torso she wore just a pale-blue towel. 'You know, you snore,' she said, reading my mind.

'You're a great mother,' I said breathlessly. The theatricality of our situation made me love her more. It had glamour, our meeting, our circumstances, our predicament. 'Believe me, you care about her so much. How many other mothers would have bothered to come down the hill in the dark? And sneak up through the basement window into the house, just so they could gaze on their little lost girl at midnight?'

I flicked on my hundred-watt idiot's grin and shone it at her and the entire crew, for we were surrounded by movie cameras, a handsome director shouting, 'That's perfect, wonderful. Cut!'

'Oh John, you fool, that was all bullshit,' she said flatly, giving me that embarrassed whine that she reserved for the very gullible. 'Isolde gave me a key, of course. I just came in a few times when you were all asleep.'

'What?'

'Three times, in fact. Isolde let me in and waited for me in the hall. We were bored. She wanted to keep me bonded with Jewels. What else is there to do in Wychwood except slave for rich bastards, or witch around?'

'But Mouse said . . .' How could I have been so stupid?

'Mouse is seven years old, and crazy. He's got no one. His mother has abandoned him. He needs fairy tales. If a ghost is his only friend then at least it's better than no one.'

'I should have realised earlier,' I said, as we gazed at one another. I felt sick with anxiety. Panicked as any father when faced with the removal of a child from his care.

'But you did realise,' she said. 'Everyone realised but no one wanted to admit it. You were all having too much of a good time.'

I thought of my early unease, exhaustion and loneliness. 'I had fears.'

'Which you turned into fantasies, so as not to have to think about them,' she said.

Not even imagination, just fantasies. I'd never be a scriptwriter; forget art, I'd be lucky even to make a good liar.

'While I've been living alone in that horrible den of iniquity,' she pouted, 'you've been dreaming about spooks and witches.'

Again I had an itch, an irritation, an unease, which I couldn't yet identify – perhaps because she was twisting a coil of soapy hair around her fingertip, and her towel had slipped down an inch.

'You're amazing,' I said.

That white towel, foam, skin. I haven't seen Hepsie for many years, but I can picture that angel still.

'Oh please! I hope you're not going to fall in love with me and confess and everything. I hate it when men do that.'

A match flared between her fingertips. In a drift of pale smoke she smouldered like a cherub on fire: she too needed to spin this meeting further into an ever more dramatic scene. Perhaps we believed that things would be fine as long as every disaster, every betrayal, had the potential to make an exclusive in a newspaper.

'I can't imagine many girls who could do what you've done,' I said bitterly.

'You'd be surprised, John.'

'There are simpler ways to get rid of babies you don't want,' I said nastily.

'But I did want her.'

'You did?'

'Sure, I could have had an abortion and no one would have blinked an eye. Now I realise that in my heart I wanted the baby all along. I didn't have an abortion because I wanted to keep my baby.'

'How convenient that you realised it just in the nick of time.'

'When I found out I was pregnant, I was too confused to know what to do. And when I said to Brian that I didn't want to abort it, and so might have to get the kid adopted, he said he thought that he could find a good home for the baby. It all happened really quick.'

'How quaint,' I said bitchily. 'And how much did you get for her?'

'Some money, yes. Expenses. But mainly Miss Moore agreed to introduce me to some people in the business.'

'And Brian, what did he get?'

'I'm not sure. He came to his own arrangement.'

'A fat introduction fee, perhaps?'

'Maybe. I got some modelling contracts and she arranged for me to meet people in TV.'

'Oh well then, it's all been worth it.'

I couldn't quite decide how to play my character, as rogue, hero, ally, or villain, so I jumped from one inter-pretation to another. I knew that in Hepsie's eyes this made me seem weak and unmanly. Women wanted their men consistent at the very least.

'Then it just spiralled from there,' she said sadly. 'Brian and Miss Moore are very determined people. Before you know it it's all out of your control.'

'Did Brian get to know Miss Moore simply so he could sell her the baby?'

'No,' Hepsie said calmly, 'he knew her already, but I think he only started working for her when he had this plan.'

'You both realised there might be money in it.'

'Brian realised that first. Perhaps I was just a little fool.'

'But then when Jewels was born, when you'd agreed to sell her to Miss Moore, and when everything was in place, then you changed your mind.'

'Yes. As soon as she was born I knew I'd made a mistake. But they convinced me to give it six months.'

'They?'

'Brian and Miss Moore. They said it was just nervousness, now the moment of handing her over was near. They said I was vulnerable after the birth. That I'd change my mind in a few months. So we agreed to have a trial period.'

'Why did you agree to six months if you knew in your heart that you wanted the baby back?' I suspected Hepsie Vine had relished not just the opportunity for career advancement, but the craziness of the situation all along: the glimpse into Miss Moore's life, the meddling with intrigue and adventure.

'We're not so different, you and I,' Hepsie said with a sorry sigh. 'Why did you agree to leave your sandwiches and your friends and come to work in the middle of nowhere for a woman you'd never met?'

'It was only for six months.'

'And look after a two-week-old baby on your own? And a crazy kid? Don't tell me you had the children's interest at heart. Don't tell me you were just trying to help out!'

'It sounded bizarre, I guess. Weird and interesting. I was offered the chance. Why not give it a go?'

'Perhaps it was the same with me. It was something different. The chance of a new way of living. So, I agreed to give it six months.'

'And now those months are up.'

'Yes.'

Hepsie stuck the cigarette in her mouth while she kneaded the suds, styled the pile higher into a wild white bouffant. The higher she lifted her arms the higher up came her towel, until it could only be inches away from obscenity. It distracted me. Made me believe our little scene. Despite the frustration I felt with her, I loved the way her chest stuck out and mouth hung a little open. As though she were caught mid-gasp, blinking. I'd always find it easier to love a girl when she was half-dressed – which means, I'm sorry to say, that despite my denials most of what the papers write about me these days is one hundred per cent correct.

But then I was trying hard to think, not just of her without the towel, but also of her whole life. If I was to be a reportage photographer I had to be able to envisage every terrible thing, even when I felt furious, or excited. But perhaps all I had was wishes and imagination. Maybe I would never have insight, empathy, understanding. Particularly, crucially, into women and their woes – and what use was any classic story without a strong female lead?

As I was thinking these lurid things I suddenly spotted my golden sports car. I felt a flash of rage. It had been moved. It was now parked, as if concealed, alongside one of the caravans. My first thought was that one of the Vine vixen had moved it in an act of mischief, and this angered me.

'My car!' I exclaimed. 'Who the hell put it there?'

'That's not your car, John,' Hepsie said with a smile. 'That's my car.'

'No it's not. It's mine!' I cried, and heard myself sound exactly like a spoilt child.

'No. Miss Moore got us both one. How do you think I've been getting up here?'

'What! It's the same colour, the same model,' I said furiously. I felt hideously cheated. My car was precious to me not simply because it was expensive and sleek, but because it was the only one around and it belonged, exclusively, noticeably, to me. It was me.

'Isn't it a wonderful drive? I've never experienced anything like it. So smooth and fast. And aren't heated leather seats the coolest thing?'

'Yes,' I muttered, looking between my car and its exact replica, hers. Now mine was not the only one in the village, it was instantly stripped of its most special quality. Suddenly it seemed gaudy and embarrassingly ostentatious.

'It's terrible to admit, but that car's one of the things that finally swayed me.'

'You decided to sell your daughter for a fast car.'

'No, not decided. Agreed to think about it. She only got me the car at the beginning of the year. When she knew I was wavering. Same time she got yours. It was necessary too, not just a bribe. So I could get up and down to Wychwood easily. Part of the deal.'

'Ah yes. The deal.'

'Just as you, the nanny, were part of the deal, John. I would never have let Misty look after Jewels on her own. In fact you, the nanny, were the main thing that swayed me, not the car.'

'It's too bizarre to be real,' I said coolly.

'It's both, John,' she said sadly, suddenly seeming years older than I. 'True and nightmarish. I've told you – that's how life is for some people. We ordinary women can't protect ourselves from those underneath disasters of life, in the way that you London men can.'

Bring on the violins, I thought, but nodded sadly all the same. She was wandering around now on the grass. Throwing her words up at the moon. Pressing her hands against her lower back and thrusting her chest forward. She didn't trust me; she didn't want to reveal how she truly felt to anyone. This could be the start of her becoming a star. The truth could be her most closely guarded secret.

'But giving away your baby. And carrying on as though nothing has happened!'

She looked at me for a long time until I was sure I could hear the rumbling drum of her pink velvet heart. I suspected she was a little proud and excited by what she'd dared to do. 'Actually I'm not carrying on very well at all.'

'No?'

'That's proving to be one of my problems with the glamorous London life – the on and on of it. There's no room to feel anything. You just have to keep going. No wonder we all love fast cars so much.'

'You look upset.'

'And that's another of my problems. I'm too vulnerable, apparently.' She stared at me. Pity: the look the wise pauper gives the idiot prince. Alongside the despair, I sensed she was also rather annoyed that everything had been revealed, forcing her into a decision before she was willing. 'That's what Cheryl Angeles, she's the manager, that's what she says,' Hepsie said quietly. 'Misery. It looks good in photos but it's no use in real life.'

For a while we looked at one another. I was waiting for her to tell me everything. But after several minutes of silence all she said was, 'I love that house,' pointing through the darkness down to Long Meadow End. 'That's why I wanted Jewels down there in her first months. It's important to keep the family traditions going. I wouldn't have accepted anything else.'

'What must your mother have thought when she heard what you were going to do?'

'She was shocked. But she'd been shocked by me before.'

'Yes, I bet.'

'And I didn't tell her until it was all decided. They'd not

seen a lot of me since I moved to London. Then, just before the birth, when I told my mum I'd changed my mind and I wanted the baby back, she was pleased. She agreed to keep an eye on you all. Isolde's been marvellous.'

'Your family spied on us.'

'She said she'd report to me on how you were doing. And how Jewels was keeping. Isolde's been telling me everything.'

'And the more Isolde told you about Jewels the more you wanted her back.'

'Yes. In fact I'm sure she told me things deliberately to sway me and get me home.'

'So now our time is up, and we're meant to return her, like a library book.'

Hepsie Vine bit her lip. I could hear her chest wheeze and noticed the ragged edges of her bitten fingernails. Not a classy look, sure, but enough for the new bad me.

'I agreed that Misty could have Jewels because I thought it was the best thing for everyone. But I can't leave Jewels. I thought I could but I can't. My mum's right: a child must be with its mother. When I look at little Mouse, abandoned and alone and going slowly crazy, I know that I'd hate that to happen to Jewels. Isolde's right. If Jewels is left alone with Miss Moore then surely that's her fate too – funny eating, pills and nightmares.'

'Oh please. Jewels has been very well cared for, by all of us.'

'But it's true! And then as she grows into a woman – drugs, gyms and fantasies. Well, I won't let it happen. Isolde's right, I should be a proper mother to Jewels!'

'Well, the fashion world's going to miss you,' I said coldly.

'Oh absolutely. Sell your shares in *Vogue* right now,' she said with an endearing grimace.

She stared at me keenly. Then looked back at the caravans. She turned to me once more, and bit her lip. Then round again to gaze towards her family. I was shot with an elating certainty that she was going to invite me inside. 'Oh God,' she said. Then I realised she was thinking this was the choice: this or that. Me or them. She was wondering what was worse, my life or theirs.

'So, you were working in a club, dancing. And you made friends with Brian,' I said. 'I just want to get all the facts right. At last.'

'I wanted to go to stage school. That's what my dream was. I'd always wanted to go live in London and share a flat with other dancers. That's how Miss Moore started out, you know. She was at a London stage school. I used to have a picture of her on my wall, laughing.'

'Then Brian told you that dreams aren't worth a bean unless you have money.'

'He's right about that, at least.'

'And you don't earn enough money as a club dancer to put yourself through stage school.'

'Actually you can do, in tips. If you're good. But you have to work very hard.'

'And you needed more money than even fat tips could offer. And then you realised you had something else to sell.'

'Oh John, you could write for the newspapers. You really are terribly sensational.'

I adored Hepsie as much as ever, but face to face she seemed more prone to irritability than I remembered from our telephone conversations. And the rigid set of her pretty jaw suggested a very unladylike determination. Alongside words Hepsie now naturally used a whole range of little gestures and wiggles to speak to her advantage. This made me newly afraid, as well as delighted by her. But I too walked and talked quite differently from how I had six months ago. Miss Moore's particular brand of femininity (a brand that I'd already decided was wretched fakery) had infected Hepsie also. Just as Brian's ridiculous, but effective, mincing masculinity had rubbed off on me. Rather than just exclaiming angrily, or smiling simply, Hepsie accompanied each emotion with a range of ripples and waves and blinks. It left her audience to decipher the meaning in her hips. It concealed the huge confusion of being a modern female. Just as Brian's wiggles and giggles allowed for secrecy. And had the potential for dishonesty.

The longer I waited, there came something a little creepy about being alone in the enormous outdoors of Wychwood with the girl who had been our ghost for so many months. I had no idea what she would do next.

'Well, I guess it's all over for now,' I said firmly, aiming for a tone of paternal authority. 'Kiss me,' I said next, reaching for the lash of a gigolo's command.

But Hepsie just played with a lock of hair and stroked repeatedly at her neck. It was a gesture of such girlish vulnerability that I wondered how she would cope with looking after Jewels.

'So that's the story,' she sighed, 'and now I have to decide if I really want to be someone in life, or if I do the right thing for poor Jewels and give back the house keys, and the car, and just become another mother.'

'I think you and Miss Moore need to meet up and talk everything through.'

'Oh no,' she cried, 'not yet. It's far too soon.'

'Beneath the pancake make-up she's a kind woman. If she loses Jewels it'll break her heart. The baby's all she's got.'

Behind me the lights had gone out in the caravan. The Vine girls were gone. Hepsie and I were almost veiled to one another by the balmy summer night, where the caramel scent of burnt roses still coiled up smokily. We were playing a game: she was hiding and I was seeking, and this is how it would always be between us – though we might for a few hot days call it love.

'I'd better go. I'm tired and I have an early start in the morning. Another shoot. On top of a crane on a bomb site this time.'

'You're going back? To London?'

'I have no choice. I'm driving down now.'

'But given what's happened now.'

'Nothing's happened *now*. I've lived like this for six months. The only thing that's happened *now* is that you know I'm the baby's mum. Why should that change anything?'

But of course it changed everything for me. I felt a gnawing emptiness that seemed to be a taste of my entire future without Hepsie and Jewels. In the black caravan I could see shadows of girls moving like fish deep underwater. For ever I would see only surfaces, endlessly tormented by the sensation of some glorious difference flickering beneath. There I'd be, poking and prodding, itching and scratching, more irritably as time went by, desperate to be allowed down into their secrets.

'But surely you'll want to get Jewels back home as soon as possible.'

'Home?'

'It'll be very hard for Miss Moore too, so we should get it

all over and done with immediately. Then you'll be free of all this.'

Now I felt like a social worker and I loathed my sensible, shallow self. I knew suddenly with a terrible clarity that I would never be an artist – never live the soaring, plummeting life of a writer, a poet or a painter, because Hepsie was right. I could not bear darkness and chaos. Lies baffled me. I had no understanding of the lengths to which desperate people would go to endure their unbearable days. Miss Moore knew too that I had never cared to enquire who I really was. Who was I? What was truly, uniquely *me*? My silken cushion of Southern privilege had weakened me, irreversibly, to need always the simple, to expect the everyday. Always to seek the sunny solution, in every situation. That's why I'd been given the job. And why duplicitous women would always want me around.

'Misty and I agreed that we'd decide what to do at the end of the summer. Don't make me rush. Please, John. I'll come and see her with my final decision in a couple of days.'

'What about Brian?'

'He's in London. He says it's up to me, what I do.' The foam had burst from her head, leaving the hair in ratty cords; she looked older and tired. But I could not, would not, let her just slip out of my life for ever.

'I guess he doesn't care now he's got his money.'

'Well, actually, he's only got half the money.'

'Oh that is a shame.'

'The deal was half the money when the baby was born and half after six months. So I guess he still does care what happens.'

'That guy's incredible.'

But that summer night I suddenly loved Hepsie Vine

despite everything. I had to have her if my life was to amount to anything beyond lazy, empty privilege. And so what if it failed? Nothing had any consequences other than how you told the tale. What was failure other than fear of how you were perceived by others? If you mastered your image, told your story correctly, worked out what you wanted, then nothing could touch you. I wanted to be ruthless, but when she smiled at me I melted and wanted to love her with every bit of me.

'I can't imagine what you've been through,' I said softly, 'giving up your baby.'

'No,' she said flatly, 'you can't imagine it.'

And with that she returned to the caravan, slammed the door and left me, alone and tiny in the vast cloud-blown dark.

Chapter Nineteen

O f course I could have run away. My suitcase was packed. I could have fled my betrayal and avoided what was to come if I had just driven to London. But what was I without bright Miss Moore? Without the children? Where would I go? Who would I be? Who would fill my days and my heart if not Jewels and Mouse? Though in my shock and anger immediately following the revelations I did on two occasions journey some way towards the South, my parents perhaps, some old friend from my abandoned BA, or a vague girl I'd once fancied who washed up in *Madame Baguette*. She might remember me. And there were the Jennifers and Jodies, those terracotta girls who went to all the parties, girls who'd learnt to kiss by watching dirty movies. They might entertain me, assuming they'd not melted away for ever in the heat of my imagination. But then that familiar irresistible longing – the same sour nostalgia that made Alex still wear the cat-piss aftershave – brought me off the motorway and back along the darkening lanes towards Wychwood.

The position of a nanny is similar to that of the child in so many ways. The obvious way of course is that you are told nothing about what is going on. So you rail along in the choppy wake of the powerful adult lives around you. The famous make kids of us all. A less obvious advantage of this position is that just like children you are often witness to situations that are assumed to be beyond your comprehension. In this way do you learn most about the world around you.

The following day, Saturday, I marched sulkily into the drawing room in early evening looking for Mouse's lost sock, only to find Hepsie sitting wet-faced opposite a sunglassed Miss Moore. It was the first time I'd ever seen the two of them in the same room. It was remarkable how sitting that way in silence, as if before an invisible chessboard, they emphasised the essence of one another. Next to Miss Moore Hepsie, breezy in a simple white shift dress topped by high leather boots, seemed younger, prettier, suddenly subservient. The older woman, over-ripe in purple trousers and a black silk shirt, revealed not only her age and experience, but a powerful adult will.

To the left sat Mrs and Mrs Vine, atinkle with that shower of cheap jewellery. Garish in their charity-shop attire, they were waiting, hands folded in laps, legs crossed, chins pulled in, like patients for the doctor. I had Jewels in my arms. At the sight of her relatives the baby was smiling and kicking her chubby legs, cooing and bumping her pretty head against my chest. I was good now at mothering, and the child loved me. The Vine women were too absorbed by the coming scene to look at me for long, but Brian, who sat by the window blank as a pot plant, saw me and nodded slightly. I hoped to detect an apology in his glance, but mostly he appeared confused, as though he only vaguely remembered me from somewhere long ago. I pictured Brian and Hepsie six months ago. How they sat, incredulous, gazing over the sparkling fairy lights, silver baubles and swags of bunting, seemingly as surprised to find themselves in Misty Moore's pinked living room at Christmas time as I was myself. Amazed that their plan to hire a friendly fool was working.

It was another year before I heard Brian's version of events. On one of our frequent nights out the following year he confessed he'd indeed decided to 'kill two birds with one stone'. 'Look, the old lonely one was past it, desperate, and looking to hire a trusty friend; the young ambitious one was gorgeous and unhappily pregnant; I just identified a market, mate. Then closed the deal.'

Mouse was in the room too. I had tried that very morning to ignore the pain of my own humiliation and explain the situation to the boy.

'So basically, the girl who I thought was the ghoul is the Biomom, right?' I told him that was correct and he smiled; the truth was a relief to us all. 'It's kinda freaky? And if the baby goes back to live with her Biomom then what will happen to you, Mummyman? And what will happen to me?' I told him that we'd all make sure he was looked after. 'Sure. Right. I'm, like, totally everyone's priority, I know that. Hello!'

Then out of the silence the grandmother turned to Miss Moore and said softly, 'The trouble is she doesn't want your life. She'd wanted fame and money for so long she'd do anything for it, but she had no idea what it was really like.'

'No,' Miss Moore said calmly, 'I realise that.'

'She just wasn't prepared for the long hours, the pressure, and most of all the nastiness and the loneliness.'

'That's because no one ever tells the truth about what this life is really like,' Miss Moore replied. Then immediately pressed her fingertips to her lips, as if astonished that her own mouth had spoken those words.

'But she promised us she'd give you her final decision by the end of June,' Hepsie's mother said. 'This can't go on any longer. It's not fair on any of us.'

Huge blocks of sunlight slipped over the farmhouse walls, and I knew that something bad was coming.

'Oh the end of June,' Hepsie laughed wildly, 'the end of my life! God, this is all such a mess! I always said to Brian it would be in the end.' Suddenly the Wychwood beauty flung her high-heeled boots hard across the waxen drawing room so they clattered against the wall. She didn't look my way, but I hoped the wild fury was mostly for me: it was what I liked best.

'Hepsie! Calm down,' the grandmother exclaimed. 'We know you're upset but think of other people for a change.'

'I wish we'd just accepted how things were, and never tried to do any of this, Brian!' Hepsie cried. Then, as if she suddenly remembered to hide herself, as she had been taught in London, Hepsie turned on a range of little sighs and flicks and pouts most powerfully to communicate her scorching sorrow.

Mouse came over to me and gripped my hand.

'I'm lonely. I miss my baby,' Hepsie sighed. 'But . . .'

'She misses the baby,' her mother said firmly, like a lawyer the Vines had hired to press their case. 'She's lonely.'

'Oh please. Loneliness isn't the end of the world! You get used to it. And we'll miss the baby,' Miss Moore cried. 'We'll miss her too!'

'But she's not yours, love. She's not yours, is she?' the grandmother said kindly.

'We're sorry for all the trouble,' Hepsie's mother said gently. 'But we're having the baby back.'

I was holding Jewels tightly; it was too much to contemplate the thought of losing her. Mouse looked up at me urgently, surely hoping that I would at last prove a man and intervene to control and restrain the women and rescue Jewels. The boy's look made me remember the heroic thoughts I'd had when I'd sat outside Long Meadow End with Miss Moore for the first time. Adventurous manly possibilities filling me, as I heard the windowpanes chattering like teeth and saw inside blue-green air moving like seawater. Hepsie was right: I was just a bag of fantasies.

'She thought she could do it but she can't,' the grandmother said, as Hepsie began to fling herself around on the sofa in emotional distress – or in imitation of such a state. Rather too obviously, I felt, Hepsie was deliberately displaying her blazing youth before the older women. Despite everything, Hepsie was behaving exactly like a young movie star. 'She has to come home before she gets into more trouble.'

'Oh leave me alone, all of you,' Hepsie said, turning to smile at me at last, simply, with that devastating young grubby smile. 'In fact,' Hepsie exclaimed recklessly, throwing herself back down on the sofa in a gesture of complete abandon, 'I really wish I'd had an abortion in the first place.'

'Oh great!' Hepsie's mother said softly. Then she pressed her fingertips to her forehead and closed her eyes.

'I might have done if he'd not convinced me I really could be a somebody!' Hepsie cried, pointing at Brian.

'Well, if you had, all this might have been avoided,' the grandmother said sternly, sighing at her daughter and then at her granddaughter. In their look I saw the difference: Mrs and Mrs Vine and Hepsie were not alone, they loved and cared for one another, and this, above everything, was the power they had over Miss Moore.

Mouse pressed himself against my leg, as if wishing to dissolve into my body. 'Gee, no kidding, they really are all nuts,' he whispered, as he looked at Hepsie open-mouthed: she was still his midnight ghost.

'I know it's going to be hard for you,' the grandmother said to Miss Moore, 'but I really think a child should be with its mother. We don't want our Jewels ending up like that poor little lad.' All eyes turned to Mouse, who gazed his mad stare back defiantly.

'No,' Hepsie's mother agreed. 'That's no life for a kid. He's proof to me that our Hepsie has to take the baby back.'

'Yes, an abortion,' Hepsie cried, stamping her foot on the floor and shouting. 'That is exactly what I wish I'd fucking done. Then I'd never have got used to things that are gonna be really hard to leave.' For several long moments Hepsie's monkeyish show of tricks created a potent way of unsaying all that had been done to her. It blew around us a mysterious anguished silence. Hepsie was either dreadfully sad, or brilliantly acting sad: I'd never quite be able to tell for sure. But one thing was certain: our love would only be possible if I never tried to know.

Miss Moore had her hand over her mouth, as if holding in all the things she wanted to say.

'I want Jewels back, but then at the same time I know I'm gonna really miss the chance to make something of myself in London,' Hepsie sighed. 'I was getting on all right some of the time. It was hard and lonely – but there were other rewards. I was really trying. But now all that work is wasted.'

I looked around at the women, who were all leaning towards Hepsie.

'Let's calm down. Do you think you could look after a tiny baby and do the modelling work?' Miss Moore asked Hepsie. My boss was displaying a measured reason that I'd not seen before. Perhaps it was the presence of Mrs and Mrs Vine that encouraged us to take things more seriously. They were ordinary adults with responsibilities in the real world and we screwballs had a duty to respond appropriately. Or maybe Miss Moore's coolness was a sudden tactical decision.

'Well, Brian says I can,' the girl replied, with that coy sigh in her voice I had heard before in determined young women. I loved it. 'He says that if you play it right a kid can actually help your image. He says that for the ambitious teenage girl having a kid is the new having an abortion, don't you, Brian?'

At the mention of his name Brian twinkled into life and nodded. Like a man on the shore sighing over a pretty sunset, while just metres away in the water a woman is eaten by a shark.

'So, Hepsie, you're saying you've considered going back to find somewhere to live in London with Jewels?' Miss Moore asked.

'No,' her grandmother said firmly, 'she's coming back here.'

'That's what she told us,' Hepsie's mother nodded keenly. 'That she wants to come home.'

'Ah, so you're moving back to this village?' Miss Moore said. 'With Jewels?'

'Looks like it,' the young one moaned. 'What choice do I have?'

'I hope you know what is involved,' the grandmother said. 'It's a lot of work with a baby.'

'And you'll have to give Miss Moore some of the money back, won't you?'

'Yes, and you'll be doing that work, madam,' her grandmother continued, raising her eyebrows at her naughty granddaughter.

Hepsie responded with a snort. As if seeing her rotten grandmother and mother together was reminding her of all that she'd never wanted to be in the first place.

'What about me?' Mouse whispered, to no one in particular. 'Where am I in all this?'

'So, you're going to live with your family?' Miss Moore said. Hepsie agreed, with a groan. 'Why?' Miss Moore whispered. 'You always said it'd drive you mad to live out here, didn't you? What about your dreams?'

'I think it's a bit too late for those, don't you?' the grandmother laughed, and Hepsie sneered, as if to say, *Dreams, dreams, dreams: Brian's right, they're written in dust unless you have cash.*

As I gazed on Hepsie and Brian memories of my betrayal returned and then my own dreams were dying all around me only to be instantly resurrected as ghoulish visions of my own unavoidable solitary future: unloved, unemployed, useless, unnoticed by the cruel world. Unless . . .

Then I began to feel excited as I watched the people in that room and remembered my own more sociable recent past: ordinary parents, school, friends. My fury with Miss Moore and Brian for deceiving me lessened. Soon it was anger with a dash of vodka. Before I'd met Brian and

Hepsie and Miss Moore, if I'd ever become an artist I'd've surely concentrated, disastrously, on the mundane, the tragic ordinariness of the everyday, the dank English poetic nothingness. Little gestures and honestly spoken words. Bleak, character-revealing moments. Realism and lost love. Because that is how my life had been, and would always be, anaesthetised by privilege, controlled by my advantage, into everlasting dullness – unless . . .

Unless, I found someone else whose life was desperate and chaotic and hopeless, and who had the courage to try and change things. I loved Hepsie all over again. I needed her passionately. Despite everything dreadful she'd done. I wanted to rip Hepsie into my arms, tear away the last of the lies. Devour every creamy inch of her. Wolf her down in the woods. Chutzpah! Yes, that's what I wanted in a woman – I'd leave the saints to other men.

'I know I complained about London,' Hepsie said at last, 'but at least there was something to *do*.'

'Oh you'll have plenty to do, madam,' the grandmother laughed. 'Don't you worry about that!'

'But it's so hard to think of giving everything else up,' Hepsie said. 'What about my career?'

'What about your baby?' her grandmother said.

'What about the money?' Brian added.

'You have to decide now, we don't have all day,' her mother said in exasperation.

'Because they're right, I can't look after Jewels myself in a hotel room, can I?' the young beauty before me moaned. 'Brian thinks I can, but that's because he's absolutely no idea what it's like with a kid, have you, Brian? He thinks you just lock them in a cupboard and go out for the night.'

Brian smiled as Hepsie pouted and I stroked my chin,

thinking. I wondered if this performance was all part of the pair's arrangement. Brian would always, over the following years, insist (and I asked and asked him about those months I spent in Wychwood) that they had never intended to request the baby back at the end of the trial six months. But I could never be entirely sure.

'Did you target Misty?' I asked him one night in a bar. I longed for him to trust me with intimate truths.

'Not exactly,' he replied.

'Hmm, well, I suppose not,' Miss Moore said. Just from the timbre of her voice it was obvious that, just like me and Hepsie, she was finding it hard to conceal some excitement. 'But if some beautiful girls manage it, why not you, Hepsie?'

'Well, they have mothers, or other staff helping,' Hepsie said. 'People.'

'Well, you can forget that, madam!' her grandmother laughed, outraged.

'If you think we're looking after your baby all day long while you go out to be photographed!' Hepsie's mother shouted.

'There's no way I'm going to London,' the grandmother exclaimed.

'That's the only reason you're coming back here?' Miss Moore said quietly, with great understanding. 'Just so you have people?' Miss Moore powered a smile at Hepsie and the girl fluttered. Something was coming, thundering towards us, unstoppably.

'People I can trust,' Hepsie clarified shyly. 'People who like me. Not just people like Brian.'

I looked at Brian. Immediately he flicked a peep at me and smiled. *I don't have to do a thing: just watch them screw it up all by themselves*. He cared nothing for any of them. One day the following year I'd be in a bar at lunchtime going over and over the details and he'd become uncharacteristically belligerent and say, 'Hey, look, don't you criticise me, man, I'm just a regular black guy doing the bad things you all expect me to do.'

Miss Moore was rattling on with her plan, '. . . so someone helps you? Is that your only reason for coming back here?'

'And I miss my sisters.'

I could hear Miss Moore buzzing like electricity as though certain her job in life was to influence the mood of sad girls. If she could not do this most simple thing, change the mind of a poor teenage village girl, then what had been the point of all the skills of public manipulation, the spinning of baubled joy, that she had spent a lifetime perfecting?

'Which? You need help with the baby, or you want to live with your family?'

'Both.'

'Really? I thought you didn't want to live in a caravan, with that lot. When you could . . .'

'What?'

'Make your dreams come true,' Miss Moore said quietly, urgently.

'Earn a fortune,' Brian said at almost the same time so Hepsie had to look from one to the other, her breathing made quick and shallow by possibilities. Her eyes blazed purple twilight again. Then for the first time in maybe a year there was a silence as each woman looked across the phantom chessboard at her opponent. I was sure they didn't see one another at all – just themselves, older and younger, their past and future terrible and inescapable.

Me? Two women: one dangerous, dirty and fresh, the other rich with breasts full of helium. I saw them together, intertwined, flash-lit, glossed, stapled into a magazine as Mouse gave a high little laugh, which rang around the room like a bell. He was right: it was an absurd story, trashy, erotic, late-night. Shot through with the scarlet force of female rivalry. But alone in my bedroom, later, it was enough for me.

'Come on, Hepsie, decide,' Miss Moore said urgently, leaning further forward like one urging a horse to the line. 'Do you just need help to be with Jewels or are you truly missing your old life in Wychwood?'

'The first reason,' Hepsie said firmly. 'I need help.'

'Of course you do,' Miss Moore said soothingly. 'It's such hard work. Absolutely, you can't possibly be expected to . . .'

A shadow slanted slowly and sharply across the room like a dark blade. Mrs and Mrs Vine began to mutter.

'So, why not live with me!' Miss Moore was grinning, then standing and holding her arms outstretched as if welcoming a phantom lover. 'You and Jewels and me, all together. What a wild time we'd have! Working, spending, travelling, shopping, gossiping – there'd be no end to our fun.'

Brian and I later agreed that it was inspired. To repackage the deal: present modern womanhood as a busy glittering adventure, warmed by hugs – forgetting the isolation Miss Moore truly knew. If Hepsie had misled Miss Moore over the sale of Jewels, then Miss Moore had just as deceptively sold Hepsie a phony lifestyle.

'What?' Mrs and Mrs Vine said together.

'And Mouse, of course,' Miss Moore said. 'The dear little Mouse must come too.'

'Freaky. It just gets freakier and freakier,' Mouse laughed. 'The ghost, the Biomom, Mrs Big Tits, the Mummyman, and me, all living together happily ever after. Hello!'

Meanwhile, Hepsie Vine was chewing on her fingertip and gazing on the carpet, a clever dumb-show of dumbness. Miss Moore stroked Hepsie's arm and grinned. She assumed her mature cunning had triumphed over the raw passion of the girl. Perhaps for her a thousand white balloons were suddenly falling from the ceiling, doves were released, mad applause and a band starting up a victorious tune. 'I'll help you with Jewels. You can do your work, Hepsie, and I'll look after you both. You and the baby. Let me care for you. Help you and support you. We'll all be so happy.'

'It'll be hard work,' Hepsie said, opening her eyes very wide. 'I'll have to be both, a model and a mother.'

'It'll be a disaster!' Brian said loudly, but privately, as though he'd rushed his thoughts straight to camera.

'It's too much work. Even for the two of you,' Hepsie's mother said. 'Neither of you are exactly hard workers, are you?'

'We'll have John,' Miss Moore exclaimed. 'Dear John will assist us.'

'Will you?' Hepsie said to me with a coy smile.

I didn't think. It wasn't my style. I just nodded idiotically and grinned.

'And other staff,' Miss Moore laughed. 'We'll pay people to help us.'

'But I'd still be her mother?'

'And we'd still be her relatives?'

'Yes,' Miss Moore nodded, 'but I'll have her around.'

'You'll still have to pay her some money,' Brian said. 'You can't wriggle out of it this way.'

'Have whatever money you like,' Miss Moore said irritably. 'As if I care about the money!'

'I'd need to be in London, though,' Hepsie said with a winning pout. 'We're not staying here in this dump, are we?'

'Oh it's a dump now, is it?' her grandmother exclaimed.

'But, you've been telling us for the last three months how you couldn't wait to come home,' her mother added sadly. Her eyes were glistening, then swelling with tears.

'She just wants it all,' the grandmother continued, reaching over to stroke her daughter's hand. 'A home and an adventure, a baby and a job.'

'So I've lost them both again,' Hepsie's mother said desperately. 'They're not coming back after all.'

Miss Moore was not listening any more. She was moving quickly round the room. 'John can come to London with you immediately, if you like, and I'll follow you down when I've packed everything up.'

Then I heard a young smile crackle, and rise up like paper catching light. 'Yes,' the girl said firmly, 'yes, if you want to look after me and Jewels in London I could try.'

'Aren't you coming back with us?' Mouse asked Miss Moore later that night. Mouse and I had hastily packed our bags, for we were to go down to Chessington Vale instantly. Hepsie had already left at great speed in her sports car. 'I thought we were one big happy family now.'

'I'd only put her off,' Miss Moore said flatly, 'and we can't risk that just yet.'

Like superstar refugees, our expensive white leather suitcases ringed at our feet, we three stood together in the brown light of the vast farmhouse hallway for the last time. Ominously I remembered my encounter with the sacked staff of Chessington Vale, in the hallway, on that first fateful day.

'And another thing,' Miss Moore said, not meeting my eye. 'It's important that she does plenty of the baby work herself.'

'I see.'

'Yes. That's right. I want her to know exactly what it's like to have a baby around when you're trying to work.'

Chapter Twenty

Summer London greeted Hepsie, Mouse, Jewels and me warmly. Everywhere I imagined photographers: despite what I knew, I hoped for them. Rich slender people were on the streets and yes, foolish idiot that I was, my heart leapt because they noticed me! That July I felt sure that young beauties walked by on the streets just to be seen walking. Glanced over their shoulders just to be seen glancing and would, in sun-spangled city parks, dance in yellow twirls that lifted their poppy-coloured skirts high as brilliant summer petals.

'It's a new start,' I'd said to Mouse as we'd sped in my little car through the dark night towards London. I was going to live at Chessington Vale with Hepsie Vine, model, actress, presenter, and everything was going to be wonderful.

'It's a freaky crazy plan,' Mouse replied, with a little smile to encourage me. 'But what have we to lose?'

'You won't have to go to school for a while,' I smiled. Miss Moore and I had agreed that as it was nearly the end of term Mouse could rest at home. It stopped us having to worry about his education. 'I might ask Hepsie to marry me,' I continued with a grin. 'One day we might even have our own children.'

'Well, just make sure when you sell them that you get a good price.'

Still, I was buzzing with plans. I was to live with the woman I'd loved from afar for so long. I imagined how I would buy her flowers and display them around the house. I would cook nutritious meals. I would arrange the furniture to make the house distinctly our own. I would fashion a bedroom for Mouse, a nursery for Jewels and order cute wooden furniture to be delivered. I would prove to Hepsie that we could handle it. Rise above the trash and laugh at it. I imagined all the things we would uniquely do, and I tried to tell Mouse. I dreamed of our future. Though I was still stunned by glamour I like to think that I was less impressionable than I had been six months ago; I no longer saw any glittering mystery in unhappiness. I wanted us to be cheerful and content and to provide stability for the children.

'We're gonna have the time of our lives.'

'Really,' Mouse said with a high little laugh that I'd not heard before, 'well, you'd better do it soon, Mummyman. Cos round here things seem to change pretty quick.'

I sped into the driveway of Chessington Vale and parked my car next to Hepsie's.

'How was your journey, sweet John?' Hepsie said when she met us at the door. 'Isn't speeding through England at night the very best thing!'

It was the early hours of the morning. She was wearing just a shining gossamer dressing gown. Her hair scrunched up sleepily. Tired, bewildered, she looked heavy-eyed and devastatingly attractive. Of course now I know the key to looking this hot was to look like a woman pretending to be a child who was pretending to be a sexy woman. Once upon a time Miss Moore had done it perfectly and, to my delight, I now discovered that Hepsie had achieved it too.

'You need to feed Jewels,' I said, and instantly I saw myself saying this over and over again in the coming weeks. Hauling Hepsie Vine back from despair and electrifying lurid adventures to our little domestic life.

The mother kissed her daughter cautiously and then handed the baby back to me. For a few moments Hepsie played with the baby's fingers and smiled uneasily.

'Come on, feed her,' I said.

'Oh you do it, John. I'm not sure how to yet,' Hepsie said, and moved around the room with the quick catwalk slink of a superstar trailed by bodyguards, as moonlight roared around us. I was sure Hepsie was pleased to see her child, but also alarmed at the thought of life with her. 'I'm just going up to get changed.'

All was replicated. I just had to focus, take it all in again. I had to be as dazzled and excited to be in the house as I had been six months ago. Dolphins were still there supporting the coffee table. Terracotta penguins still crowded round the wide chrome TV. The rocking horse gave a quick snort of disdain, and for a moment the fairy-flashing tree was there too. Atop it my darling, twinkling with a silver wand. I was certain Hepsie Vine could, before too long, be a very successful actress, if only I could stop her occasionally being so honest.

'Who are all these guys?' Mouse said loudly as another dusky stranger called a greeting into the room.

'New staff.'

'I thought you and freaky Brian were the staff.'

'Not any more.'

'If you're not the staff, who are you?'

'I'm the family now. They're the staff.'

'No kidding. It's like that staring game,' Mouse whispered to me very seriously, as we stood alone together in the living room at 4 a.m. waiting for the young mother to reappear, 'the loser is the one who blinks first.'

We waited. No one passed by. I noticed there were more mirrors in the house than on the first day I'd arrived. Or perhaps I just hadn't noticed mirrors before. I turned to one and looked at my face. For some time I'd sensed I was becoming as pathetically preoccupied with controlling my image as those in whose circles I moved. It had started. Now that I was returned to London, without my fantasies and fears about Mrs and Mrs Vine to take attention away from myself, I saw how changed I was. Recently I'd begun to glance at myself like a girl, I looked at my own copper-tanned body for several long moments every time I removed my clothes. I sniffed my wrists and armpits like a dog snouting up the arse of another mutt. I worried deeply if my outward appearance did not meet my inner expectations. Was the very me-ness of me altered for ever by my six months with Miss Moore? Brian's flirtation with female-ness worked because of his excessive masculinity, but what about me? You could carry off being pussy-whipped only if men envied you in other ways.

Mouse looked up at the ceiling. His jaw dropped and he closed his eyes. He could hear the ghost clomping around overhead. Immediately I wished Brian would appear. I needed his advice, for I had to jolly things along for Mouse, and cheer up Hepsie. Like Brian had perked things up with Miss Moore in those early days. Bubble baths, oils, dresses, all these things helped, but it was more than this. For Miss Moore's sake and my own, and most of all for Mouse and little Jewels, I had to find a way of bringing beauty into Hepsie's life. Though I could not imagine how to do it without lies. I feared that Brian was right: it was difficult to be both honest with women and make them happy.

Hepsie returned in a floaty coffee-coloured dress and kissed us all. Then she inhaled, took her baby firmly in her arms and led us around. She seemed unaware that it was not even dawn as she wove through the empty rooms. I decided, with a thrill, that in the last six months Hepsie's nights must have been indistinguishable from her days, and I imagined all the nocturnal London fun that soon was to come my way.

Hepsie showed Mouse his room at the far end of the first floor. Swagged, gilded, cushioned and stencilled, and undoubtedly all furnished by Brian, or a man like him. Or a man like Brian had pretended to be. Mouse's room was the opposite of Miss Moore's room in Wychwood. Money and gross luxury were belching in every corner. My own room, I'd soon discover, was the same. 'It's even bigger than I imagined,' I enthused as we wandered on and on.

'This stuff's what she's worked for all her life,' Hepsie sighed, running a finger over a bronze sculpture of a young boy positioned on the landing.

'And what she was willing to give up,' I said.

'Yes, in exchange for this cute bundle,' Hepsie said, and squeezed Jewels' toes.

I remember particularly Hepsie's bedroom. Especially her unforgettable bed, wide and high with long pillows. And the bedside table where an ashtray overloaded with stubs rocked on a pile of glossy magazines.

'Just think that I used to live on a farm, and yet I turned everything round, and look at me now,' Hepsie said, twirling through the room. She wore tears like diamonds on her pretty cheeks.

'Cool in heatwavey London,' I said, grasping her from behind and pushing myself into her.

'Let's order some champagne.' She was bouncing the baby uneasily against her rangy hip. 'It's like England's a completely different place to what it was six months ago.'

'Yes, it's hotter,' Mouse said.

'We need to feed Jewels before we do anything,' I said, and after a moment's hesitation Hepsie took the child over to the bed. Carefully she placed one pillow on top of the other against the high wooden headboard. Outside a wash of pink morning was spreading over the sky. Hepsie settled herself, wriggling her slim shoulders to mould a comfortable space. At first she seemed uneasy with how to position the baby. I went to help and soon Hepsie tucked Jewels into the arc of her elbow and began to feed her the bottle. Bubbled sucks rose and popped around the quiet room. Hepsie looked so small on the big bed: hospital, I thought. That is how the pair of them must have looked in the beginning, without Brian, Misty and me.

Later on when Jewels had fallen asleep, and Mouse had been taken to his room, a servant brought us a bottle of champagne and I ran Hepsie a bath. En suite and icy white, it was the biggest bathroom I'd ever known. Hepsie gazed at me, me at her. We were both trying so very hard to be in love in those first hours that it made our chests ache. 'You're gorgeous,' I said firmly, taking her in my arms. 'We're gonna have such a brilliant time. I've got all sorts of ideas for the house and candles and oils . . .' I kissed her.

Over her shoulder I saw brushes of all sizes and many cartridges of lipsticks. I saw an assortment of purple, green and blue pats of eye shadow strewn over the thick carpet. Tiny mirrors caught darts of golden morning light.

'When I met you, Hepsie, you were just a country girl, and now you're an almost star.' I spun her round and kissed her madly again. Wildly I wanted her. She pushed me away, laughed and sank on to the bed with a cry.

While Hepsie took her bath I stood at the high window drinking champagne and listening to the slow splashing of the model washing away her secrets in the white bathroom. On and on I waited. Every few minutes a dark silhouette would rise over the white walls. I wondered how long it would be hot like this. When it would cool. If it would be windy or still tomorrow. Thunder or storm. How long it was since we'd had rain. Boredom and denial expressed itself this way in several of the men I knew, my father certainly – that constant preoccupation with the weather.

Most days in the first week we left the house for a walk and were happy. Hepsie had mostly settled into the mothering and now fed, changed and bathed Jewels quite happily. I felt enormously relieved to be free of my responsibilities. In her expensive pram, we wheeled Jewels around the London streets looking in shop windows and making jokes about what we could buy if we could be bothered. Twice photographers snapped us. Mouse and Jewels, Hepsie and me. Hand in hand in sunny summer. Hepsie kissed me and hugged me. I knew she could have been pretending; I just hoped there was genuine passion in her pretence, like those high-crying actresses on chat-shows who declare, 'My movies are always best when I'm in love.'

On one occasion we were definitely recognised by a giggle of pretty girls, who stopped on a Kensington pavement and gasped just to look on us. 'It's not even her baby. It's Chinese, isn't it?' I heard one whisper as they hurried along by the side of us to look in the pram.

'Is the baby definitely Chinese?' another girl gasped.

'Is that why she doesn't want any photos of it except these for that magazine?' her companion replied, curling a thin red lip as she gazed a freezing stare over our little party.

When Hepsie was working I took the children on bright days out: Hyde Park, the Zoo, Oxford Street, the London Eye, the *Cutty Sark*, we covered it all in wide smiles. If Hepsie got a night off, which happened once that first week, we went to an expensive restaurant and giggled at the other guests. We praised one another and laughed loudly and flung ourselves back in our seats glamorously. We decided all the other diners in the place were our extras, discreetly rhubarbing while we stars spoke the thrilling script.

Today I realise that such seemingly innocent star-struck fantasies gave me – and Miss Moore, Brian, and Hepsie – the disorientating illusion that everyone was under our control. No one could exit the set till the end of our scene. Or offer a look, or utter a line that wasn't written down exactly in our screenplay.

But when I was alone without distraction my pleasure began to dim. I was often dizzy in Chessington Vale that July. It was hard not to be nauseated by the furniture, for a start. Still, I thought my fainting feeling was a combination of the delayed vertigo of my trip to the North and the giddy height of my more golden life. I remember us in those early summer days flooded with late-afternoon sunlight. When I lifted the heavy frame on her bedroom window we could hear the chirp and crash of birds nesting. But the air made no difference to the temperature and one afternoon Hepsie shouted into the telephone and demanded some new servant send up a fan.

To my initial relief Hepsie had, on our second evening there, announced that she wanted Jewels' cot in her own room, and she declared that she would be the one to get up in the night when Jewels cried. Soon, however, she was increasingly tired and irritable from working during the day and caring for Jewels at night.

The fan didn't so much as cool a red fingernail, but just tinkled on madly. 'Your bath's ready,' I cried out. Over and over like a barrow boy I cried out those lines, for I ran Hepsie a bath every day. Ringed it with candles and scented it with oils.

'Thank you, John,' Hepsie said. 'Keep an eye on Jewels.' Sighing, she wandered into the bathroom, and then hugged me, though it was more of a sudden squeeze that she used to stop herself falling to the floor than a true embrace. She threw her clothes off next. She was much thinner than she had been a month ago. And her body, naked, was of course startling, but scrawny and child-shaped. Up I lifted her chin and saw that the girl's eyes glistened. To a truthful man this might have indicated tears, but looked at in another way it implied a foggy wash of desire. This was how she had got through her days in London and how Misty had once got through her career too – learning to turn a look of pain to a look of yearning. You had to know what you'd got to sell in this world, and then go to town.

*   *   *

'He's back,' Mouse called out from the hallway early on our third morning. The boy's voice was quiet and flat, his tone one of ominous inevitability.

Brian had arrived.

'Oh and a puppy,' Hepsie said as she rushed to the door, and I saw a tiny creature pulled out of Brian's pocket. It was sleepy, bald, tan suede, then suddenly squeally and new as Jewels on that first day when she had squirmed pig-like on the rug.

'It's not just a fucking puppy,' Brian grinned, 'it's a chihuahua.'

'Do they sell them for charity outside supermarkets?' Hepsie said sadly. 'Five for a pound?'

'A pet!' Mouse cried, more delighted than I'd ever heard him. 'That's so cool.'

The dog was the perfect little touch of foolish beauty, the distracting false note that I should have thought of. Where had other men learnt how to please and pacify women and children? Age must teach you it, I decided, for when I looked at Brian he had the controlled masterly poise not of a flaky fashionista but of an older and wiser man.

'How you doing, babe?' Brian said to Hepsie as he kissed her on the cheek.

'Oh OK,' she said hesitantly, 'though I sometimes think I'm not doing either thing well. I'm too tired to be a good presenter and too busy to be a good mum. But I'm trying to make it work.'

'Excellent,' he said and patted her on the bottom.

The dog gave Hepsie and Mouse and me a distraction over the next few days. Just as Brian's first idea of a Jewels, then the actual Jewels, must have distracted Miss Moore all those months ago. Brian had entertained Miss Moore in

Wychwood because he thought he could make money out of it. And now he was entertaining us.

Some nights I felt disappointed with my new life and needed to get away from Brian and Hepsie and so went out into the hurtling metropolitan evening with the little dog in my pocket to buy bottles of champagne and hundreds of cigarettes. I hoped, left alone with Hepsie, Brian could convince the girl to cheer up. To go on reading the revised, more heart-warming, script. The version that now required the main character to be both a fearless fashion model – and a tender mum. As I walked I became plagued by guilty thoughts of what had happened to Hepsie and Miss Moore. I worried it was unforgivable, though exactly what and why I couldn't quite decide. Once, for a single second as I pounded my heels along the hot paving stones, I thought I might run on and on all the way out of London and never return. I even tried to lose the little dog in a pale park. But it came after me yelping, and courage to wring its tiny neck deserted me. I returned immediately with the pup and the booze, running up the stairs towards Hepsie and what I feared was the ennui and manipulation that was my future. Of course, as Hepsie predicted, it's turned out to be nothing so romantic.

'Oh champagne and the pup,' Hepsie laughed, running up to the door beside Mouse and throwing herself into my arms, and in a single gulp she was changed into a fantastic red glittering dress.

'Doesn't the little devil look cute!' Brian laughed. He was right: we needed the ridiculous clothes and endless booze to keep us breezy, to stop us feeling ashamed, and slipping back into the guilty despair of our first meeting in Chessington Vale.

'She looks amazing,' I said. Brian had dressed her up for me, and I was grateful to him.

And after midnight in the dust-shot living room, drunk on champagne, Hepsie gave us a most memorable performance. She danced for Brian and me. There was no sign of Jewels. Then the light came soft and orange and somewhere music started up on the street, a gentle lilt of jazzy tunes. Surely the notes were calling, urging us to forget everything. We had only one life. Only one chance to find out who we truly were. I drank more and more. Miss Moore was right: loneliness wasn't that bad when you got used to it. Misery was actually no more than a feeling. Guilt was entirely a matter of opinion and morals were private matters. On and on Hepsie danced in slow dips and turns. I had only Hepsie. She was trying to make it work. She was the dirtiest, truest, most dangerous thing that after nearly twenty years in the world I'd been offered. I had to hang on to her. And time passed and Hepsie stood on the white sofa and peeled away her red gloves, then stockings, like a bloody rind. Then half naked she wiggled and sang to us. She was a true professional. We all drank more. There was laughter. Brian and several of the cleaners arrived with jugs of cocktails, which were shot on request into frosted tumblers and immediately exploded to head-stars on impact. I liked the feeling, and drank on till I feared for Hepsie's top notes – sure they would explode the sequins on her matching G-string into a thousand night-spangling ruby pieces.

'The baby's awake,' a little voice screamed. And when we turned the music down and the lights on Mouse was standing there in the doorway, red-faced, holding uneasily the wailing Jewels. He looked at me and Brian desperately as the plump baby flailed in his thin arms. And at the cleaning staff sitting in a ring around Hepsie watching her dance.

Mouse was in his pyjamas and his balaclava, crying.

Chapter Twenty-one

M iss Moore called me for the first time early the next evening. I was in a Soho restaurant with Mouse. Hepsie and Jewels were back at Chessington Vale. We'd had a silly argument about the dress Hepsie had chosen for the outing. Feeling it too plain and frumpy for the little beauty, I'd foolishly suggested she find something more startling to wear. 'There might be some photographers there,' I'd said. 'You want to look your best, don't you?' Hepsie threw herself on the sofa and sobbed that she had nothing decent to wear. Her despair seemed indulgent and this angered me. After six months in isolation in Wychwood I was desperately keen to get out of the house to play. I wanted urgently to forget my regrets in smoky places with fashionable people. Impatiently I suggested Hepsie take a look for an outfit in Miss Moore's closet. 'Oh God, this is all so trashy,' she'd cried. 'You go out and get photographed if you really want to, but leave me here in peace. I've had enough of being ogled by strangers. I need to rest.'

'It's all done,' Miss Moore said calmly, after I'd asked her if she had everything packed. 'But why aren't you at home with Hepsie and Jewels?'

'Oh well,' I said anxiously, for I was still eager to please her. 'I thought she ought to know what it's like to have to stay in with the baby while everyone goes out.'

'Good idea,' she said quietly.

Mouse had laid down his knife and fork and was watching me, open-mouthed. I felt a chill.

'How do you know I'm not in the house?'

'Because I'm watching the house.'

'You are?'

Behind me the room was swimming with a greeny nightlight as smoke drifted in time to jaunty piano music.

'Mrs and Mrs Vine aren't down here, are they, John?'

'I hope not,' I said, and glanced quickly round the room to where tall, silvered waiters marched though a thunderclap of pans and cutlery.

'I noticed earlier this evening that the light was off in their caravan, and I got this terrible feeling that they'd come down here. I've been keeping an eye on her and there's no sign of the family. I can see her right now.'

'You can?'

'She's gazing over the garden, holding Jewels.'

I could picture it exactly, for this was how Hepsie often spent the early evening when she was not working, pacing with Jewels before the window, back and forth, dreaming.

'She's just fed her,' Miss Moore said.

This reminded me of another argument Hepsie and I often had. To my great disappointment Hepsie had declared that she did not like to go to restaurants. She preferred to stay in and cook for us all. She was a good cook, but I was very frustrated by how much time she spent in the kitchen making special little pots of goo for Jewels and elaborate pies and cakes for Mouse and me. The food was heavy, wholesome and old-fashioned, as if prepared by a busty, aproned housewife, and after eating I felt lethargic and forlorn.

'Why are you bothering with this?' I'd exclaimed the previous afternoon when she placed another huge meaty meal before me. 'We could pay people to do this shit for us! Or preferably just go out.'

'I like to do it, John,' she said, obviously hurt by my remark. 'It's called caring for people.'

'She's so unhappy, don't you think,' Miss Moore continued. 'She's looking just like I expected: trapped, frustrated and bored. I can see her. Watching everyone else in the city going out and having fun. I can see her talking to Jewels right now. She's explaining everything, John. Nuzzling Jewels gently and saying what she's decided she has to do. She looks so worn out. As if she's been up all night making her decision.'

A gang of pretty women burst through the door of the restaurant. Around them the air had a cut-glass chill. They smiled at me and I smiled back and winked. This was the busy, spotlit beauty I wanted now. The thought of returning to unhappy Hepsie sank my spirits.

'And intelligent. I knew that as soon as Brian showed me the photographs of her. In fact that's one of the reasons I agreed to Brian's suggestion. I really thought I was doing her a favour. Hepsie's still too young for all this responsibility. She should be out having fun and learning about life.'

'She seems to find London tiring.'

'Of course that's exactly what I thought at first. When I came down here at seventeen I thought I'd not last a month. She just needs someone to explain to her that this is normal.'

'Are you going in to see her?' I asked uneasily. Summer night sparkled outside the restaurant. Evening traffic was busy. Cabs rumbled in a queue.

'Oh God no, I don't want to startle her. This is the crucial time. She has to come to her resolution alone. That's the mistake we made last year. Brian had me take the baby too soon. But rather than me going up to the haunted house, Hepsie should've come down here for the first few months. Then she'd have made the decision much sooner. Has she told you what she's decided to do?'

'No,' I said. 'She's told me nothing.'

'I spoke to her mother yesterday. They've been most friendly to me. They said they'd not heard from her either, except once when she rang her mum for some recipe.'

The truth was that after just one week together Hepsie and I rarely spoke intimately, mostly we bickered. Hepsie was teary and remote, spending most of the time either baking late at night in the kitchen or alone in her bedroom with Jewels. I'd tried to cheer Hepsie up with gifts and saucy notes but she came in from work each day more miserable than the last. Rather than allowing her to revel in the clothes and the attention, her lifestyle seemed to serve only to make her anxious and exhausted. 'Just let me change,' was the first thing she'd say when she walked through the door, and I knew it was not a casual remark, it was a desperate plea.

'I can see her now and she's explaining it all. Saying what she has to do. Poor thing, it must be hard for her; that's why I'm staying here, to support them both.' Again I could see Hepsie. In the darkening light. Gazing over the fertile summer garden, crying, longing for home.

'Do you want Mouse and me to come and meet you? It

sounds lonely out there in the street, watching the house.' A woman who all her life has been looked at, now hidden in the street, gazing up at a yellow window, where an unhappy mother and child are silhouetted.

'I'm never lonely when I'm watching Jewels. The thing about Jewels is that she makes me want to try to be a better woman. Why's no one talking about how hard it is these days to be a good person?'

'Do you want to come and meet me and Mouse and have some food?' I felt I should try to keep her talking. She sounded unnaturally light and breezy, terribly certain that everything was going to be all right. 'You never really explained why you wanted Jewels in the first place.'

'Well, life can be empty, John. Ordinary people don't know how lucky they are. To live a simple life with Jewels, you don't know how excited I am!'

'But you can change without Jewels, without any baby,' I laughed. 'You're a star. You're free to do anything you like.'

Mouse leant more keenly towards me then, and I felt the importance of this moment as one must when negotiating with terrorists. 'But I'm sick of being so free, John. I don't want to have to make choices every day. I want to do things because I have to, not just because I want to. Jewels needs me. Oh I think she's asleep now. Hepsie's swaying more softly, and now she's lifting the girl on to her shoulder. Oh and she's covering her back with a blanket. And oh now . . .'

Outside the restaurant I noticed the traffic had halted in a jam. Two men were out and shouting at one another; pedestrians were stopping to look.

'I just mean that you don't need a baby in order to do what you want to in life.'

'I think she's taken the little girl to the cot now. I can't see her any more. But wait, look, she's coming back, and Hepsie's looking out at me. You're right: she looks so tired. It reminds me of the first time I met her at the train station. Brian arranged it. Hepsie was a few months pregnant and still dancing in a club. She looked so young and tired, and I thought, hell, I'm sure old enough to cope! And I had the money and no ties and nothing to lose.'

'Why didn't you just have a baby of your own?'

'Oh I tried, John, for many years. But it's not as easy as you might think. Look, she's got her face almost pressed up to the glass now, and she's moving in that agitated, hand-washing way, like she's urgently searching for something in the street. I can feel her frustration.'

'Can she see you?'

'Oh no. I'm keeping hidden behind this tree.'

'Well, make sure you don't scare her, peeping about like that. She might think you've come back for other reasons. It could ruin everything. If she gets startled she could just run off.'

Mouse was shaking his head slowly.

'John, you know even if she did see me I don't think that she would recognise me now.'

Chapter Twenty-two

'All you have to do is get seen and then just convince them that you are going to work really, really hard. If they like you then they'll give you a chance but the key is never quit. I mean, you might have to do some really menial things at first. I mean, there are people, I *know* people who are making half a million a year just from adverts. It's not ideal, sure, but if I had to, I'd do it. Wouldn't you?'

It was the early hours of the morning and we were in Central London somewhere, drinking. 'Quick, let's go out,' Brian had said when Hepsie and the baby were asleep. I was delighted that Brian had asked me to accompany him. Now Brian was drunk, and consequently being more honest than I'd ever heard before. I was thrilled to be his confidant. It was two days after the call from Miss Moore and I'd heard nothing from her since. I'd not told Hepsie that she'd been watched. And Hepsie had not confessed any decision about Jewels.

Mouse was out with us as he'd refused to stay at Chessington Vale without me. He feared Miss Moore would return and there'd be some dreadful climactic scene. Mouse had declined to sit at the table and so was sitting underneath it, occasionally gripping my ankle with his sharp fingernails.

Beyond its reputation as the chicest celebrity haunt, the place in which we sat was just a regular expensive restaurant, soaked in brandy, panelled in mahogany and spicy with the linger of cigars. I had intended to tell Brian about the call from Miss Moore but I feared he'd just laugh, and I was keen to banish my reputation as a gullible fool.

'I actually think the reason why most people fail in life,' Brian said to no one as he finished another hazy cocktail, 'is because they just aim low and keep cautious, or even have no aim at all and just fire off in all directions wasting their energy. Whereas I know exactly where my target is.' Here he pinched his thumb and index finger together and mimed the throwing of darts. 'And that's the top. Christ, man, do you know that we live in the fourth richest country in the world? It's true! Doesn't it make you feel a real failure, being basically a babysitter, when all around you people are making a *fortune* and going to parties and being adored? I don't know how you manage to keep calm. Some days I can't stop thinking about it . . .'

And slowly bright things were emerging through the blue fog. I knew he'd said the same thing to poor little Hepsie Vine, and she had repeated this purple advice to me on that first fateful day. And before the year was out I'd repeat it to some hungry girl and she'd tell her children and they'd tell theirs.

'What will happen to Mouse?'

'. . . and I just think well maybe I'm still where I was one year ago because of a total lack of daring in my life. Do you think so? Some days I feel like such a failure because I haven't made enough of my life and . . .'

'But you're doing really well,' I said. 'What with the magazine column and the style advising and . . .'

'Oh look over there! It's the owner!' Brian exclaimed. 'I've read all about him. He's what's made this place. He's absolutely the most sumptuous fucking chef in the whole of London.'

'Oh take me to all the places Misty goes,' I cried later, and soon I was deep in a purple night during which I did not hear a bird or see a star or feel smudged by the dark, only illuminated by it, as growling cabs hurled rainbowed puddles at our feet. I felt an unmistakable romance at having dined after midnight in London, and relief at being away from the ragged dogs of Wychwood. Free to think nothing of poor Misty Moore but to go unnoticed in the night's neon hurl; that busy, loud, mindless ease, which we all found most comforting as Brian played the tourist guide for Mouse and me. Trailing us through Soho and Covent Garden until sometime later we landed in a ginger-glowed restaurant from where Brian called 'some people': models, dancers, stylists, men and women with good skin.

Being around young, rich, beautiful people calmed me, and it made me wildly happy too. Yes, I was relieved to be away from Hepsie. Glad not to have eaten a steak-and-ale pie thick with gravy. I was pleased that I had dared to have such a radical haircut. Delighted that I no longer wore a stained woollen jacket from a charity shop and stank of patchouli oil and rolling tobacco. And soon, as though I had just clicked my fingers, shining women arrived from all over the city to be at our side. And, even if they were all strangers with not a teardrop of tenderness between them, unease wasn't so bad when you'd had a drink. Some of the women were still young enough to wear their beauty plainly, others looked as though they'd had to be polished very hard for a long time with a soft cloth. But everyone had, just like Misty, perfect teeth seemingly fashioned from tiny cubes of porcelain. After a few more drinks I particularly liked the way Brian greeted the newcomers like lost lovers. 'It's only styling for now,' I heard him say to a girl who held her sharp golden chin pointed to the ceiling, 'but who knows where it will lead. I don't rule out acting at all.' And then without us trying or signing a cheque we were snowballing it through the summer city. Picking up new wonderful slender friends as we went. Until a large gang of us, Mouse too, slunk through the city from dark expensive club to screeching smoky bar, where customers glanced at our beauty, as though that night we were crafted of the finest treacle and all eyes stuck to us.

I knew Brian was a heartless bastard, but I admit also to being delighted not to have to glimpse anyone old or poor or bitter for the entire evening. No whining babies or their weeping mothers. No pastry. No washed-up stars (I hadn't forgotten, and wouldn't for a long time, the lost tone of Miss Moore's voice speaking from behind a London tree). This was the freedom money had bought the famous, and I wanted to buy it too. Not to have to mention old age, poverty or ugliness. I nodded to myself in drunken acknowledgement of how exciting unkind people often were. How alluring the heartless. How potent the combination of sex and cruelty, and how nasty men often did so well with nice women. Generally cruelty, callousness and malice were seen as bad qualities, at my school at least, but I was starting to see, when carefully played in the right hands, what joy and excitement they could deliver also.

Again, later, we sank down side by side into a club, and

over sofas I sprawled with strange and beautiful girls. Far off, ever-sleepless Mouse played madly on a games machine.

'Where did you get that hat?' I heard Brian coo.

'This thing!' a scorching woman cried. 'God, I've no idea. I don't even remember what I'm wearing. We had to leave in such a hurry I had no time to choose. We were only told we had to come at six o'clock. It's a real fucking drag, actually.'

'I'm sure I've seen it in a magazine,' Brian continued sweetly.

'Oh probably,' the girl muttered.

'My eyeballs hurt,' Mouse said to me, shouting to be heard above the noise.

'Have you ever thought of modelling?' an ex-footballer, who at some point must have joined our party, asked me later. I snorted in imitation of embarrassment. 'No really, you're a good-looking guy. Why not come into the salon sometime and I'll introduce you to some people?' And I took the business card he offered me because I was drunk and it was London after midnight. I had dined with handsome people in a superior restaurant, in one of Europe's finest cities, and yes, I might just become a top international hair model. Stranger things had happened already. 'I have other bits and pieces here and in the States,' he said, 'film stuff, music, TV; perhaps there's other things we could collaborate on. Looks like I might have some great opportunities coming up in the near future.'

'Sure,' I said coolly. Already I was reclining in my silver trailer with a frosted ice pack over my beautiful green eyes as Brian cast spells over Hollywood and carved up the film business. It got so dark I could just see slices of yellow light,

247

like rips in a black curtain, and I thought of Hepsie and her little daughter asleep.

'I know!' Brian cried. 'Let's do what Misty does.'

'Oh yes,' a beautiful trim stranger agreed, her laugh brittled with irony, 'let's do everything that Misty does.' This was the same girl who had told me earlier that she worked as a 'trend analyst', as I'd told her about my recent fashion shoot in New Orleans.

'Last photos I saw of Misty Moore she was looking really *old*,' someone said with a shudder of revulsion. 'And I think she's set the cause of women back fifty years.' All the women agreed gleefully that she was a traitor to her sex.

'We want to go lap dancing,' Brian shouted, bouncing up on the seat. 'That's what Misty does.'

'Lap dancing! Lap dancing!' And the other women around began bouncing too until we were all jumping like beans and someone clicked their red-nailed fingers and we were in a cobalt velvet booth overhung with tiny pools of silver light. A brown girl oiling herself around a golden pole. Brian cheered and clapped and the bright women of our party stuck out their giggling tongues as if to lick the sticky beauty clean. All that night's glittering girls swirled in the same matching G-strings, a tiny red, white and blue Union Jack picked out in sequins.

Brian seemed to know lots of people in the club. It was very busy and Mouse got trampled in the crush inside the door. I had to pull the poor boy out from under a crunch of drunken men. I danced. Later I discovered Mouse sleeping heavily, drugged, I wondered, under a pile of coats. The dancing girl, sweating licks and kisses, boogied wildly on and on until she reminded me of a garment going round and round in the washing machine and it was coming light again.

'Chessington Vale!' someone cried. 'We want to stay there.'

'The ghastly pile that's in all the magazines!'

'Oh yes,' a lean Brazilian girl agreed coolly, 'let's go to Misty Moore's house. I'm so dying to see it.' Perhaps she was not Brazilian, though the girl wore a tiny tight replica of the country's banana-yellow football strip.

'I heard it's really vulgar,' someone laughed.

'Even better!'

'Yes, it's a complete state, so everyone says.'

'Hardly surprising. She's not exactly known for her *taste*.'

'Hey, but perhaps it's meant to be like that.'

'I suppose we could,' someone sighed, the tone in her voice suggesting she was giving up a front-row seat at a Milan catwalk for the chance to play bingo in Peckham.

We stepped from the growling cab and Chessington Vale stood in the pinking morning light. Not like the luxurious chilly hotels of my early dreams but like a flickering suburban brothel. I noticed how the two golden sports cars were parked side by side in the drive, like smart company cars outside company headquarters. Inside there was no sign of the depressed young country mother and her baby so we all danced and kissed, and then a skinny red-eyed man who was standing in the hallway with a somnolent crowd of thin-lipped women said wearily, 'We have to call out Brian's name.'

'OK,' I sighed, and we did until Brian appeared at the top of the stairs in one of Misty's floaty red dresses, laughing down at us. Triumph radiated from that sharp black face. He wore a long blonde wig in the exact fashion of her hairstyle, and twenty tons of make-up.

The wig was really hers, I later discovered when we were living together. If she needed to go out in public without spending an age in the bathroom she'd scrape her hair up in a knot and slip the wig over. When Brian wore it, the effect was that, despite his bulging muscles and gleaming black skin, for a moment he truly resembled her.

That was it: the remembered look. The glare of defiance and challenge that I had seen on other men's faces. Men whose stare in train carriages made my heart pound. Lean, pink-scalped, baby-faced men dressed as skinheads with nose rings, tight denim jeans, in steel-capped boots whose piercing stares both shocked and elated me. Serenely angry men whose refusal to make their intentions clear dissolved all our boundaries, sending us down in freefall. People being what they had decided to be, rather than what they had been told to be by their parents and teachers. It was rather astonishing – and for one who had been a good son and a good pupil it was all still, despite the last six months, rather intimidating.

'Call me to come down, you people, and I'll come down.'

'Come down, Brian,' we droned in unison.

He pouted, struck a pose, raised one shoulder, and turned his head from left to right slowly, glowering with the vicious sultriness of the drag queen.

'Again,' he mimicked. 'Call my name again. Louder!'

'Come down, Brian,' we yelled.

He trotted down the stairs with arms outstretched, his little finger raised as if he was drinking tea politely. There was clapping and laughter that I felt sure would rouse a furious Hepsie. 'Hello, London! Isn't this the dogs?' Then he put on a short dumb show: twirled and impersonated Miss Moore with eerie accuracy. He made leaps and bows that a Bolshoi ballet dancer would have been proud of. There were whistles and cheers. Still no fiery teen mother appeared to rage at us. Then Brian clutched his heart, groaned, gasped and to a chorus of giggles collapsed in a scarlet pool of rippling chiffon. 'I've been crushed to death by the weight of my own hairspray,' he cried.

I stayed up all night talking to the ex-footballer about opportunities in television and didn't see Hepsie until the next morning. She was predictably furious when she woke to find hungover models and bruised beauties lying as if slaughtered around the house.

'I couldn't sleep last night for listening to the noise you lot made,' she cried.

'So why didn't you come down to the party? We had a great time.'

'Are you mad? Why would I want to spend my free time with that bunch of idiots?'

'Actually there's some great people here. Your business is all about contacts, so you should meet them.'

'Er, I've got a baby to care for, in case you'd forgotten.'

'Oh don't start.'

'Don't look away when I'm talking to you!'

Hepsie Vine was no longer just a sexy apparition but a true woman with hunger and anger. It would be a full-time job for us both, being in love. But I still thought that it was within our reach. Sure, she was darker, deeper, than I had ever imagined, but still my eyes whizzed to the size of country moons just to gaze on the half-naked child-beauty.

'Do you think my body's all right?' she asked me on Monday afternoon as she stepped naked out of the bathroom. Exhaustion and a slumping unhappiness were the most instantly noticeable features of her body.

'It's perfect,' I smiled. I was on the other side of the room, gazing out of the window, looking urgently over the street, checking for forty-year-old women hiding in the trees.

'Oh I know it's not perfect. But it's *all right*, I think, don't you? Look very carefully.'

Mouse was there and he looked at Hepsie. He'd tell me later he believed that she was happiest as a mother when she was the ghost, coming quietly in the night to check on her daughter. Now she was real with a busy job in the daylight world and corporeal female flesh to attend to, she was miserable.

'I'm looking, honey,' I said, turning away from the window. I frowned, hoping to amuse her, but she was looking down and round at her bottom.

'Modelling is a big change from dancing; it's more demanding. You have to get your body totally right. What do you think I should change? In order to get on in show business.'

Again she stood completely naked before me and performed a routine that I felt she had done a thousand times before. That it was all practised annoyed me – though I knew she was trying to be the woman I wanted her to be. She moved round very slowly, her arms outstretched, watching me over her shoulder, and pushing her bottom back a little so her spine hooked. I felt tired and keen to get out to a restaurant.

'Nothing. You're perfect. I love you. Let's go.' The more self-aware she was the less attractive she was to me. Or perhaps it was just that now that I had her I wanted her less.

'I know it needs some work. I know Miss Moore has a much better body than me. But then she's not had a baby, has she?'

'Spooky,' Mouse said, as he looked on her. He was surely thinking how thin and pale she looked, how almost like a ghost she was becoming. 'She can't breathe. She's suffocating. If Hepsie doesn't get out of here I think she'll die,' Mouse would say to me that night just before he went to sleep.

'So it's not surprising I've still got some way to go,' Hepsie continued. 'Give me a few months at the gym and a few injections here and there.' She spoke now in a whisper. Her eyes were large and frightened. I could see the breathless rise and fall of an anxious heartbeat.

'Don't change anything,' I said as the sun went down.

The moon rose. On and on I looked at her eagerly. Mainly because I was the only adult male there and I'd discovered enough about women that year to know that, if she was to come out of the kitchen and become who we wanted her to be, she needed someone to look, always. Brian was right: nowadays that's all women wanted from men. It was a woman's world and we had to take what scraps we could. Still, looking and serving could be a lucrative profession, for there was money in it – as Brian had discovered. Yes, that would be my role too from now on, to look at Hepsie whenever she needed it, and ensure that look was always the right look. Men of my generation had to wait, to look attentively, in the correct way, until they were called upon to perform some further humiliation. Only Brian had resisted this. Yes, Brian had carved, most marvellously, from our servitude a powerful plan. For this I admired the guy, despite how he had deceived and ridiculed me.

253

'When I think of all the shitholes I've lived in in London, and now here I am . . .' It was Monday evening. She had slumped her head against the wall of the hallway in Chessington Vale and closed her tired eyes. 'Then it's all been worth it,' she said, sliding down the wall so she was sitting with her head in her hands on the floor.

Chapter Twenty-three

'Y ou're a clever little thing,' I said to Hepsie on Tuesday afternoon, when I had taken a cup of tea to her room. 'Here you are with your baby, living in London, people from all the poor countries of the world helping you, waiting on you, in fact! And there you are going out to be photographed every day – if you can be bothered.'

'I've had to be clever,' she replied without enthusiasm.

'Well, don't give up now. Come on, get dressed.'

We argued more fiercely than ever nowadays. I imagined how the staff below must have heard us and smiled. Just as I had heard Brian and Miss Moore on that winter's day six months ago. And thought how thrilling and glamorous their unhappiness had seemed. Of course we had not told the staff that Jewels was Hepsie's child, or that I was the nanny. We told them nothing. All was secret. I discovered for the first time the intoxicating power of not telling anyone what you were up to. They'd have to work it out for themselves, perhaps with a bit of help from the tabloid newspapers. Indeed they must have wondered if we were lovers. I know they whispered about us when we were not in the room. They definitely speculated about our dazzling lives, because when peeping round a doorway I'd heard them.

Other days I panicked: perhaps our misery was no longer enchanting, our tears no longer gems. Hepsie was certainly less appealing than she had once been, now that she was always so busy with Jewels. She continued to cook and this infuriated me. And I woke up one morning and imagined with horror that her skin smelled boozy and her fleshy lips were dry and torn into a wet blister in each corner. I told her I loved her. I hugged her and praised her and she didn't resist my kisses. But by the end of that week Hepsie had moved bedrooms. She said she needed more rest if she was to be fresh-faced for work. It was all right to feel tired, but to look tired was career suicide, she said. 'Plus I want more time alone with Jewels, so I can make up for all the months I've lost.'

'You'll have plenty of time for that in future. Right now what matters is that you establish yourself.'

'I'm too tired.'

'Oh great. That attitude's really gonna make us a million.'

'Perhaps it's living in a mansion,' she sighed. 'I'm exhausted just walking up to bed.'

'Then perhaps you'd rather live in a little caravan.'

'Maybe, yes. There's more to live for than big houses and money, John.'

'So speaks the girl who sold her daughter for a fast car and a job in London.'

'You know, I think worrying, about money and the house, is what made my dad and granddad shoot themselves. Maybe I've been making the same mistake as they did.'

'But you used to want this so badly. And you're doing so well. You could be huge.'

'So what? What's the big deal about using your face to make people buy things? Lots of money, that's all you get.'

'It's about much more than just money, it's about purpose. The purpose of your life.'

'But I have a purpose, John. I have Jewels now.'

'But surely you need more than that. Do you want to be another single mother? You need – meaning. A job.'

'No, I'm not sure I do any more. Last year I was seduced by people telling me how pretty I was and how much money I could make if I just gave up everything else and focused completely and worked hard night and day.'

'You have to believe you're worth it. That's your problem, you're too humble. You're losing your hunger. You'll never compete with this attitude.'

'But meaning and purpose and worth, they're not things you can buy. So what's the point of having the money?' she said urgently, turning and gesticulating passionately. 'That's what I've realised, John. No matter how much money I make, or how much Miss Moore gives me, the purpose and meaning of my life will be down to – well, love.'

'But I love you! You are gorgeous!'

'And I'm a human being too, John. With feeling and thoughts and memories. And when I remember what I did with this little girl when she was so tiny I feel so terrible. And this makes me think of my own mother and all the pain I've caused her.'

I tried to divert Hepsie with lingerie, gossip and trivia. I blew hundreds of pounds on tiny designer knickers, but each time after she'd unwrapped the gift she wandered soon away from me and returned to Jewels. I purposefully didn't mention the baby. I kept Mouse, and even the little dog, out of her way. I made sure that we didn't speculate about Miss Moore's arrival (though I checked for her regularly from the windows). Or wonder when Brian would pop out from behind a wardrobe brandishing the perfect cute gift. Hepsie wanted only privacy. She was not resting. The constant clatter of the staff below didn't help. Her new room was on the third floor of the house. It was en suite but sparsely furnished, which seemed not to bother her. She had the whole of the third floor to herself. She insisted that the staff did not come up there unless she asked because she was so tired.

Sleep was a problem for us both, though drinking helped me a little. On the Thursday afternoon I remember clearly how I went up to her new bedroom as the sun was slipping towards the pavement and the room's fatty light was turning afternoon blue. Up there I was wiltingly hot: dying on the hottest day of the year. A slight breeze made the fleshy curtains pulse. There was the stench of musky sweat and cigarette smoke and, everywhere, meat. The smell, I discovered later, was the stench of the bowls of dog food she set up around the room. Hepsie had asked the cleaner not to work up there so she had some solitude. 'I just want one place where I don't have to pretend any more,' Hepsie cried. 'Please.'

The next day when I thought she had gone to work I found her and Jewels embracing in the bed far away in her high room.

'Are you ill?' I asked her. 'Why aren't you at the studio?'

'I just get a bit nervous,' she said sadly, 'and it makes me sick. I can't possibly go to work. In fact I don't think I'll ever go again.'

'She's sick,' Mouse said to me.

I confessed to Mouse that, to be honest, it was all a bit hard to deal with: one day I had to love her for her strength, the next day for her weakness, equally every time. But perhaps this was the lot of the modern man.

'Listen to me carefully, Mummyman, she's totally sick. And the reason is she's unhappy.' Then Mouse repeated, more slowly, 'Mummyman, this isn't about you. She's sick.'

Each hour more eagerly during those final sun-drenched days I began to itch for chilled booze to arrive. Six months of life with the sad millionairess and champagne, beauty, luxury no longer excited me; I just got irritated, then annoyed, if I didn't receive the things I wanted, or had paid for, quickly enough. Though Hepsie and I still kissed, conversation eluded us. Later I would admit that we had nothing in common. Most days she was smiling and frowning simultaneously, as if at any moment a perfect rainbow would arch over her face, resting a pot of gold on her delicate shoulder.

'Repeat these words after me, Mummyman, *Hepsie is sick and we must help her.*'

Mouse was right, she was sick and she was unhappy.

I often thought of that first December day. Brian's wiggling gait, Hepsie's sparkling tears. How I'd heard the tinselled chandelier shudder at its own tackiness. How the sugared confection of cushions, rugs and huge white leather sofas had made my teeth ache. I'd wanted trashy heartbreak right from the start, and now I had it. But I mustn't panic: to make it work required control – the key was not to feel the sorrow but to work with it. For the last six months Brian had ensured the women kept their secrets. I needed to learn to do that too. In the future I needed to create a powerful persona around women that said, *I understand everything, you need tell me nothing.*

Instead, though I had no right to ask anything about Jewels, on Friday evening, moodily I said, 'What about Jewels' father?'

'Are you mad?' Hepsie exclaimed.

'Don't you have a duty to tell him what you've done with his daughter?'

'Are you kidding?'

'Who is he?' I'd been brooding on that village boy Wayne. Who, once, in a strange village in the sparkling countryside, had freed a trapped baby from a golden sports car. 'You owe him some information. And the rest of us. None of us knows what you're going to do next.' Tears filled my eyes as I spoke and I turned away.

She looked so desperate and I wanted to love her but I couldn't think of anything to say that was both true and would make her happy. We couldn't even touch each other tenderly any more. I felt so many sad things and yet didn't know how to speak any of them. Worse, in the last six months I had learnt to distrust plain honesty, fearing I'd be quoted, and my words misconstrued then used against me. So I stayed silent and turned away and just watched the clouds moving over the summer sky as behind me the young girl hunched over her baby.

Of course today I know from my own experience that inconsistency, volatility, unpredictability is required of stars. Tottering on the edge, as the audience below gasp in fear of your imminent fall, is all part of the show. Often that week I tried to love her more and we performed the kind of sex that was 'a scene', 'a steamy romp', 'a session'.

Every time afterwards I felt strangely nostalgic, like when seeing a sunset and being aware that you've not captured it on film. It was true: now I had Hepsie desire for her came more slowly. It was frustrating. I had to close my eyes and imagine her to want her. Secrets, fantasies – so lurid and strange – I was pleased that Hepsie and I were so deeply incompatible and she would never read my mind.

'I'm too unhappy,' she said to me before we had even finished having sex. 'I want to go home.'

'Aren't I enough for you?' I said, raising up on my elbows to look at her.

'I don't think you love me,' she said sadly. 'Do you?'

'Of course, I do,' I cried. 'I'll try harder. I love everything about you.'

'I think men like the *idea* of me. They don't know me, or really want to know me.' I truly had no idea why Hepsie made everything such hard work. If she'd only relax, we could work it out. But I could say none of this so I just stroked her hair. 'It's this lifestyle, John. The endless exhausting working, the constant fixation with money, the self-obsession that's so essential – well, I think it makes it impossible to be truly in love. Sex yes, this yes, but not love.'

I got out of the bed and went to the window. I couldn't think what to say. She had to hide her feelings, decide not to say what she felt, or see what she saw. Concealment was our only hope. 'Miss Moore was homesick once,' I said. 'When she went away to dance with the Bolshoi.' I could see Miss Moore there in the snow amidst the onion domes, twirling.

'I'm missing everything,' Hepsie continued, dressing quickly as though she'd come to some sudden urgent resolution that required her to get away from me immediately, 'not just home, I'm missing being free and relaxed and unnoticed. But most of all I'm missing having the longing to fall in love. And yes, dreams are one thing, but memories matter more, and if I carry on like this then for my entire life I'm going to be unloved, unloving and plagued by guilty memories. Just like her.'

'Well, we have to make sure we avoid that,' I said.

'That's the difference between men and me,' Hepsie said softly. 'You lot think life's about avoiding trouble. I've learnt you just have to cope with it when it comes.'

'I thought we'd solved all the troubles,' I said irritably. 'We've almost got everything. Recognition, respect, riches; it's all just a step away if only you'd cheer up.'

'No,' Hepsie said calmly, taking her clothes quickly from the wardrobe and folding them into a pile. 'I've told you, if we stay like this our troubles are only beginning. I want to go home with Jewels. This is no place for a child. There's strangers everywhere, it's not safe. She's not happy here, she misses the countryside and her family. She doesn't get any fresh air. No, I can't pretend Jewels isn't my responsibility.'

Again silence. I wondered later if this was the moment she had carved for me to say just the right thing to change her mind. 'But what about me?' I cried, hoping to shoot forth a thrilling climactic moment of romantic challenge that would stir and excite her. 'I love you! Don't leave me. I can't live without you!'

Hepsie smiled and bit her pretty lip. The excited determined look reminded me of Miss Moore's thrilled smile when she'd invited Hepsie to live with her in London. 'Then come with me to Wychwood,' Hepsie said. 'If you love us, you don't have to leave us.'

She was staring deeply into me with that powerful look of defiance that I'd first fallen in love with. I almost asked her to marry me then, but it was the end of the story, not the beginning and I had changed from the man I once was.

'You, Jewels and me could all live together. As a proper, ordinary, decent family.'

'Well,' I said. 'We could.'

'You could get work in Wychwood. There is work around if you're willing to graft. I'd work too so we could save some money. My mum could have Jewels during the day. I might even go to college and get qualified.'

'Hmm,' I tipped my eyes to the floor and stood very still. She was too strong for me. The terrible truth was that, in order to be the man I fantasised about being, I needed weak, compliant women. I tried to imagine myself going off with Hepsie into the sunset of a decent life, but instantly I pictured myself skulking off to Southern cities secretly after midnight, texting sex messages to lap dancers from my car.

'I might train to be a teacher. Something useful. At first we could live at the caravan, so it wouldn't be too expensive. It'd be chaos, with my gran and all the girls around us, plus the baby, but at least we'd have each other.'

'Yes.'

'Then, when we'd saved up enough money, we could get a little place of our own in the village. Think about it. It's a chance to change everything.'

'Let me think about it.'

When I gazed away from her to the black windows I didn't see her reflection or mine, but I understood what Miss Moore had seen in the windows of Long Meadow End: an azure lagoon in the shady lily pond, luminous tangerines hanging from the branches of the chestnuts, dogs big as crimson bears, melons like suns in the elms, bananas sharp as sickle moons, red and orange parrots splashing like cocktails against the dark glass, and bright budgerigars blazing to and fro over the black grass.

Chapter Twenty-four

I called Miss Moore early the next morning and explained the situation. She was quiet for a long time and then said, 'This was always my fear. She's got beauty and she's got brains but she hasn't got stamina.'

'She doesn't want it enough.'

'No.'

'She thinks it's all bullshit.'

'Yes.'

'Perhaps Brian could speak to her,' I suggested. 'After all, he persuaded her in the first place.'

'Brian? Do you think we'll ever see Brian again?' Miss Moore replied in a puzzled tone.

'I've not heard from him for a while,' I said. 'Perhaps we could call the magazine.'

'Magazine!' she cried.

'Where he has his column,' I said anxiously. 'That's what Hepsie said.'

'Oh,' she laughed, 'you mean he can read and write?'

'What shall we do?'

'The only thing left to do: appeal to her parents.'

The next day the Vines arrived in their dusty truck, Miss

Moore in her expensive car. The problem was immediately obvious when Hepsie raced down the hallway to greet her family: Hepsie was loved; she was wanted as a daughter, a sister and a mother, and she had a home to go to.

'Oh it's too hot. Please just stop bloody asking questions,' Hepsie Vine was shouting as she came down into the living room half an hour later.

She was a determined woman and hated having to admit defeat on anything. I noticed that she wore a decorative yellow flower in her glossy hair. She did not even seem to notice Miss Moore, who stood in the room plainly, wearing neither make-up nor perfume, no high heels, shades or fingernail polish. Something in my look must have excited or startled Hepsie, because as I stared at her she turned away quickly to conceal her face. She moved so swiftly the decorative yellow flower fell from her hair and hit the polished wooden floorboards with a soft bounce.

'Here, let me get that,' I said, stooping down to collect the bud. But before I could reach it Hepsie's foot (shod that day, I cannot, ever, forget, in a super-high-heeled red leather boot) ground down upon it, crushing it to a dark slime. 'Just forget it,' she cried, 'it's just some stupid silly thing my sister brought me from home.'

A searing dart of rejection burnt a hot hole in my heart: she swatted me away like a bluebottle. Fiercely, I wanted her once more. It was hard to explain, but I most liked her, and I certainly only fancied her, when she was both damaged and strong, and, crucially, unavailable. I looked at Hepsie, and thought of Miss Moore and of Isolde, and had a moment of horrible understanding: I would probably become – for I was soon to be *twenty* – the seedy sort of guy who only fancies women he can't have. Schoolgirls, nurses, lesbians, nuns. It would intensify as my waist doubled and my dreams of art receded with my hair. It would doubtless end in chronic loneliness – websites, more and more sensational, as my only friends. Don't say I didn't warn you, my young self tells me daily.

Behind Hepsie and her mother and grandmother stood the rest of the Vine girls, scowling. No one looked at Miss Moore, plain in her jeans and T-shirt. Mouse had raced towards Isolde in a crazy stumbling zigzag and she'd scooped him into her arms. Now she was nuzzling his neck and pulling off his balaclava in one deft move. He clung to her vulnerable and unpeeled. She kissed him over and over on his pale messed-up head.

'The boy doesn't look too good,' the grandmother said quietly.

'Homesickness. I always told you it was a real thing, but no one would listen,' Hepsie said sulkily. Now she had made her decision she'd regressed to the naughty Wychwood teenager she'd most enjoyed being.

'I can't believe he's still here,' Isolde cried. 'Hasn't anyone tried to find his family yet? You, John, you should have done it. He can't stay here with you two jokers for ever.'

'Yes, I should have done it, but I forgot.'

'John's been kinda busy,' Mouse said kindly.

'Well, leave it with me,' Isolde said. 'I'll make sure you get home.'

Mrs Vine put her arm around her daughter supportively and I noticed those hands again. Leathery cushions of red skin around the knuckles, fingernails that were dirty and torn. Hands raw from working in the real world – the world that could still be mine if only I had the nerve to take a chance.

'Do you want me to find your mum?' Isolde chatted on, bending down so that she was face to face with Mouse. The boy nodded. 'OK, big man, I'll track her down and get you two back together.'

She did. Three weeks later Mouse left Chessington Vale with his tearful American mother and I never heard from him again. Though I often think nowadays of getting in touch. At other times I hope that he remembers us all as nothing more than blurry ghouls from a strange dream.

'. . . and that's it. I can't stand the phoneyness of it all.'

I looked at my girl drifting round the room in that shapeless yellow dress that finished, correctly, just above the knees. If I went with Hepsie to Wychwood, perhaps I could live usefully in the world too. I hadn't entirely ruled it out. I could train as a nurse. Do good, love and be happy. I remembered the England of hay bales, and summer wheat and drystone walls and a rise of land with a scribble of black trees bending in deep wind and home cooking and family meals. I looked at each of the Vine women and imagined spending my life with them, losing my shallow life in their deep waters.

'I guess you just weren't cut out for it,' Miss Moore said to Hepsie.

'Actually it was getting to know you that changed everything for me,' Hepsie said quietly. 'You were nothing like I hoped you'd be. And that big empty tasteless house – oh I hated it. I couldn't risk ending up living like that – all alone.'

Yes, I should leave with Hepsie.

Much time passed. I served tea in cups with matching saucers, each trembling with a little silver spoon. When Miss Moore and Hepsie looked particularly distressed I chattered mindlessly to cheer them up. Still I waited, as if expecting the breeze to decide my future for me. Jewels was passed tenderly between her grandmother and great-grand-mother. The dark Vine sisters declined to sit down and instead stood around the room at various points like tiny guards. The girls' messed-up hair, clinking jewellery, cheap clothes, suspicious eyes could not obscure their beauty, which flickered a jittery candlelight over us all. I've spent the last ten years searching for another woman with that exact firelit look.

Occasionally one of the girls would go up and stroke the arm of their elder sister. Mouse stood close to Isolde, his hand holding hers. Celeste gazed out of the windows at the city. Perhaps this was the legacy of my time with the Vines: I'd never be able to look at pretty women again without wishing I was good at photography.

I turned my attention back just in time to catch Hepsic rising up in fury from the sofa, exactly as she had six months ago, as uneasily as a new foal on her pretty, endless legs. 'Oh God, I've made such a mess of everything. I'm so sorry,' Hepsie cried. Then lit a cigarette and slowly blew a smoke ring, into which she hooked, with a bride's coy smile, the third finger of her left hand. 'But I'm certain. Now we just have to see what John wants to do.'

She might want to be ordinary – and might even be capable of a simple honest life – but like me in the last six months she'd been struck by lightning. It was unlikely she'd ever be able fully to conceal her difference. Perhaps she would be for ever cursed, like me and Brian and Alex and maybe all the finest of my generation, with the constant possibility of another life. Imagine being suspended in the agonising nothingness between the fast-car adverts and the news of bombs, wars and disease. Hung for ever between fear and longing. I sometimes wonder if this is how Hepsie lives now too. I often imagine her and Jewels warm in their caravan, watching my TV show. Remembering the young, real me as they laugh and cry with my dastardly screen character.

Miss Moore rested her elbows on her knees and put her head in her hands. Then Hepsie said quietly, 'Is John coming with us or not?' A heavy wringing scent was making it difficult to breathe. It was coming colder, as if the planet only had hours left.

'Take all my money,' Miss Moore whispered, as though it was the thing she wished most to be rid of in the whole world.

'I've told you, I don't want to be someone who sells their daughter.'

'Seriously, have as much of it as you like.'

'I want to be someone else.'

'Who do you want to be?' Miss Moore laughed incredulously. 'I know exactly what kind of girl you were before I met you!'

'Well, what about you!' Hepsie shouted, pointing now at Miss Moore. 'Calling everyone darling and poppet and sweetie. It makes me sick! Oh yeah, it doesn't take away what kind of woman you are. And how you started out.'

'I did everything through hard work.'

'And look at you now. Look where you are now! You're rank. Everyone thinks so. I'm not happy. This life is nothing but drinking, working and flirting.'

'What else is there?' I asked, because Brian was no longer there, so it was my job to supply the breezy questions now.

'It's a man's life,' Hepsie replied. 'That's why it feels so trashy. I want more than that, I'm so homesick. But we could be happy, John,' Hepsie cried dramatically, wandering over to me and placing her hand on my shoulder and squeezing. 'Come with us,' she whispered, pressing her soft cheek against mine. 'I don't want to leave you here. Come with me and be happy.'

Miss Moore sighed and looked at the ceiling.

'So what are you going to do?' Hepsie said to me when her family were all in the van and we were alone in the living room. Hepsie had Jewels held firmly against her hip and a large bag over her shoulder. 'She won't need you here any more because Isolde's going to get Mouse back to his mum any day now. Isolde's determined.'

I looked past Hepsie at the expensive furniture, imagining the bright disco swirl of the tree lights twinkling over the white leather sofa. The only sign that the entire Vine family had been in the room an hour earlier was a single brown chicken feather fluttering on the arm of the sofa, and on a velvet cushion, silver strands of dog hair flecked like blown dandelion clock. I wondered if I could immediately forget them, or if they would haunt my dreams more fiercely than when they had breathed over me in the night.

'Are you going to come with us?' Hepsie said gently.

'I might do,' I said, 'but first I think I need to get her settled and then . . .'

'John, you do what's best . . .' she said kindly. 'Jewels will never forget you.'

'I'm going too,' Mouse said. 'It won't be long now, my mum's coming for me, isn't she? Very soon.'

I stroked the boy's head and smiled. 'Miss Moore needs me,' I said shyly, 'at least for a little while.'

'Do you mean you need her, John?'

271

I laughed and said, 'No, I mean she's lonely and I feel sorry for her. I'll just make sure she gets over this.'

'Are you going to live here?'

'Oh God, no,' I laughed. 'I'm going to get my own place in London.'

'An apartment,' she smiled. 'How about a warehouse apartment?'

'I think that'd take more money than I have,' I said. 'And anyway I'm not sure it's me.'

'Oh I'm sure she'll help you out. Money is the one thing she does have.'

'I want to earn my own money.'

'Why not get a job on a magazine?'

'Look, I'm just going to stay around for a couple of weeks so I'm sure she's all right. Then . . .'

'Perhaps we'll see you in a couple of weeks then.' Hepsie gathered her things around her and kissed me quickly on the cheek. 'I'm not angry with you, you know. I'm grateful for all you've done for Jewels. And I think if things had been different we really could have been in love.'

Before I had the chance to embrace her and make a more moving farewell speech about love and separation, Miss Moore appeared behind us. 'Can I just say goodbye to Jewels?' Miss Moore said, and Hepsie nodded and handed her the baby. Miss Moore held the child against her chest and closed her eyes.

'She'll miss you both,' Hepsie said.

Miss Moore inhaled the breaths of the baby like some much-needed drug. 'I'm sorry about what I said before. I think you're wonderful, you know,' Miss Moore said to Hepsie. She reached out then and stroked a finger along the girl's cheek. 'Thanks for giving me those six months with Jewels. You're doing the right thing.'

'I think you're wonderful too,' Hepsie replied.

'Yep, it's been kinda freaky but fun,' Mouse said to the ghost. 'Goodbye.'

'You'll be back with your mum soon, Mr Mouse. Everyone back with the right mummy soon, yeah?'

Miss Moore nodded. 'I hope everything works out for you, Hepsie. If you need anything, let me know.'

Hepsie nodded and smiled. The two women embraced, and when they pulled apart both were crying.

'Oh I nearly forgot,' Hepsie said, 'here's the keys to the house and the car.'

'Keep the car,' Miss Moore said, 'as a thank-you present. You'll need it for Jewels. It's the least I can do.'

What generally wasn't understood, I realised later, about Miss Moore was that she knew what others thought of her, and in fact she thought it too. Shame was part of her identity, and guilt and lies, and she'd been playing with all of these things, and exploring where they led. And as Miss Moore held the child and I smiled sadly at Hepsie and Hepsie raised her eyebrows at me, sunlight blazed around the place, gilding us all so starkly, showing us all so clearly in the glare if anyone wanted to see. Mouse leaned over and gave Jewels a little last kiss too. The baby giggled at the boy.

'It's a happy ending,' Hepsie said.

Chapter Twenty-five

S o what if it ended in ruins, it was just an idea, and I was
young and still had my glittering life ahead of me.
Mistakes were the only way you learnt after all, and I
needed to learn about life if I was to realise my full
potential. Nothing mattered other than what I wanted to
do right then, for following my desires in every instant had
its own daring integrity. I'd just stay a month until everything was settled. Perhaps Hepsie would call each week and
I'd entertain her with witty stories of my time in London.
Perhaps I'd hook up with Brian and see more of the dark
side of the city. Miss Moore would introduce me to influ-
ential people. I still had to phone the ex-footballer who'd
called me handsome and offered me a job in TV.

There was a mirror at the bottom of the stairs and when
the Vine family had gone Miss Moore came quietly up to
me. She stood at my side. Mouse slipped in at the back of
the room and he watched us watching ourselves.

Yes, I looked at the two of us, transformed. I had a
different colour, weight, scent and clothes than at the start
of the year. Yet despite everything that had occurred in the
last six months we still looked like we were advertising

something that the world would want to buy: serious but handsome, sexy but melancholy.

'You should phone people and tell them you're back,' I said to her reflection.

'Yes,' she replied, as if talking just to herself, 'I forgot I was making my comeback,' but I didn't see her go to the phone, and just as no one had called us in Long Meadow End, no one called us that day in Chessington Vale. So unnoticed were we that I imagined the house had floated out to some place where communication was impossible, even though somewhere the staff worked. I inhaled and tried to sniff the lingering of Vines in the house, the hot stickiness of the girls. But they were as gone as if they had never been there. It was only when I closed my eyes that I could see them burning there before me as clearly as before, and before that.

But now I had to make sure that ahead of me was tomorrow, not yesterday. I turned to the left and then to the right and posed, fiddled with my sunglasses, and Miss Moore eventually managed a little laugh, which pleased me greatly. We were still looking into the mirror. In a way we were an exact fit of the kind of rich, vulgar, miserable people that I'd hoped six months ago to meet during my time with Misty Moore. But I had understood so little then, had seen only the crass rush of those busy lives, nothing of how it was when you stood there in silence listening for instructions from sunbeams.

Despite the cleaning staff, the house, particularly in our private rooms, was dirty. The legacy of my time there with Hepsie. I had lots of work to do. Later, as I cleaned, rooms would turn around me, as though we were the statues and the house the living thing. But I remembered my tendency towards the garish. So perhaps I did have a grain of the artist in me. Yes, to me a rich woman was still a million-airess, a spot of sadness heartbreak, sorrow tragedy, lust love, and a forty-year-old woman and a handsome man, both alone in a big quiet house, the most poignant sight in the world.

Just when it was becoming strange that we were still there in front of the mirror, staring, still and silent and utterly alone, the tiny hairless dog appeared, scuttling through the hallway, yelping. I had my first job: care for it. Find it a bowl, a blanket and food.

A NOTE ON THE AUTHOR

Helen Cross was born in 1967 and brought up in East Yorkshire. She is the author of the critically acclaimed *My Summer of Love* (also published by Bloomsbury) which won a Betty Trask Prize. Helen currently lives in Birmingham.

A NOTE ON THE TYPE

The text of this book is set in Linotype Sabon, named after the type founder, Jacques Sabon. It was designed by Jan Tschichold and jointly developed by Linotype, Monotype and Stempel, in response to a need for a typeface to be available in identical form for mechanical hot metal composition and hand composition using foundry type.

Tschichold based his design for Sabon roman on a font engraved by Garamond, and Sabon italic on a font by Granjon. It was first used in 1966 and has proved an enduring modern classic.